Lloyd F. Ritchey

the Kellsburg VAMPIRE

Wildgrave
www.wildgravepublishing.com

THE KELLSBURG VAMPIRE

A Wildgrave Book

ISBN 10: 0-9985785-3-3
ISBN 13: 978-0-9985785-3-8

www.wildgravepublishing.com
www.lloydritchey.com

Published in the United States of America

Printed in the United States of America.

Acknowledgements

The author wishes to express his thanks to the following persons who generously offered their opinions and/or expertise in helping to polish *The Kellsburg Vampire* into its final form: editor Alan Gooding, Christine Ritchey, Stephen Ritchey, Cy Brinson, and Harry Myers. Thanks also to artist Aüsome Rex for his stylish "Electric Skull" logo used inside this book's covers.

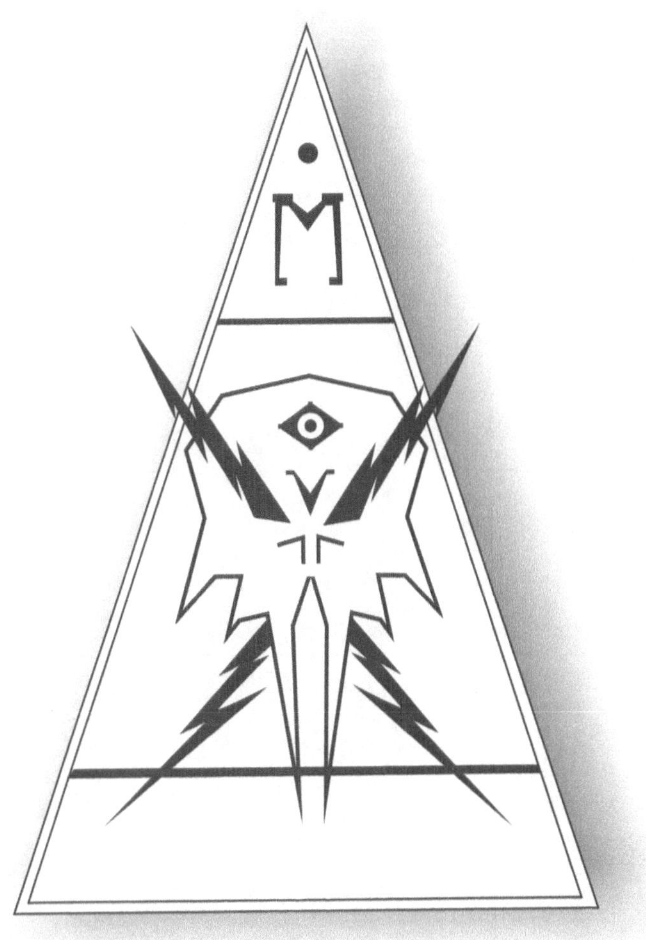

Part One

Forbidden Doors

1

Johnny Helstrom downshifted his mountain bike and coasted to a rattling stop. The steel gate loomed before him, its massive frame suspended between brick columns and secured with padlocked turns of heavy chain. Beyond the gate's rusted bars, a concrete bunker glared at him from a single shattered window. Creeper vines webbed its mottled gray surface like distended veins.

Signs screwed to the columns carried a faded warning:

KEEP OUT

U.S. GOVERNMENT PROPERTY

Kip braked on Johnny's right, his bike's knobby tires chattering through the shale mantling the road's cracked and buckled surface. He lifted his Yankees baseball cap and swept a tangle of blond hair from his eyes. "Awesome," he said, pointing at the bunker. "It's one of those machine gun things."

"It's called a pillbox. That slit underneath the window is the gun port." Johnny plucked the water bottle from its holder and eyed the contents: half-full, and the morning was already sizzling in the August heat. West of their position, towering clouds were drawing close, their turbulent undersides scudding low enough to stir the surrounding forest of pine and spruce. He should have watched the weather forecast; a real Special Forces soldier would have done so.

He walked to the gate and looked up at the spiked bars. "This thing's gotta be twenty feet tall, and there's no toe-holds."

The chain link fence, stretched tight between steel posts and crowned with spiraling coils of razor wire, ran from either side of the support columns and vanished into the swallowing woods.

Kip knelt and began tossing rocks from a low area beneath the fence. The soil had eroded, and the retaining beam had sagged and crumbled. He pried out a loose wedge of concrete and sent it clattering down the steep embankment. "We can get under."

"There's not enough room for the bikes."

"Don't deer hunters get in? They probably have a secret entrance."

"Hunters don't go inside. Nobody does."

Kip rotated his cap, pointing the bill forward. "So, we walk."

A bigger opening might exist, Johnny thought, but they could search all day and never find it. "Yeah," he said. "We'll leave the bikes and go under."

Lying on his back, he squirmed beneath the fence and tugged the packs behind him. Kip followed, his skinny form maneuvering quickly through the narrow gap. They were wearing camouflage shorts and T-shirts, and as they picked their way across a wide expanse of thorn vines, the black barbs clawed at their exposed arms and legs.

Kip swiped a thread of blood from his calf. "Ow. I'd rather walk through that razor wire."

The thorns finally released them into the shadow of the woods. The old entrance road curved across their path and quickly vanished, the trees piercing its ruined surface having buried it long ago under a carpet of pine needles and decaying limbs.

Johnny unfolded his army surplus compass and let the needle

stabilize. "We go north-northeast."

Kip glanced at the sky, his hand shielding his eyes. "It's gonna' rain like crazy."

"A little rain won't hurt us. Besides, we could get inside one of the buildings and wait it out." Johnny wished he had chosen another day to explore. But he had to be tough. This was his mission. He had planned this reconnaissance for days, poring over ancient newspaper articles and Internet photos of the wrecked buildings.

The North Ridge Air Defense Base was considered dangerous, the subject of tall tales and stories about trespassers disappearing inside. After some mysterious disaster closed the base back in the sixties, the military had destroyed the roads and topped the fence with concertina wire. But if he and Kip pulled off this adventure, Spencer Middle School would be talking about them for a year. And his dad—Engineer Sergeant, 10th Special Forces Group, Retired—would be so proud. Once he got over being pissed.

They walked through thick woods for perhaps a half mile, Johnny constantly checking the compass, lining up on a distant tree or rock outcrop. He had almost forgotten about the weather and looked up as a hissing breath of cold air dropped from the sky. Threads of lightning flashed and wormed through lowering clouds and a dull boom rolled from the west, spooking a dark knot of crows that burst croaking and cawing from a nearby aspen.

Kip stopped and looked around. "Where are the buildings? They're supposed to be near the entrance."

Aligned north a moment ago, the compass now pointed south. Johnny carefully zeroed the bezel, but the needle suddenly wavered and swung left. It was as if a great magnetic snake were slithering around underground, tugging the needle as it moved.

Kip nudged up beside him and reached for the compass. "You

poser. Don't you know how to use that?"

"It's not my fault—"

The ground burned blue-white and a cannon-loud *crack* blasted the woods.

Johnny forced himself to remain calm. "We'll just head back the way we came and look for the road."

Another brilliant flash, followed by a stunningly loud report, brought him to his knees. Somewhere a branch crashed, and a frigid downdraft lashed his body, knocking him sideways. His teeth began chattering, partly from cold, partly from fear, and he found himself running away from the storm.

"We're gonna' get hit by lightning," Kip shouted, his voice verging on panic.

"Stay away from the trees."

"We're in the *woods*, dumbass."

A cascade of roaring silver tumbled from the sky and raced toward them from the west, churning the landscape into an impenetrable gray blur.

"Hail! It's huge!"

They yanked off their packs and held them aloft, shielding themselves as ice stones the size of golf balls smashed through the wildly gyrating trees. The missiles sliced into Johnny's exposed fingers and flashed beyond the pack-shield to pummel his shoulders.

Kip's shrill voice cut through the din. "Look! Over there!"

A stubby, rounded structure jutted from the ground a few feet away, startlingly out of place in the storm-darkened woods. Inset into the small dome was a door of riveted steel with a wheel in the center, like a submarine hatch. Johnny slung the pack over his arm, grabbed the wheel with both hands, and yanked it back and forth. The mechanism finally gave, and the door opened with a stiff shudder. A flash of lightning revealed a narrow chamber and a black hole through which dropped a rusted metal ladder.

"Go on." Kip yelled. "Get inside."

Branches cracked and split, the thrash of falling ice and staccato booms of thunder merging into a continuous roar. Johnny grasped the ladder and swung into the hole, felt his feet touch the first step leading down. Driven by a shrieking wind, hail banged hollowly against the open door and rattled into the cramped space like shrapnel.

Kip pushed into the chamber behind him. "Move," he said. "I can't get all the way in."

Threads of water trickled from Johnny's body and vanished into the black void below. An odd, oily mix of odors rose through the open shaft. He withdrew a sturdy aluminum flashlight from his backpack, clicked it on and pointed the beam down. "There's a tunnel," he said. "It's only about ten feet below."

"I'm not going in there."

"I know what this is. It's an air raid tunnel, in case the enemy bombed them. And they connect the buildings. We could follow it—"

"I'm still not going. Snakes could be down there."

"Shut up about the snakes, okay? Look, I'll go first." Johnny climbed down the decayed steps, holding the flashlight precariously in his right hand. He dropped to the tunnel floor, his Nikes puffing up a cloud of dust. "It's dry. Come on. There's no snakes or spiders or anything."

The concrete passage was cylindrical, about eight feet across, with no cracks or indications it might be unsafe. Light bulbs in protective metal cages hung at intervals from the curved ceiling, but Johnny didn't even look for a switch; the power had probably been shut off for fifty years. He stepped aside as Kip crept down the ladder and landed beside him.

Above, the wind keened past the open door, the sound accompanied by cone-shaped ghosts of lightning flickering down through the overhead shaft. Johnny's flashlight beam probed the tunnel's length and melted into darkness. "Let's go this way," he said, nodding to his left.

Kip dug a flashlight from his backpack. "I'm not so sure—"

A baseball thudded to the floor and rolled against the tunnel wall. Kip retrieved it, blew the grit off, and stuffed it back inside its zippered pocket.

That stupid baseball. Kip took it everywhere. It was like a talisman or something, just because it was autographed. "Come on," Johnny urged. "If we don't see something cool right away, we'll go back." They'd come this far, and he wanted to keep his friend moving before he flaked out and they had to return with nothing to show for their effort. And no *way* was he going to explore the place alone. He moved deeper into the tunnel, the jittering beam of Kip's flashlight joining his own.

They had walked perhaps a hundred yards when the tunnel abruptly ended. Centered in the obstructing wall was another gray, hatch-like door. It squeaked and moaned on its hinges when Johnny tugged the wheel, but opened easily. Cool air rushed to meet them from the darkness beyond.

The beacon of Johnny's flashlight lanced into deep, open space. Sounds of the creaking hinges echoed from the walls of a huge chamber. "Oh, wow!" he said as he stepped across the threshold onto a metal catwalk. Kip brushed up beside him, and both flashlights danced into gloom.

Twenty feet below, louvered machines studded with dials and switches clung to the walls, and consoles with old video monitors, dark and silent, huddled in raised islands across the floor. Cage-like copper coils big enough to hold a tiger gleamed dully in the center of the room, rising to metal poles that vanished into shadows high above.

Kip leaned forward against the railing. "Beam me up, Scotty." He cupped his hands and shouted a loud "Hey!" the distorted echoes slapping back in quick succession.

"Shhhh!" The reflection of Johnny's own whisper sounded eerie, as if someone on the opposite side had admonished him to be silent.

Kip held his hands out. "What?"

"I don't know. Just don't."

The place gave Johnny the major creeps. But, he thought as a shiver raked his spine, this was going to be awesome. He retrieved a small digital camera from his backpack and brought the viewfinder to his eye. The flash exploded, its light instantly devoured by the overwhelming dark. "I need more pictures."

They clattered down a dizzying spiral stairway and stepped onto a dusty concrete floor. More of the submarine-style doors, all of them shut, were inset here and there along the room's curving perimeter. High on the opposite side, two rows of black glass looked out from an observation or control room.

Johnny focused his camera on a hulking machine and triggered another flash. "This is just awesomely cool."

Kip dragged his fingers across the grimy surface of a console. "Looks like they left in a hurry."

Chairs were overturned, and old papers, coffee mugs, and moldering jackets lay scattered around the room.

"Look at that," Johnny said, his flashlight circling an enormous sliding door on their left. "That's where they bring in the big machinery and stuff."

Railroad tracks emerged from beneath the great door and traveled in recessed grooves toward the room's center. Above the rails, chains and hoists dropped down from the shadows, quiet as spider webs.

Johnny approached a bulkhead door straight ahead. "Let's check it out."

As he reached for the wheel, Kip piped up: "Behind door *A* is the beautiful blond babe. Behind door *B* is—"

"Shut up, you emo."

"Yess, Masster."

"Very funny."

"You have no sense of humor."

"Don't you wonder why those people left in such a hurry?"

"Oh, I know. Because a huge Frankensteen monster…and if he came in here, I'd"—Kip made a batting motion with his arms, his flashlight slashing spirals of light across the dark chamber walls—"Ka-bam. Outta' tha' park."

"Screw you. I give up." Johnny grabbed the door's latching mechanism and turned it.

The door groaned open with little effort, revealing concrete steps that fell some ten feet to a wide tunnel. Elevated on stubby trestles above the tunnel floor, the railroad tracks emerged from the main chamber, followed a sharp curve to the left, and arrowed into darkness beyond the flashlights' reach.

Johnny froze. "Listen!"

"Oh, God, what *is* that?"

A moist, deep-throated growl issued from the tunnel and echoed ominously in the still air. The boys flinched back and shot their flashlight beams deeper into the tunnel, probing for the source. The lights flickered from the surface of water rushing within a broad channel and danced across a high, arched ceiling blackened with mold. A hundred feet ahead, beyond a steel handrail, where the lights began to fade, they could see a wide circular pool at the convergence of three canals.

At the pool's center, the water spun around and around, spiraling into a hole of infinite darkness. The funnel's silken mouth widened and contracted every few seconds, making a hollow grumble that made Johnny's neck hairs stand on end. "A whirlpool," he whispered. "That's making the growling sound. It's, like, a big drain or something."

"Dude, I do *not* like this."

Johnny forced his courage up, went down the steps, and began walking alongside the canal, its liquid voice murmuring a vague warning.

"Come on," he said, "Just one more door. I want to find something I can take back...a souvenir."

Kip heaved a sigh and joined him, his flashlight flicking nervously across the tunnel's gray walls. "Yeah, sure," he mumbled. "Let's jump in and go for a swim."

About twenty yards into the tunnel, they turned right and climbed a series of concrete steps to a steel door standing halfway open. Riding a faint current of dank air, the smell of burned machinery, chemicals, and mold drifted from the dark room beyond.

"It's a lab," Johnny said as he stepped inside.

Their flashlight beams glided across rows of electronic equipment and gleamed from tables loaded with tall glass cylinders and coiled chemical apparatus.

Kip wandered into the forest of instruments. "Gnarly," he whispered. "*Look* at this stuff."

"Be careful."

Johnny walked between two long tables, fascinated by the glassware and interconnecting electronics. A fat container, resting at eye level, held something suspended in liquid. Leaning in close, he pointed his light into the amber murk.

The bulbous object inside had convolutions and ridges like a strangely eroded landscape. He jumped back as the shock of recognition hit him. "Brains," he whispered, fear building like a tidal wave. He swept the flashlight along the table, the beam illuminating row upon row of similar vessels, each filled with the same amber fluid, each with a wrinkled gray mass drowning within.

He started at the sound of Kip's voice. "Totally *sick*." Kip was rattling and clinking through instruments and lab tools.

Johnny's own voice came out high and strained, terror constricting like a claw on the back of his neck "Let's get out of here..."

"Check *this* out." Kip stood on the opposite side of the long table, arm extended across its top, cradling something in his hand: a glass cylinder sealed with a metallic cap. Johnny lifted it gingerly and held it before the flashlight.

Suspended within the tube was a curved disk of plastic or glass about two inches across. A number of stiff, silvery filaments of varying length, some about four inches long, stuck out of one end of the disk, giving it the appearance of a jellyfish with a flattened body and straight, skinny tentacles.

"Great souvenir," Johnny said, his fear forgotten. "I'm gonna" keep it." He unzipped his pack and stuffed the tube inside, then pointed his flashlight at the nearest fat jar resting on the table. "Look."

Kip leaned forward and peered into the container, screwing up his face as he registered its contents. "Gross!" He stepped back, his flashlight beam glinting from the identical rows of fluid-filled jars. "What were they *doing* in here?"

Then the light came to rest on another object in an open space beyond the lab bench—a metal table beneath a cluster of dead overhead floodlights, a disturbing bulk covered by a rotted sheet stretched upon its surface.

Although the rational part of Johnny's mind was sending powerful signals to flee, to run, to exit the door, up the stairs and through the tunnel to freedom and light, a siren's voice of curiosity drew him on. Heart thudding in his ears, he walked closer, swept his light along the sheeted mass, and stopped as the beam glinted from a silvery metal contraption at the uppermost end of the table. The apparatus resembled an oversized helmet, but with odd attachments and wires that coiled into it from some kind of electronic device.

And inside the dark cavity of the helmet, brightened by the flashlight's trembling beam, rested a grinning human skull.

Johnny's guts froze. He was looking at an operating table, and a body was strapped to it, its fleshless head pinned and pierced by the helmet, or machine, or whatever it was. The agonized jaw yawned wide. Black filaments branched from the hollow eye sockets, as if someone had taken charcoal and scrawled heavy lines branching like veins over the forehead, back along the temples and from the screaming mouth.

"Oh shit." Kip's voice came out in a constricted, high-pitched chirp. He backed away. "What *is* this place?"

Johnny stood paralyzed, too frightened to remove his eyes from the ghastly apparatus and its tortured remains. Scenes of horror erupted into his conscious thought: Dr. Frankenstein's lab, dead bodies rising to eat the flesh of the living, reanimated corpses with murderous intent...

Then, a terror beyond his wildest nightmares—

With a sudden *snap* and a bright, lingering flash, beyond the bared teeth, inside the darkened helmet with its wires and screws and metal rods, the skull glowed from within, from where the brain should be— glowed orange and red and flickered like an enraged thunderhead.

It happened so very quickly, and Johnny screamed, his body involuntarily twisting to run. Then he felt Kip's fear, heard his terrified wail from the opposite side of the lab table, and looked back. The skull rattled against the metal pins, the cranium pulsed with reddish light.

And through the black eye sockets something phosphorescent came.

"*Run!*"

But Kip was trapped. His only route to freedom was past the operating table and its terrifying burden.

"I can't get out!"

"Jump over! Jump over!" Johnny swept his arms across the black countertop, sending glass vials, jars, test tubes, and electronic parts crashing to the floor. Kip bounced halfway onto the high surface and struggled to pull his body across, his arms making a frantic clawing, swimming motion. Johnny reached out and grasped at his friend's hands. From the corner of his eye he saw the glow moving, heard it pop and sizzle, heard a skittering sound like rats or crabs. "*Come on!*"

Kip's feet met the floor and he bent down to make a leap; then the glow—bright enough to throw stark shadows from the tables and wiring and coiled glass tubing—crept across the floor toward him.

"It's on me...*on me!*" Kip belted out a sound like Johnny had never heard in his entire life, one that made the best screams of horror movies and war films seem phony and contrived, and collapsed into the blue aura throbbing at his feet. There rose a hissing, snapping sound, like he was being burned alive.

"*Kip!*"

Then Johnny saw more of the candescent forms scurry from beneath the table, swarming after *him*. He turned and fled, galvanized by the most consuming terror he had ever known. He almost collided with the door as he pelted through the opening and down the concrete steps.

His left heel lost traction on the damp concrete surface and he fell. The sharp steps hammered his back, and as his arms flew outward to slow his descent, the flashlight leapt from his hand. He felt himself roll across the narrow walkway, and realized with horror that as he crawled after the flashlight and his hands and knees dropped onto a steep incline, that he was tumbling toward the canal's dark, rushing water.

Cold engulfed him as he plunged in. He forced his head above the surface, coughing, gagging, feeling the tenacious grip of the current. The flashlight's hazy greenish eye raced away below him, glaring up from the depths. The light suddenly made a rapid pinwheel spin that briefly illuminated a smooth, transparent, tornado-shaped tube before it winked into a hole of utter blackness.

Then he heard the growling, sucking noise.

He turned and swam with every furious ounce of strength he could muster, kicking and thrashing against the relentless current. His hands struck the concrete ledge, grasped, clawed, lost purchase. The funneling sound grew louder. The whirling black tube drew him closer.

And in an interminable, agonizing moment of blind, shrieking panic, he began to spin, the hollow vacuum-roar thundering within his chest, his explosive screams strangled into stuttering liquid sobs as the vortex snatched him down.

2

Clutching a coffee mug in one hand and a sheaf of warrants in the other, Sheriff Greg Colvin stared through his office window and watched hailstones detonate across the unprotected cars in the courthouse parking lot. He wondered if all eight of the department's cruisers would be afflicted with ice-induced craters. Fortunately, his car was beneath one of the protective awnings so generously provided by the county.

A cannonade of thunder pounded the old building's granite walls, rattling the windows and vibrating the floors before rolling off in a wave of descending grumbles.

"Sheriff, I still can't raise anyone," came the crusty voice of dispatcher Margie Pruett. She had turned around in her seat, radio static raging in the background, a disgusted look on her face and a cigarette cradled between the first two fingers of her left hand.

"Margie," Deputy Rick Lewis said, dropping a stack of folders on his desk with a pop, "Try again. I'm sure that tender voice of yours'll cut right through."

She cackled. "Beats smoke signals, Tonto."

Colvin wrinkled his nose. On humid days, the cigarette smoke interbred with pungent ghosts from the liquefied chewing tobacco that once fermented in the ancient building's plentiful brass spittoons. Cigarettes in the courthouse were not strictly legal, but Margie was the best dispatcher the Grayson County Sheriff's Office ever had, and everyone winked at the offense while she puffed her way toward an early grave.

Colvin handed Lewis the warrants. His deputy was full-blooded Apache, tall and slender, with a head of thick black hair he wore braided into a ponytail. Margie was Navajo, short, round, with an energetic personality and an attitude primed for mischief. These facts, combined with their generally obstreperous personalities, mixed as a catalyst for politically incorrect gibes.

"I'll be gone for an hour," Colvin said. "You two lovebirds can anchor the office."

Lewis stared at the paperwork. "Trade you, Sheriff."

"Pass."

Lewis heaved a resigned sigh. "Greg, don't you ever miss, you know, the city, want to move back, see some real action?"

"Hell no. I prefer the bucolic quiet of the small town. I'll never go back."

Margie fired up another cigarette, her plump face breaking into a grin. "Don't ever say 'never.' Never is a shit magnet. If you say it, it'll be on your plate next morning."

"Well, thanks for that eloquent bit of wisdom. I'll keep it in mind." Colvin shook his head. The department could definitely use some decorum.

***

Wearing a broad-brimmed hat and a tan raincoat with SHERIFF in bold reflective letters across the back, Colvin slogged hunch-shouldered through the downpour and climbed into the cruiser. He adjusted the radio's squelch, receiving only garbled interference.

Modern FM transceivers were supposed to be virtually immune from ordinary static, but radio and cellphone reception was an intermittent proposition in Grayson County. Superstitious people attributed the problem to the old military base north of town, but the idea was ridiculous; the base had been abandoned long ago, dead for some 50 years.

He backed out into the torrent, thankful the hail and wind had diminished, and drove down Main Street toward the highway, wipers at maximum. In five minutes, he found what he expected: a wreck at the confluence of two county roads by a steep curve cut into the hillside.

An suv had clipped the guardrail and upended in a gravel ditch funneling runoff into the Tehuec River three hundred feet below. A state trooper's car was already there, light bar slashing blue stripes up the vertical sides of the canyon. A line of flares glared and hissed against the flooded pavement.

Colvin toggled on his overheads and pulled up behind the trooper's vehicle. As he lowered the window, one of the officers approached and leaned in close, rainwater streaming off his hat. Colvin knew the man—James Skeller—a thirty-something, by-the-book trooper who had once been a local and accepted the state job to broaden his horizons. "Your communications gear working, Sheriff?"

"Nope."

"We need an ambulance. There's a man and a woman. She's cut up pretty bad, unconscious. We're afraid to move either one of them."

Colvin shifted the cruiser into reverse. "I'll take care of it, James."

A mile south, Colvin pulled into Big John's Gas N' Go and dialed Grayson Medical using the pay phone. The rain settled into a drizzle as he walked back to the car, and the sky was brightening to slate gray, the dark cumulonimbus mass of rain and hail dragging southeastward. As he slid into the driver's seat, he keyed the mike, and Margie responded.

"Static's gone, Sheriff."

"Five minutes earlier, you could've saved me fifty cents."

"Got a ten-hundred from PD, in Cielo"

Cielo was a tiny, working-class town eight miles northwest of Kellsburg. It had been thrown together in 1942 to serve the old North Ridge Air Defense Base and was now sustained by tourism and Los Alamos employees who preferred seclusion bordering on isolation.

"Whose request?"

"Coroner says it's a strange one, Sheriff. They want someone with forensics experience."

Margie quoted the address and Colvin pulled onto the two-lane county blacktop that wound northwest into the Los Cabrisos Hills, toward Cielo. He glanced at the dashboard clock: 3:35. The rain had stopped, and high-altitude winds were tearing ragged holes in the somber sky, allowing a few fleeting rays of pale sunlight to sweep through.

Ten minutes later he parked in front of a white, one-story bungalow, one of hundreds constructed when the base was running at full tilt, before the disaster had shut it down tight. A Kellsburg police cruiser and the coroner's unmarked car occupied the short, narrow driveway that led to the decrepit house and sagging garage.

The front yard was overgrown and the clapboard house was in bad need of paint, the only color provided by a slash of trumpet vines clinging to the porch railing and arch. A few curious neighbors, old and decaying to blend with the neighborhood, stood in the next yard, sheltering beneath umbrellas and watching with frowns and pursed lips.

Colvin walked onto the creaking porch and through the front door, which had been propped wide open. The odor constricted his windpipe.

"Nice smell, huh, Sheriff?" The young officer stood a few feet away, his nose scrunched in distaste.

"What the hell *is* that?"

The officer tilted his head. "Down the hall. Back room. Farnsworth and the Chief's there."

Colvin crossed the living room, his steps rattling the shelved bric-a-brac as the uneven floor bounced beneath his weight. A doorway at the end of the hall opened onto a small den furnished with an outdated television, a worn La-Z-Boy recliner, and a card table with four folding chairs.

A flash blanched the dimly lit room as Coroner Jim Farnsworth triggered his camera. Gordon Leinway, Kellsburg's portly police chief, stood with his hands thrust deep into his pockets, forehead pinched in a frown, his stare focused on something beyond the recliner. Colvin stepped around the big chair, his eyes finding the source of the pungent, chemical-animal odor that permeated the house. "Jesus Christ!"

After twelve years in law enforcement, the last four as Sheriff, he thought he'd seen just about every form of physical insult that could be wrought upon the human body. But this was a new one.

The Chief finally spoke. "It's Catherine Klatty. At least we think it is."

The wreckage of a woman's body lay in a twisted heap between the recliner and an ancient, floor-model radio, one with a big round dial and an arched wooden cabinet. Klatty (if it *was* Klatty) was slumped forward as if she had tottered from the chair, her spine bent backward at a severe angle, head mashed against the base of the speaker grille. A skeletal hand lay across the cabinet in a frozen grope for the controls.

Her skin, still appearing soft and supple, sagged like a loose sack against the skeleton, as if the underlying mass of fat and muscle had been magically stripped away. Partly charred clothing—a short sleeved blouse and flowered dress—draped in oversized folds across her frame, indicating there was no more substance to her torso than there was to her skull and arms. Klatty was, quite literally, a bag of bones.

Colvin bent down and studied the collapsed face and outstretched hand. He narrowed his eyes and frowned. Wormy black lines, thinly coated with a translucent substance, bled from Klatty's splayed fingers, crawled across the radio's wooden surface, and converged on the volume knob. More tracks, heavier than the ones from her fingers, radiated from her glistening eye sockets and gaping mouth, crept across the speaker grille, and merged with the dark trails branching into the radio. "What do you make of these marks?"

"No idea," Farnsworth replied. "Thought you'd have some theory."

Colvin flinched as a zag of lightning from the departing storm flickered into the room and reanimated the grisly skull with fluttering shadows. He stood and turned to the coroner. "How long…?"

"Probably dead less than a day. Hard to be more exact because of the condition of the corpse, which is impossibly abnormal anyway. What's odd, too, is there's no insects."

"A neighbor made the call," Leinway added. "Said she visited Klatty last night around eight, and she was fine then. Klatty didn't answer when she called around two this afternoon. The neighbor, Gail Norton, got worried when she didn't answer an hour later. Used her key to get in, saw the body, freaked out, and called Kellsburg PD at three o'clock. Officer Terrance answered the call." He stared at the body in silence. "Looks sorta' like, what do you call it—spontaneous incineration."

"Spontaneous human combustion."

"Yeah, that."

Colvin's gaze went from the corpse to the radio, and the hairs on the back of his neck took on a life of their own and came erect, sending a chill creeping along his spine. He remembered rumors about Catherine Klatty. Her husband died in 1962 during the disaster at the military base. His body, along with several hundred others, had never been recovered. The woman had gone a little off her rocker, thinking she could still hear her husband's voice calling out to her late at night on the radio. There was a cruel, singsong rhyme children had taunted her with for as far back as anyone could remember.

> *Crazy, Crazy Cathy Klatty*
> *Husband died and she went batty*
> *She says she isn't lonely, though*
> *'Cause she hears him on the radio*

"That radio," Colvin said, his eyes lingering on the instrument's tall wooden cabinet. "Is it still plugged in?"

The coroner looked behind the set and followed the cord to a point where it disappeared behind the television. "Yeah. It's still in the wall. And there's another wire…"

"An antenna wire."

"Yeah, I guess. It goes up, maybe into the attic. What of it?"

"I don't know." Colvin bent and peered at the volume knob, where the black trail from Klatty's fingers led.

"You think she was electrocuted or something?"

Colvin stood and shrugged. "See if you can pull that plug. And be careful."

The coroner worked the plug back and forth. "I think the thing's welded in there, like from a short circuit. Maybe that explains why some of the lights don't work. The radio shorted and blew a fuse. These old houses probably still have fuses."

"I'll check that." Colvin walked down the hallway into the kitchen, which looked like it had the original cabinets and appliances from the 1940s. He found the fuse box on the wall inside a small pantry. One of the fifteen-amp screw-in fuses had, indeed, blown. The label on the cover said den/bathroom.

He returned to the den. "Yeah, it's the fuse."

Chief Leinway scribbled in a small notebook. "So, you think maybe lightning hit the antenna, or zapped the wiring, and killed her?"

The coroner hunched over the body, pointed the camera, and triggered another flash. "Never heard of lightning doing anything like this before."

Colvin thought for a moment. "I suggest bringing in a specialist—an engineer, or somebody with the power company, somebody who might be familiar with...electrocution." He turned to leave and the police chief fell in step behind him.

"Craziest damn thing I ever seen, Greg."

"Saw."

"Huh?"

"Grammar."

Colvin paused in the hallway outside a bedroom door and turned to Leinway. "Mind if I have a look?"

"Help yourself. We didn't find nothing suspicious."

Klatty's small bed was neatly made. A bedside table held an ivory-colored windup clock, a box of tissue, and several medicines in prescription bottles. He looked in the tiny closet, where dresses and overcoats hung in a neat row. Finally, he turned to the cedar chest at the foot of the bed. On top rested a tattered photo album. Colvin opened it and thumbed through the pages: wedding pictures of a smiling, youthful bride and groom—probably Catherine Klatty and her husband, William—a little girl and boy at Disneyland, assorted relatives, friends. Then, pages of yellowed newspaper clippings dated 1962.

Headlines screamed about the tragedy at North Ridge Air Defense Base, how a series of explosions had blown the hell out of a dozen buildings, including the hospital, and killed hundreds. One clipping included a long list of the missing. William Klatty was underlined.

Colvin asked Leinway, "You remember that kid's rhyme they used to sing?"

"Crazy Cathy Klatty?"

"Yeah."

"Spooky. Kinda makes you wonder if this is some kind of wacko prank. Like maybe they substituted somebody else's body…"

Colvin gave the chief a look.

"Or not."

"Let me know when the ME makes his report."

Leinway nodded. "Good luck with the referendum."

"Thanks, Gordon. Give my regards to Shirley and the kids."

Colvin left the house, glad to leave the stench behind him. The radio clipped to his belt squawked as he stepped from the porch, and he heard his number called. "Sheriff, two twelve-year-old boys reported missing since morning, both with addresses in Tanglewood."

The nominal waiting period for adult missing persons was twenty-four hours, but a missing kid could trigger the Amber Alert in a heartbeat if the circumstances were right. He waved off the three local news hounds lurking in the yard, ducked beneath the yellow tape, and climbed into the patrol car, trying to shake off a creeping sense of foreboding and the image of Klatty's shriveled corpse, with its groping hand and lightning-shadowed skull.

3

The two-lane road wound around rolling hills bristling with lush stands of pine and spruce. Round, sand-colored boulders bulged from frowning granite cliffs, the landscape highlighted in soft patterns by shafts of sunlight sweeping through the dissolving clouds.

Colvin pulled into the Tanglewood entrance, drove west for two miles, and turned northward again, heading onto a wide lane that wound into the ritzy part of the development. Tanglewood was an unincorporated resort six miles north of Kellsburg, beyond the city limits. The Sheriff's department was the only provider of law enforcement there, and local volunteers handled fire and emergency services. Kellsburg would have died long ago if not for Tanglewood, and Tanglewood existed because of the leafy hillsides and the crystalline waters of Lake Arrowhead.

A large ranch-style house, framed by tall pines still shedding their burden of rain, sat at the end of a U-shaped drive. Colvin could see a broad deck that offered an expansive view of the lake, whose slate-gray surface was still chopped and darkened by the passing storm. He pulled up behind a silver Mercedes station wagon nosed into a carport to the left of the house.

The missing boy's mother, Joan Helstrom, greeted him from the porch. Standing beside her, a big German shepherd growled a warning. She uttered a command, and the dog fell silent and sat down, his baleful eyes still fixed on Colvin.

Helstrom's slender body was poured into a turquoise and black jogging outfit. Short, black hair curled slightly forward below her ears, framing an attractive, oval face marred by worry. She snapped her cellphone shut and held it out, exasperated. "I can't reach him," she said. "He doesn't answer, even when the signal goes through. Johnny's been gone since nine o'clock this morning—he and his friend, Kip, riding their bikes. He was under strict orders to return by noon."

She ushered Colvin inside. The house looked more like an upscale, permanent home than a vacation house; a parlor grand piano sat at one end of the wide living room, an arched stone fireplace at the other. A polished oak stairway curved up to a second-story landing that wrapped around three sides of the room. Colvin glimpsed a deep, open area beyond the landing, and hallways leading off into the remaining upstairs.

Mrs. Helstrom was prepared. She held out a four-by-five-inch photo of two swim-suited boys clowning on a wooden pier behind the house. Johnny was broad-shouldered, muscular, with medium-length black hair. Kip was small-framed, with light blond hair that brushed his shoulders.

"I've been speaking with Jennifer Hawkins," Helstrom said. "She's Kip's mother. She...well...she has a bit of a drinking problem. Anyway, she hasn't seen them either. Johnny was supposed to be at Kip's all morning, then both of them were supposed to come here for lunch." She glanced down at the German shepherd, which had followed them inside. "And Max, he's a highly-trained dog. He goes everywhere with Johnny. They're inseparable. But this morning he was closed up in the backyard."

Both fathers were away on business and wouldn't return until the following day. Colvin asked the usual questions: what clothing were they wearing, where did the boys usually hang out, who were their friends, and had anyone seen any suspicious persons in the area. He looked up from his notes. "I'll put a bulletin out, drive around, starting at the marina—"

She interrupted. "I just thought of something. I think I saw him wearing his backpack. He wouldn't take it unless..." She motioned. "Please come with me, to his room."

He followed her upstairs and down a carpeted hall into a large bedroom that looked out onto the lake. Posters of rock bands, sports heroes, and movies covered the walls. Military posters joined the mix— Air Force, Special Forces, SEALS.

On a table near the window, toy soldiers and an array of miniature armored vehicles raised their weapons in frozen battle. In a separate theater, *Star Wars* figures squared off against alien monsters creeping over a realistic landscape of rocks and sand.

Helstrom opened the mirrored door to a wide closet, and Colvin saw several camouflage jackets hanging beside jeans and shirts. A pair of black, lace-up boots was parked neatly beside a row of scuffed sneakers. "I was right," she said. "His backpack is missing."

"Would he have gone camping?"

"No. But ..." She looked around the room, as if searching for something. "That military base..."

"North Ridge?"

"He's been talking about it for months...how great it would be to explore."

Colvin walked to the boy's desk and looked at the computer, a late model with a wide monitor—better than the one in the sheriff's office.

The winking light indicated the computer was in sleep mode. "Mind if I have a look?"

He tapped a key and the screen lit. Colvin studied the image for a moment, then scrolled until he found a caption. "This is a satellite photo of the North Ridge Air Defense Base. Looks like it's from one of those Internet sites." A notebook rested beside the keyboard. Colvin flipped it open and halted on a page labeled NRAD. "This sketch shows compass bearings, pathways, streets, buildings."

Helstrom looked over his shoulder. "Oh my God. You don't suppose..."

"Well, you said his bike's gone, backpack too."

Her frown deepened. "That would be just like him, to go in there. We warned him about that place." She shuddered. "With this storm..."

The two-way crackled: "Sheriff, hikers found a young boy in the Tehuec River." There was a sharp intake of breath from Joan Helstrom, and Colvin waved her silent. "Ambulance is en route to Grayson Medical."

"Roger. Did you get a name?"

"Negative, Sheriff. The child is unconscious." The boy's description followed: dark hair, blue eyes, about twelve years old. Had to be Johnny Helstrom.

Colvin turned to Mrs. Helstrom. "Come on. I'll give you a lift."

***

The two-story Grayson Medical Center was tucked into a hillside on the west side of Kellsburg, two blocks off County Road 4. Thanks to a handful of wealthy patrons, the hospital was well staffed and had an excellent trauma unit.

Johnny was in a shared room on the second floor. His face was pale and bruised, his eyes obscured by knots of black hair curling across his brow.

A tube from an IV rack snaked down to the boy's left wrist. He looked up as Joan Helstrom cried out and rushed to his side. "Mom," he murmured. He hugged her with his free arm as she kissed his forehead and stroked his tousled hair.

Dr. Carol Myerson stood at the foot of the bed, her curvaceous form swallowed by the unflattering white coat. She lowered a clipboard and smiled at Colvin, then looked at Mrs. Helstrom. "He's been awake for a few minutes now. Lots of scrapes and bruises. No broken bones."

Myerson pulled Colvin aside. "He's got a mild concussion, was semiconscious when they brought him into the ER. Hikers found him at the riverbank. Apparently, he nearly drowned."

"I need to ask him a few questions."

She glanced at her patient. "Just for a minute."

Colvin pulled up a chair and the boy turned to face him. "Your friend, Kip, do you know where he is?"

"Inside…"

"Inside where?"

Johnny's eyes flicked to his mother, then back to Colvin. "I don't know."

"You and Kip entered the old air base, right?"

The boy nodded. "We crawled under the fence. Left our bikes, walked. I used my compass, but it kept wiggling and we got lost. We went about half a mile, east, I guess. Then the storm came up and we found this, like, concrete thing with a door. We went inside." His eyes darted downward. "We walked through a tunnel into this huge room with all this equipment, then a smaller one. I picked up some junk, just for souvenirs, and took some pictures." His voice tightened. "And Kip saw this table...and a body." The boy's face twisted with some horrible memory. "Something started glowing. We ran, and Kip screamed. And then I fell into the water and got sucked down..." He looked up, eyes pleading, brimming with tears. "You're gonna' look for him, aren't you?"

"Sure. Right away." Colvin stood and turned to Joan Helstrom, who was shaking her head in disbelief, as if her son were suffering from hallucinations. "We'll get a team together, search the grounds, see if we can find that tunnel." To Johnny: "You said you took some pictures."

"In my backpack."

Colvin pulled the still-damp backpack out of the closet and poked around until he found the camera. Then his hand closed around a glass cylinder. He lifted it out and stared at the contents: a strange, curved disk with a mass of thin, rigid wires jutting from one side. "What's this?"

"That's from the room...inside the tunnel."

He held it up for Carol Myerson to see. Her brows knitted, and she shook her head, puzzled. "Odd looking. It's hermetically sealed, padded against impact. Looks electronic."

Colvin pocketed the camera and stuffed the cylinder back inside the pack. He turned to Johnny. "I'd like to borrow this too, okay?"

The boy nodded.

Colvin left, toting the pack, and called his office from the nurses' station. "We may have a kid lost on the old North Ridge Air Base," he told Deputy Tom Grove. I want you to round up a search party. I'll call Judge Haywood and get a warrant just in case the owners have a problem. See if Tex Kaleb and his dog are available." There was dead silence at the other end. "You still with me, Tom?"

"Yeah, Sheriff. But the old air base...wow."

"Not afraid, now, are you, Tom?"

"I'll get right on it, Sheriff."

Colvin hung up and checked his watch. By the time he got a team together, it would almost be dark, and with the reputation the North Ridge base had, it was the last place on earth he'd want a kid to be lost.

4

The intercom buzzed just as Marty Berringer completed a masterful shot with the new Guerin Rife hybrid putter. He watched the monogrammed Titleist silently arc across the maroon carpet and click home into the tumbler ten feet away. Satisfied, he leisurely twirled the five-hundred-dollar club, rested it across his shoulder, and punched the intercom button. "Ellen," he said. "I'm taking lunch. No calls...no visitors."

"Well, you'd better take this one, Mr. Berringer. It's Mr. Kendron."

"Thomas?"

"None other."

Marty dropped the club, pulled his leather chair close to the desk, and lifted the receiver. He leaned forward, brows pinched in concentration.

"Mr. Kendron?"

A dry voice, almost a whisper, hissed into his ear. "Marty, I need you to take care of a little matter for me."

This was extraordinary. In Marty's two years with Kendron Technologies, he'd not seen or spoken with the Old Man, nor had he met anyone who had. Thomas Kendron was eighty years old, still corporate president, and rumor had it he was plugged into more tubing and electronics than the Space Shuttle.

"As you may know, Marty," the voice continued, "this company owns a property in New Mexico that was once the North Ridge Air Defense Base."

"Yes sir...I think—"

"A child wandered onto the property today and is missing..." The voice faded, replaced by a deep gasping sound. *Is he on a respirator?* The dry crackle began again: "We've been handed a search warrant permitting the local authorities to enter the property."

"I see..."

"We want to cooperate, but"—his voice dropped to a growl—"the property is still quite dangerous. I want you to stop them from entering. Tell them we're working with proper authorities to conduct a safe search."

"Yes, sir. But what about Stephenson and Coleman? They handle your real estate."

"I need someone more resourceful. Someone who can handle legal matters with a modicum of tact. Someone I can trust to control matters."

"Control?"

"Liability to the company. Toxic. Dangerous. I'm sending others with you to help with matters, and as your personal protection."

Personal protection?

"Meet them at the helipad in two hours." Kendron hung up.

Marty dropped the phone into its cradle, cast a wistful glance at the golf ball nesting in the overturned glass, and heaved a long sigh. This was absurd. If he was being groomed for a major position with the company, this visit to Podunk was a hell of a way to prepare him. He'd been snapped up by the company right out of Harvard Law, and for the last two years had been bored out of his skull with minor legal matters. He'd never been invited to a board meeting, never met any of the really big dogs. If the pay and perks weren't so high, plus the promise of better things to come, he'd have left months ago and joined one of the big Manhattan firms.

***

An hour and forty-five minutes later, starving for lunch, Marty was strapping himself into the middle seat of the company's posh Bell 430 helicopter, its rotors beating a slow rhythm as it perched on the rooftop forty stories above 45th Street.

A frowning man in a white lab coat trundled toward the chopper and loaded two aluminum instrument cases into the rear compartment. As he climbed into the front passenger seat, Marty leaned forward, extended his hand, and introduced himself.

The man returned Marty's smile with a sour look. "Dr. Carl Heim." Instead of accepting the proffered handshake, he snatched a pen from his coat pocket and began scribbling in a small notebook.

The left door opened, and Charles Sweeney, clad in his usual pinstriped Armani, swung into the cabin, sat down beside Marty, and smoothed back a few errant locks of immaculately coifed gray hair.

Marty was taken aback. Sweeney was KT's legal Rottweiler, usually busy fending off attacks by the FTC and disaffected users of the company's products. Why was this powerhouse needed to help shoo some small-town goobers off the company's abandoned property in the middle of nowhere?

Sweeney offered a handshake. "Glad you're aboard, Berringer."

"I'm surprised the company is sending in the hotshots."

The senior attorney consulted his Rolex and looked forward. "These choppers are too damned loud for conversation. I'll fill you in when we reach the airport."

As the pilot twisted the throttles up, two burly men wearing KT blazers and dark glasses—*bodyguards?*—strapped themselves into the rear seats.

Marty's gut lurched as the helicopter lifted up and forward, gliding toward the edge of building. He frowned; the assignment was getting weirder by the minute, and he wanted answers.

— 5 —

Colvin unrolled the plans across the conference room's scarred oak table and weighted the corners down. The first page showed the North Ridge Air Defense Base boundaries. NRAD was roughly square, about three miles on each side. The river feeding Lake Arrowhead formed the eastern border. To the west and north were deep woods. The southern boundary approached Kellsburg, Tanglewood, and the old Cielo military housing development, the one where Catherine Klatty lived—before someone, or some *thing*, converted her into a wrinkled mass of skin and bone.

Two roads entered the base, one on the north, coming from Perrin, the other on the south side, leading into Cielo and Kellsburg. Both of the long entrance roads had been destroyed years ago by the military and were now impassable. The two kids, according to Johnny Helstrom, had followed the southern road on their mountain bikes, entered the base, and walked roughly east for a half mile before stumbling into a tunnel.

The next page showed a map of the grounds and structures. On a separate sheet, Colvin made a rough drawing showing building placements and distances. There wasn't time to make a copy of the huge map and reduce its size for field use.

Deputy Rick Lewis stumped into the room. "The G-Med chopper is tied up on a run into Albuquerque, and the one at Los Alamos is in maintenance."

"Go out of state if you have to. I want help by tomorrow morning."

Lewis slapped a folder onto the table. "Here's the search warrant. I had a copy made for each team, in case, you know, Kendron Technologies gives attitude. Oh, yeah. Parnell interviewed Kip Hawkins' mom, Becky. Said she was drunk as a skunk, didn't give a frack about her kid's whereabouts. The old man is in Chicago. He's flying in tomorrow."

Colvin nodded, tapped the elevations. "There aren't any underground structures here."

"That's all the county had."

Colvin handed the Helstrom boy's waterlogged camera to the deputy. "See if forensics can get the images off this. If they can't, take it to the university. They've got a computer department. Make it a priority."

Lewis slid a Post-it note in front of Colvin. "I finally got through to Kendron Technologies. Here's the number for a Philip Dodgsen, one of their top guys. Total asshole. Says he'll only speak to you and that no one can enter the base."

Colvin snatched up the paper "You think you'd get some cooperation, especially since it's a lost kid." He walked to his office, pulled the chair to his desk, and punched in the phone number. A secretary answered, and Colvin drummed his fingers on the desk as five long minutes dragged by, eating time he needed to find the missing boy.

Finally, a deep brusque voice answered, and Colvin began calmly explaining the situation. "Mr. Dodgsen, two young boys wandered onto the North Ridge Air Base this morning, and we believe one of them—"

Dodgsen interrupted. "Sheriff Colvin, do not enter the North Ridge property under any circumstances. Your warrant is irrelevant. The property is too dangerous."

"What dangers?"

"Much of that is classified. But for now assume toxic substances."

"What about the tunnels..."

"That's all I have to say."

"Mr. Dodgsen, a child is lost on your *toxic* property—" There was a click and a buzz, and Colvin was talking to a dead line. He stared at the receiver for a beat, then spoke under his breath: "You, sir, just made a very big mistake."

***

An hour later, Colvin and Deputy Frank Parnell hooked up the department's ATV behind Colvin's cruiser and headed north on State Highway 501. A mile past Tanglewood, Colvin pulled onto an unmarked blacktop road and drove eastward, toward the river. He swerved around the rotting barricades and warning signs and parked in front of a high chain-link fence obscured by a heavy overgrowth of vines and trees.

This was the outermost perimeter of NRAD, the first of two fenced boundaries enclosing the property. The entrance road, which had been bulldozed and blasted into a crumbled mess, angled through the gate and vanished into the dense woods beyond. The road inside the fence had been purposely destroyed in 1964, and the base sealed off. Peppered with mature trees and riddled with craters and broken slabs of asphalt, it was totally useless.

A pickup stopped behind Colvin, and deputies Lewis and Grove climbed out, banged metal ramps onto the trailer, and rolled four Honda ATVs onto the ground.

Grove walked up to Colvin, his eyes on the shattered road. "I'm not sure even the Hondas can drive through that crap, Sheriff."

Colvin lifted the big bolt cutter from the cruiser's trunk and walked toward the gate. "We're about to find out." The massive gate had sagged and twisted between its rusted steel posts, leaving a gap just wide enough to have allowed passage of the two kids and their bicycles. Colvin placed the cutter's jaws across the hasp, heaved, and the steel gave way with a snap. With Grove's help, he muscled the gate open.

There was a chugging sound as a battered and smoking pickup truck labored up the road behind them. The brakes squealed as it ground to a stop beside Colvin's car. A door creaked open and a bearded man in coveralls and a grimy undershirt stepped out and graced the asphalt with a brown squirt of chewing tobacco. Behind him, a huge bloodhound launched from the cab, its tail wagging in big circular arcs. The man tugged the leash and approached Colvin with an extended hand. "Howdy, Sheriff."

"Thanks for coming on such short notice, Mr. Kaleb."

"Ain't no problem, 'specially if there's a lost kid."

"It's about half a mile to the second gate. You ever driven one of these ATVs?"

"Got one myself. Jake's used to ridin'. He'll set just fine." Kaleb scratched his beard and squinted into the woods. "Main problem is whether the rain warshed the scent away. But if it's doable, ol' Jake'll do it. Won't you boy?" He cast a loving look at the dog, which wagged more furiously.

Colvin signaled the deputies, straddled one of the Hondas, and cranked the two-stroke engine to life. "All right. Let's get started."

They rode single file through the gate and into the wood, keeping the destroyed road to their left, grinding in low gear through the grasping brush. They passed beneath the sunlight-robbing boughs of older trees, and the ground cover finally thinned, inviting faster travel. Colvin led the way over a hill, wrestled the ATV through a watery pothole, and braked. Here was the second gate.

A dying sun painted the ragged clouds crimson and reflected red and gold from rainwater pooled in the artificial craters. The wood was fading to black, its long-fingered shadows groping ominously across the ruined entrance road. Colvin dismounted and stared at the angry, vine-shrouded guardhouse; the flattened concrete dome and horizontal gun slit reminded him of a WW II pillbox.

There was a crunch of footsteps as Lewis walked up beside him. "Jeez, would'ya look at that? Those kids had more guts than I would."

"They went through here," came Parnell's voice. He was holding up a stiff flap of fence. To his right, bicycle handlebars glinted through the brush.

Colvin used the bolt cutters again, this time the heavy lock requiring all his strength to break. The chain rattled free from the steel frame and the gate shivered open on rusted hinges. He cupped his hands and shouted the lost boy's name into the darkening woods.

Only the echoes sighed back.

Colvin pulled the compass and GPS unit from his pack, took a bearing, and led the others through the entrance. Stopping beside the bunker, he flicked the beam of his flashlight through the shattered window. Wind-driven leaves and pine needles had piled several feet deep, smothering the rusted shells of a metal desk and chair. The odor of mold and decay wafted from the interior. No sign of disturbance.

Parnell walked to the fence and untied a cotton sack stuffed with Kip Hawkin's clothing. Kaleb took it and opened the sack wide before Jake's eager, snuffling nostrils. The dog buried its muzzle in the proffered items, making a rapid series of sniffs and grunts as he locked in the smells.

Kaleb released several feet of leash, and Jake immediately began tracing a zigzag pattern, nose to the ground. "Seek, Jake. Seek."

The group walked behind Kaleb at a distance sufficient to keep their own scents from contaminating the faint trail. After twenty minutes, Colvin checked the GPS. They were six-hundred yards northeast of the gate, and Jake was still going strong, tugging Kaleb first one way, then another as the dog's amazing olfactory system sifted and sorted the odors rising from the rain-soaked earth.

Fallen and splintered limbs and the occasional uprooted tree were evidence of the furious storm that had passed through the area earlier that day. Now the quiet air had chilled, and a creeping fog rose from the ground. Odd, Colvin thought, that even the sound of crickets was absent in this part of the woods.

Colvin again held the compass beneath the flashlight's beam. The instrument indicated magnetic north with the same precision as the GPS unit, its steel needle steady and constant; Johnny Helstrom must have been mistaken about his own compass's erratic behavior.

But as Colvin watched, the needle began to oscillate, swinging quickly right, then left. It finally stopped about thirty degrees east of its former position. The Helstrom boy was right: something *was* interfering, pulling the needle off track. If the two kids had intended to go northeast, toward the administration building, the wandering compass would have instead pointed them straight for the old medical complex.

Grove was watching over Colvin's shoulder. "Maybe there's a pile of metal underground or something..." He stopped in mid sentence. The needle jerked, wavered, then began rotating again, this time to the west. "What the *Hell*?"

"Shit," Colvin muttered, looking down at the GPS. "Now I can't even get the satellites."

There was a quick rustle of footsteps and the jangle of dog tags as Kaleb, his flashlight beam slashing erratically through the fog, approached at a trot. He and the dog had done an about-face and were headed back, Jake straining at the leash. The bloodhound's tail was tucked between its legs, its tongue lolling, eyes wild and white.

Kaleb slowed as he passed Colvin, a deep frown cleaving his hirsute face. "Somethin's wrong here, Sheriff...real wrong." He restrained the dog, both hands grasping the taut leash, his body leaning against the animal's insistent pull. "Jake's spooked somethin' awful. Don't know what got into him. Never seen him act like this before." Kaleb looked back over his shoulder as he hurried on. "I'm done here, Sheriff. I'm real sorry."

Lewis joined Colvin and Grove, their flashlights melding into a bright pool of light on the forest floor.

"We're screwed," Colvin said. "There's no way to navigate, and if anyone gets lost out here, they're just compounding the problem." Lewis looked around, studying the terrain. "We can set up camp by the gate," he said. "Take it slow until things clear up."

"That would work." Colvin thought for a moment. "I'll take Frank back with me. We'll have search teams organized by mid- morning, and maybe we'll have a helicopter." He unsnapped his radio and keyed the mike. Margie Pruett's voice scratched back, distorted beyond intelligibility.

Like the squad-car radios, his portable was an FM digital, not easily affected by random static. Now it hummed like a high voltage power line, the sound rising and falling in a disturbing, repeated pattern.

He stared into the enveloping night. *Yeah. What the Hell.*

6

he headlights punched through the gathering fog and illuminated a rust-stained sign: **KELLSBURG SUBSTATION**. Beyond the chain-link fence, towering high voltage insulators, transformers, inductors, and capacitors loomed through the haze like robotic ghosts.

Senior lineman Ed Danforth pulled the big truck to a stop and handed the gate key to his assistant, Jerry Martin, who was dribbling crumbs onto the seat as he finished off his second bag of nacho-cheese chips. Martin wordlessly took the key, climbed out, and unlocked the gate, swinging it wide. Danforth gunned the truck through, stopped, and listened.

No sixty-cycle hum or soft sputter of electrical energy came from the system. There was only the hollow soughing of deep woods and the patter of water as the station shed fog-borne moisture.

The control board back at the main station had indicated an open line, which probably meant a lightning strike had blown the arrestors or tripped a breaker. With this substation down, a hundred homes in Tanglewood and Cielo were dark, occupants impatiently waiting for the electric power they took for granted. People also took linemen for granted, Danforth thought, the guys who worked in every conceivable weather condition, day or night, wrestling with energy that could blow a man to vapors before you could blink.

No matter. He'd retire in two years and spend the rest of his days on the porch of his lake cabin, fishing and listening to every sporting event played on the planet.

Martin climbed back inside. "It's quiet."

Danforth drove to the right, the tires crunching over the gravel drive. "The main feed is on the west side. We'll pull the plug, then check the system." His assistant was young, just learning the ropes, so Danforth always laid out the plan. "If we're lucky, we'll reset, kick it on, and go home."

He stopped beside the squat tower that supported the lightning arrestors, then climbed out and played his flashlight over the massive porcelain insulators. "No sign of a flashover, but we'll have to put a meter on it."

They walked to the disconnect lever, cranked the circuit open to isolate the system, and threw the heavy grounding switch. After Danforth backed the truck into position beside the arrestors and swung the stabilizers into place, Martin climbed into the yellow polyethylene bucket at the end of the elevator boom. There was a moan of hydraulics and the arm swung out and started rising, lifting him alongside the bushing. Martin bent toward the connection, his flashlight beaming a gauzy yellow column through the fog.

Danforth jumped as a series of staccato *cracks* rippled from the row of big transformers hulking in the dark on his left.

Violet light bloomed in the moisture-laden haze, accompanied by a sizzling hum—the sound of high voltage current arcing from cable to cable. The hairs rose on the back of Danforth's neck.

Martin shifted inside the bucket. "What the hell was *that*?"

"Get down! Get—"

A sickening rasp of electricity split the air above Danforth's head. A blue-violet light suffused the fog like lightning through a thunderhead.

Martin belted out a wavering, high-pitched scream.

Danforth groped frantically for the control, his hands shaking. "*Oh God, Oh God...*"

In his thirty years as a lineman, he had never witnessed an electrocution, never gotten careless, never had a close incident. He and Martin had followed procedure to the max, had thrown the correct switches, taken the right precautions, but...

He yanked the joystick and the bucket descended ponderously through the fog and shuddered to a stop three feet off the ground. Ropes of electricity buzzed and hummed from the overhead bushing and groped the air where Martin had been moments before.

Danforth flew to the basket, heart hammering. "*God, God, God!*" A stench hit him as he stared into the basket's dark interior—ozone and burned flesh. Moans drifted from the limp figure curled inside.

He leaned forward and grasped Martin, then yelped as his fingers sank through the oily gore that had been his partner's left arm. He staggered backward, goggling at the basket, frantically swiping his hands across his coveralls. Fifteen feet above, the electric arc doubled back and hummed and sputtered and corkscrewed downward along the insulator's finned surface. It was heading straight for him.

Danforth ran to the cab, withdrew the stabilizers, and vaulted in. He gunned the engine and swerved toward the gate, accelerating over the rough gravel as fast as he dared.

His words exploded into the mike: "*This is Ed Danforth. I got an injured man...*"

$$=\!\!=\!\!=\ \ 7\ \ =\!\!=\!\!=$$

r. Carol Myerson reached across the mound of paperwork and punched the intercom button. Distorted by cheap electronics, Dr. Floran's *basso profundo* rattled into the room: "Carol, I think we need you on this one."

"Good evening, Dr. Floran. What have you got?"

"A man with very deep electrical burns. Since you've had experience with trauma of this nature, I was hoping you could offer some insight. We're in ER Two."

That the arrogant Dr. Charles Floran would ever admit to needing assistance was almost traumatic *per se*. "I'm on my way."

She rode the elevator to the second floor, donned a mask and scrubs, and pushed into the operating room. Dr. Floran was hovering over the patient, hands clasped behind his back, a frown pinching his tanned forehead. Nurse Betty Aldrich glanced up, her eyes offering a grimace above the green surgical mask. Under the watchful eye of the anesthesiologist, vital signs beeped jagged lines across the monitor. A peculiar, unsettling odor permeated the room.

Floran's gaze remained fixed on the patient as Carol moved closer. He slowly folded back a serum-soaked gauze from the unconscious man's upper body as he spoke. "His name is Jerry Martin. He was working a high voltage line an hour ago and, well, as you can see…"

Carol had seen plenty of traumata: wrecks, burns, machinery accidents. But this chilled her blood. The sight of grotesquely injured faces, torsos, and limbs required a degree of mental detachment; you tried to remain calm and assured when confronted with emergency-room horrors. And this wasn't the bloodiest or goriest she had witnessed—it was the most ghoulish.

Martin's left arm was sheathed in smooth skin that stretched in a normal manner across the biceps. But then it abruptly sagged into a thin, translucent membrane that clung loosely to the underlying bone. For some reason, this was far more unsettling than seeing a limb mutilated by a wreck or a runaway machine.

Dr. Floran was watching her, gauging her reaction. "Pulse and respiration are slightly elevated, and he has a highly erratic EEG."

She glanced again at the monitor, which showed a pattern of relative quiescence followed by wild spikes similar to those produced by an epileptic seizure. "We need to estimate how much current he received. Then we can estimate depth of penetration, organ involvement, skin grafts, future tissue loss, and so forth." Her eyes roved over the victim's torso. "I don't understand how a man could sustain such a massive dose of electricity—enough current to burn the flesh from an entire limb—and live."

Carol bent forward and examined the destroyed arm more closely. A small amount of amber serum oozed from the healthier tissue, the blood vessels and arteries apparently having been cauterized by the searing electric charge.

The patina of flesh sheathing the bone below the elbow was uniform, not ruptured or torn. But the muscle, fat, nerves, and sinews within had disappeared. This was odd, totally inconsistent with what she had observed in similar cases. It was almost as if the man's arm had been thrust into a vat of flesh-eating acid that showed a preference for muscle and nerve tissue, leaving the skin relatively intact.

Her eyes shifted to the area above the elbow. "See this? These purple tendrils across the biceps, leading across the trapezium and into the neck..."

Dr. Floran nodded. "What do you think?"

She frowned. "I'm not sure. Perhaps the current followed the veins—burning."

"And your recommendation?"

"Amputation," she said, pointing to a spot halfway up the biceps. "Two inches above the conspicuous trauma. We'll get a path report on a section and a full-body MRI, see what those purple lines are and how deep they go—"

Carol jumped as a long, haunted moan escaped Martin's throat. His eyes flashed open and fixed on her. The EEG displayed jagged lines indicative of an impending seizure.

His chest heaved as he shouted in a desperate, grunting voice: "Its coming...COMING...NO!...NO! Disconnect—*Now!*" His torso convulsed and bucked upward against the restraint; his legs and right arm thrashed violently as he tried to rise.

Carol lunged for his shoulders. "Sedate him!" Martin's eyes, boring into her own, held a terror bordering on madness. The anesthesiologist worked frantically at the intravenous tubing that had ripped free from Martin's remaining arm.

The man shrieked as Carol and Aldrich threw themselves across his body. "*Disconnect me!...Dis...*"

Carol turned her head, searching for Dr. Floran. He had backed from the table, eyes bulging. She yelled at him. "Get help!"

"I don't understand. He's fully sedated. He's—"

"Get some help, *dammit*! We can't hold him."

Martin's head snapped backward against the pillow. His mouth yawned and flooded the room with a wail that froze Carol's blood. The heart monitor went into overdrive.

"He's in V-tach!" Carol turned, hit the defibrillator switch and grabbed the paddles. The monitor suddenly hummed and flashed green-white as smoke boiled from the machine's cooling vents. Carol dropped the paddles and backed away. "What's going on...?"

Martin screamed. "Noooo...coming...*comming!*"

The overhead fluorescents fizzled and strobed. Sparks shot from the monitor. Martin convulsed violently. His right hand clawed at the electrodes dotting his head and chest. As he raked the wires away, neon-blue threads of electricity snapped from the electrodes and forked across his body.

Carol collided with Aldrich as she stumbled backward. The doors behind her flew open, and two attendants rushed inside. "Good God," one said. "What's..."

A crackling hum joined Martin's screaming.

Carol slammed through the swinging doors into the hallway and stopped before the crowd of nurses, doctors, and patients gathering outside the room. "Shut off the power...the electricity! *Somebody!*"

Behind her, Aldrich and the attendants burst from the room. As the doors swung shut, Carol glimpsed an aura of pulsating light, growing in intensity, radiating from the examination table.

No more screams issued forth. The room exhaled only a throaty hum and a searing electric crackle.

It sounded almost as if something were feeding.

8

Colvin's radio squawked: the dispatcher's voice fighting its way past the infernal blasts of static. "Ten-seventy at Grayson Medical. Fire truck is en route."

"Roger that. On our way." Colvin ignited the cruiser's overheads and accelerated down Highway 501. They had just left the search team at North Ridge, and the ATV was still riding on its trailer behind the car. The small vehicle's motor had refused to start, and they were bringing it in for repair. He turned to Deputy Frank Parnell. "It's gonna' be a long night."

Ten minutes later, he swung into the hospital parking lot, cursing under his breath at the jumble of emergency vehicles blocking his path. The fog had thickened, and the flashing lights mixed into a dazzling blur that discouraged navigation. "Take the car," he said to Parnell as he stopped and climbed out. "Drop the ATV at the county garage and meet me back here."

Inside the lobby, two firemen in SCBA gear nodded as he passed them. Evidently, the crisis had been contained. He smelled no smoke, only a disturbingly familiar stench—the same odor that had permeated Catherine Klatty's house earlier that day.

Bright lights flared from his left: the News Eleven team. His heart fell when he saw Commissioner Long step up to the mike. "Our splendid fire department, as well as Police Chief Gordon Leinway, answered the call within minutes and have everything under control." Long glanced at Colvin as he walked by. "And I see Sheriff Greg Colvin is finally arriving..."

"Up yours, you grandstanding nitwit," Colvin muttered. Another fireman opened the stairway door and walked into the lobby, tugging off his gloves. Recognizing him, Colvin flagged him down.

"Jim, what's going on?"

The fireman shook his head. "Man you wouldn't believe...some sort of weird fire or something."

"Where?"

"Second floor, east end."

Colvin bolted up the stairs and opened the door onto a hallway jammed with patients, most of them on beds and gurneys, waiting for the elevator down. Nurses and paramedics hovered over the more serious cases. Despite the absence of smoke, the foul odor thickened the air. Beyond the nurses' station, the hallway lights were out, but Colvin could make out a group of cops and medical personnel standing outside a room.

He threaded his way past the congestion and came up beside Chief Leinway. A light flashed in the darkness: the coroner's camera at work.

Leinway nodded at the operating room. "Check *that* out, Greg."

A cop stood aside as Colvin brushed past him and through the door. The sight hit him like a freight train. Wan illumination from a portable emergency light barely folded back the room's shadows. Instruments, cardiac monitor, and EEG had been knocked to the floor. Jim Farnsworth was moving about quietly, recording the scene with his digital camera.

But what stopped Colvin in his tracks was the body. It was half risen above the seared bedsheets in a frozen lunge. The skeletal arms reached outward as if grasping at something unseen. The hands were opened wide, fingers arched into bony hooks. The mouth shouted its silent scream, the dark eye sockets stared, and the brow, crafted of rigid folds of reddish and desiccated skin, frowned menacingly, as if the ghastly remains were preparing to leap from the bed and snatch Colvin in a deadly embrace.

He flinched as the coroner fired off another strobe. "Sonuvabitch."

"Yeah," Farnsworth said, lowering the camera to his side. "Déjà vu all over again."

"How did it happen?"

A female voice sounded behind him: "I was here..." Dr. Carol Myerson stood in the doorway, her arms folded tightly around her chest. Her clothing was disheveled, her attractive face marred with fear.

"His name is Jerry Martin," she said. "He's a lineman, and his partner brought him in two hours ago. Said he was working at a substation. His right arm, it..." She shuddered, swayed, staring at the lineman's grisly form.

Colvin gently guided her back outside. "I'll see you in your office, Carol. Right now I want to examine him up close." He turned back and edged toward the bed.

"Be careful, Greg."

He crept forward into the nimbus of danger that throbbed from the corpse like a repelling force. "Klatty," he whispered as he observed the reddened and charred folds of loose skin clinging to the skeleton. *Just like Klatty.* But in this case, the lineman's body had apparently been subjected to greater heat.

Colvin stared at the skull and the glistening black ribbons that branched from the eye sockets, down the shoulders, and across the bed. Then he noticed something new, something he hadn't seen on Klatty's body—a small crater in the center of the man's forehead, where more of the carbon-like pathways converged.

He traced the branching lines with his eyes, and another thrill of apprehension shot through his system: the tracks left Martin's corpse, burned across the wall and floor, and entered the electric outlet beside the bed. As he bent even closer, he could see a translucent substance coating the black pathways. The tracks were virtually identical to those leading from Klatty's destroyed body into the controls of her radio. He exhaled, suddenly aware that he had been holding his breath, and looked up at Farnsworth. "Jim, you got a sample kit?"

"Yeah."

The coroner disappeared for a moment and returned with a plastic toolbox. Colvin selected a specimen jar, scooped a small amount of the viscous substance into the container, and screwed the lid tight. The slime-like material, he noted, had a faint amber hue. He surveyed the room one last time and hurried through the door.

He found Carol slumped on a chair in her office. Her short chestnut hair had curled forward across her forehead, shading her eyes. She looked pale and drawn. When she saw him, her mouth twitched a brief smile. He cleared his throat. "I'll just ask a few questions," he said softly, "then you go home, get some rest."

She looked down as memory of the event distorted her features into a look of horror and anguish. "We could have saved him, Greg. I was examining his arm, the one that received the electrical burns, when he suddenly screamed and was engulfed by—I don't know—electricity, or some type of energy, or *something*." Her gaze found Colvin again. "He was unconscious, heavily sedated. But then somehow he rallied and became agitated, just before the...attack...occurred. And that's what really frightens me. He said—screamed—'It's coming…It's coming.'"

"Any witnesses to the first injury, the one at the substation?"

She brushed the hair from her eyes. "Another lineman, Ed Danforth, saw it happen. He drove Martin in the repair truck and met the ambulance on the road."

Colvin phoned the electric co-op from Carol's desk and left an inquiry about lineman Danforth. He turned to leave. "Carol," he repeated. "Go home."

She stared past him, nervously tugging at the lapel of her lab coat. "I feel like a fool, reacting like this. But it's just hard to get that image… out of my mind."

"You want me to drive you?" he asked. (The question, he thought, sounded more like a plea.)

"Can't. I have rounds to make." She paused, her expression seeming to brighten a little. "But maybe you could see me later. I'd like that."

Colvin stood there for a moment, nodding, his smile conveying an instant "Yes." Then he said, "You sure you can't leave?"

"I'll be alright"—she gave a humorless chuckle—"I have drugs."

Colvin crossed the fog-dampened parking lot, which was still choked with fire trucks, news vans, and police cruisers. His car was in a nearby slot, and Parnell climbed out. "Margie called. That lineman, Danforth, left for the substation. Said he'd meet up with a crew from the power company."

Colvin swung into the driver's seat. "Good. Because I want to see that station for myself."

***

Heavy fog rolled across County Road 4, and Colvin slowed the cruiser to a crawl as he looked for the entrance to the old Kellsburg substation.

Parnell tapped the windshield. "That's it," he said, indicating the hazy bloom of light off to the right.

The sign drifted into view, and they turned onto the gravel entrance and drove through the open gate. Two big Mesa Electric Co. trucks were parked at the eastern end of the substation, engines idling, their spotlights illuminating a pair of tall white insulators rising through the fog. Colvin parked beside the trucks and they climbed out.

Four men, partly obscured by shadows, turned to face him. Colvin could tell by their postures that a confrontation was in progress. As he drew closer, he could see their features and Mesa Electric logos on their jackets. No one was smiling.

A gray-haired man with a ruffled shirt and a slight sway stood apart from the others. "Well, hal'luja. Here's th' Sheriff and a frien' come to straighten out this shit."

The man on Colvin's right extended a hand. "I'm Marvin Ham—"

"He's Marvin Hamlek," the inebriated one said. "Marvin's gonna' get it, get with it..."

Hamlek rolled his eyes. "I'm the engineer for this area." He introduced the two younger men as Bob and Eric, technicians. He pointed to the gray-haired man, whose sway seemed to have worsened. "And this illustrious member of our team is Ed Danforth."

Danforth scowled. "Wanna' get the hell out of here." He looked up at the insulators and shuddered. "Somethin's bad wrong here."

Hamlek shook his head. "How can we help you gentlemen?"

Colvin raised his voice over Danforth's mutterings. "I was hoping you power company experts could tell me what's going on with the electricity."

"Well, regarding the injury to our lineman, it was carelessness. Jerry was working up there"—he nodded toward the insulator overhead—"and they must have left the system hooked up to the main feed..."

"No sir! No sir!" Danforth spat. "Went by the Goddamned *book*." He swept his arm out and pointed. "Opened the main feed, closed the ground circuit. See." He took an uncoordinated step.

The two technicians, carrying electronic instruments and flashlights, left the group and headed for the rear of the substation. Parnell followed.

"So," Colvin said, "all this power is turned off?"

"It is now."

"Was then, too." Danforth growled.

Hamlek's voice rose. "No way a high voltage current could exist unless the switch was still making contact."

"These stations, they don't store electricity?" Colvin asked.

"Impossible. The capacitors are in parallel with inductors and bleeder resistors. They can't store electricity."

Danforth interrupted again, an angry squint in his eyes. "It came from over there, like I said." He pointed north and lowered his voice. "Musta' come from the old lines somehow..."

Colvin looked. At the edge of the floodlights, beyond the fenced enclosure, a tall shape leaned through the mist like a drunken scarecrow. "Is that another transmission tower?"

Hamlek snorted. "Well, yeah, but those old lines have been dead over forty years. The cables don't even reach the substation. Hell, you see, this substation was built back in the fifties to serve the military housing off base. The base had its own power plant and supplied electricity for this entire area. When they shut the base down in sixty-four, they had to bring in power from Mesa Electric." He paused and darted a glance at Danforth. "Nope, the accident here was a result of worker error."

"You are full of SHIT!" Danforth spat.

Hamlek rounded on Danforth. "Tell me, Ed, were you drunk when you and Jerry came out to work on this?"

Danforth stared at Hamlek for a moment, then screwed his face into an angry grin. "Of course, Marvin. I always work high voltage when I'm shitfaced. That way, if my ass shorts a thirty-KV line, I don't feel it. Now, if you gentlemen will excuse me, I think I'll go and puke my guts out." And with that, he staggered behind one of the big transformers and noisily vomited.

The two technicians and Parnell emerged from the shadows. One of the techs handed a clipboard to Hamlek. "It's like Danforth said, boss. A shorted lightning arrestor tripped the breaker, and the system's disconnected."

Hamlek started writing. "Well, I gotta' get a new arrestor installed so folks can have their power back

"Just one more thing," Colvin said. "Could a power surge, or maybe lightning, get inside a building and...injure someone?"

Hamlek sighed. "Look. That didn't happen here. If you want answers about the effects of lightning and high voltage phenomena— they can do some pretty weird things—I suggest you contact a scientist. We only keep the power going."

Danforth wandered back from behind the metal box, the fight having left him for what Colvin knew was going to be one hell of a hangover. He looked the bedraggled old man over. Despite Danforth's unstable and malodorous condition, he wanted an interview. "We'll drive him home."

They left the substation with Danforth sprawled in the car's back seat, the windows cracked open, and the ventilation on high. Colvin turned onto the blacktop county road and headed for the highway. "What can you tell me, Ed?"

There was a long pause, then: "I raised Jerry up in the basket to check the arrestor, like I said. Line was dead. Stone cold dead. Then all of a sudden…zap…*ZZAAP!*" Danforth belted out the last word with such force that Colvin twitched in his seat. "I lowered him quick as I could," Danforth continued. "Then it started comin' down the insulator stack. If we hadn't of left, it would've got me too.

"And then, back at the hospital…" He paused for a long moment. When he finally spoke, his voice became distant, carrying an emphatic note of horror. "It was like it got a taste of him, then came through the electric lines to find him to…finish its meal." He fell silent.

"Where did it come from?"

"Don't have any idea. Maybe it was hidin' there in the substation, waiting for a victim. Only other way is maybe from the old power lines, but they're not even connected up, you know, the lines from the old NRAD base."

They parked in front of Danforth's house, not far from Klatty's neighborhood, and helped him from the car and onto a couch in his living room. "I'm leavin'," Danforth mumbled as he slumped against the cushions. "Leavin' an' never comin' back."

Colvin delivered Parnell to the courthouse and pointed the cruiser toward Cielo, hoping Doc Pritchard would be alert and sober. He picked up the cellphone and connected with Doc, the transmission mercifully clear. Doctor Ralph Pritchard: good friend, unofficial Grayson County Historian, official man of wisdom. Closet alcoholic.

Maybe he could illuminate this growing nightmare.

— 9 —

The creaking three-story mansion, built for a mining-company executive in the 1920s, perched at the end of a pine-shrouded drive at the apex of Estate Hill. Viewed through the veil of shifting fog, the old place was spectral, a ghost of yesteryear drifting the currents of time.

Colvin knocked, and Doc Pritchard opened the door after a long wait. He pumped Colvin's hand and smiled. "You should have knocked harder, Greg. You know my hearing's a bit degraded. If I hadn't looked outside and seen your car, I wouldn't have known you were here."

Pritchard looked the same as always: rumpled, outdated coat with a ratty tie loosely knotted and pulled askew, heavy wisps of white hair badly in need of a comb, and a salt-and-pepper mustache too large for his narrow face.

"Hell, Doc, if I'd hit it any harder I'd have busted it off the jamb. Put in a bell."

Pritchard turned and ambled into the dimly lit main room. "C'mon back. I've got the maps all laid out for you." Each time Colvin visited, he marveled at the home's construction: the tall ceilings, precise joinery, and lavish use of hardwood. A hundred years ago, such material was plentiful and builders thought nothing of using great solid slabs of it for every reinforcement and decorative purpose.

Inside the darkly paneled office, the wide oak desk and side table carried a burden of books, binders, and papers. The place smelled stale and looked tired.

Pritchard paused and looked at Colvin, as if reading his thoughts. "Since Effie died, I mostly live in just a few rooms. Ought to sell this old house and buy a bungalow down in the valley."

"You've got too many happy memories here, Doc. This place has good vibes for you."

Pritchard shot Colvin a sideways glance. "Speaking of quality of life, when are you going to ask that lovely Dr. Myerson out for a date?"

Colvin looked away. "Come on, Doc, we've been out a couple of times, and it's always ended poorly, always interrupted. It probably just isn't meant to be. Besides, I'm her senior by seven years."

"She likes you, Greg. Asks about you every time I'm at Grayson Med."

"You still doing all that charity work?"

The doctor smiled. "Don't change the subject."

"It's only been six years since...I lost Annie and James." Colvin paused, wincing from the memory. "And besides, I'm just a sheriff."

"Bah. She knows quality when she sees it. Handsome guy like you—"

"Now we're into embarrassment."

"Well, I know when to shut up." Pritchard turned to the desk. "I gathered some old maps, stories, photos. You asked about underground tunnels and caverns, but I haven't found anything to support that." He rifled through some bound pages and yellowed newspaper clippings. "Doesn't mean there aren't any, though, because so much was classified. They may have kept the tunnels a secret."

Colvin lifted a faded blueprint off the desk. "What else did she say?"

"What?"

"Carol."

Doc snickered. "Oh. Well, now. I don't remember. You'll have to ask her yourself." He paused, then looked at Colvin. "Her parents were divorced, you know. Earned her way through med school. She got a scholarship, and Kellsburg offered her a loan-for-service deal. It paid some of her expenses in exchange for three years practice in Grayson County. She stayed because she liked the people."

Colvin nodded thoughtfully and tucked the information away, deciding not to become further distracted. "Who would know?" he asked. "About the tunnels, I mean."

"Well, the military, of course, assuming you could get the information."

"They're giving us the runaround, and the Freedom of Information Act would take too long. I need something now."

Colvin's eye was drawn to an elevation of the North Ridge drainage system. "Here's something," he said. "The Helstrom boy claims he was sucked into a whirlpool. He was found about here." He tapped the map. "Maybe he was swept into this pipe and discharged into the river. I'll make a wild speculation that, since he wasn't underwater long enough to drown, that he was sucked in not far from the outlet, which I will locate tomorrow. I'll concentrate the search for a tunnel entrance along here." He indicated an area west of where Johnny Helstrom was found.

"How long someone could survive inside that pipe would depend on all sorts of things, like whether the pipe had air in it, how fast the water was moving, and so forth."

"Of course." Colvin thought for a moment. "The military did the excavation, but there's no pictures, and no names of construction personnel or any companies involved."

Pritchard hefted a thick binder. "Let me show you something strange." He dug through the bound items and pulled several photos from their protective sleeves. "The disaster was supposed to have culminated in a series of explosions—an ammo dump or something. They said it released toxic materials. Folks assumed it was nerve gas or biological weapons, but nobody was talking."

He dropped a black-and-white photo onto the desk: an aerial shot of a large building with a heavy plume of black smoke funneling from its gutted roof. "This is the hospital complex. Notice that only the hospital is burning." He dropped another photo. "This is the same complex with more buildings on fire. *But*, the picture was taken a day later." Another photo hit the desk. "And this...this is a broad aerial view taken a week later. It's the only one I've seen that shows the entire southeast quadrant of the base. You can see the hospital and the damaged buildings. The ammo dump, you'll notice, is still intact."

"So, you're wondering why the ammo dump wasn't destroyed."

"Yes. If the accident was a result of munitions, why did the hospital blow up first?"

Colvin rubbed his eyes, fatigue sapping his powers of deduction. "You mind if I take these with me?"

"Sure. Go ahead. I've been collecting history of this county for some forty years. It might as well serve some purpose."

Colvin collected the photos and maps and turned to leave. "Oh, yeah. I almost forgot. If you don't mind, I'd like your opinion on what this might be." He reached inside his coat pocket and withdrew the glass vial he had taken from Johnny Helstrom's backpack.

Pritchard took the cylinder and held it beneath the desk lamp. He rotated it for a moment, frowning, started to hand it back, then looked again. His eyes grew wide, and Colvin thought he saw a flash of fear. "Where did you get this?"

"The boy said he found it inside a tunnel. Said there was a body on an operating table." Pritchard's face blanched. He swiped his hand across his mustache, staring unblinking at the object. "What's the matter, Doc? You okay?"

Pritchard didn't answer, but jerked the desk drawer open and snatched up a magnifying glass. He examined the cylinder at various angles beneath the lens, turning it before his intense gaze. Finally, he looked up at Colvin. "If this is what I think it is, you've stumbled onto something."

Colvin stared. "What?"

"Follow me."

A narrow staircase at the rear of the house led up to the third floor. Pritchard took the steps slowly, then paused, breathing heavily. "It's my arthritis. I don't climb so well anymore." At the top, he walked down a short hallway and entered a room beyond a heavy wooden door. He fumbled in the gloom and flipped a light switch. Two dim wall sconces illuminated a space crammed with antique furniture, filing cabinets, and storage boxes, all coated with dust.

"I apologize for the mess," Pritchard said, "but I rarely come up here. I use it like an attic."

He poked around in a dark corner, lifting boxes aside. "Now, where did I put it?" He turned, then: "Ah. There you are." He bent down and lifted an olive-drab metal container fitted with handles. Colvin thought it looked army surplus, something that might have contained munitions.

Pritchard set the box on a round oak table in the center of the room and yanked the chain on an overhead lamp. He pried up four clamps that held the lid tightly shut. There was a brief hiss of air, and the lid popped free in his hands. A foul odor exhaled from within the dark confines, a reek that Colvin instantly recognized. Pritchard reached into the box with both hands and hesitated, wrinkling his nose. "Phew. You'd think, after all these years, especially after using a desiccating agent, that the stink would subside."

He lifted gently, producing a round mass wrapped with stained and moldered cloth, and began peeling away the covering. After a moment the object was exposed—a human skull—which the doctor held out and rotated into the light.

Colvin's skin crawled. The skull was almost devoid of flesh, here and there bits of hair and skin still clinging to yellow bone. But this was not what sent shivers coursing along his spine. It was not the shadows that twitched in the hollow eye sockets, driven by the swinging overhead light, or that the skull reminded him of Klatty's sagging corpse viewed in the glare of distant lightning—it was the forehead, into which a centered, two-inch diameter hole had been precisely cut.

Pritchard held up the glass vial. "May I remove this?"

Colvin nodded, dreading the coming revelation, and the doctor popped open the vial's mouth. He teased the contents from its cotton padding and rotated it beneath the magnifying lens, the long, thin spikes that grew from the thing's base glinting in the wavering overhead light.

Pritchard set the magnifying glass aside and gingerly inserted the device into the hole in the skull's forehead. "A perfect fit, centered in the frontal squama. Even the screw holes match."

"Where did you get that skull, Doc?"

"No one knows I have it. Sam Mayfield found it in the mud down at the river and brought it to me, oh, about twenty-five years ago."

"You should have turned that in."

Pritchard swiped a hand across his ample mustache. "There's a reason."

"And?"

"It's the second skull…"

"There's *more*?"

"Only one that I know of. They found it in the woods just outside the old air base, near the river. The forehead had an opening just like this one. The sheriff—that would have been Ted Newberry—turned it into the FBI. They took it, and we haven't seen or heard anything since."

Colvin sat down in a dusty chair. "What are they hiding, Doc? What were they doing at North Ridge?"

Pritchard looked down at the skull, its violated forehead now penetrated by the strange metal device. "I don't know," he replied, almost in a whisper. "But it scares the hell out of me."

10

Colvin crunched across the gravel driveway toward his car, heavy mist brushing cold and damp against his skin. He paused and looked back at Pritchard's house; the fog had choked the building's features into shadow and hazed its lights into an alien glow. Maybe it was just fatigue, he thought, coupled with the unnerving events of the day, but he had a chill feeling that something ominous was gathering, creeping in with the heavy atmosphere. He felt uneasy leaving Pritchard alone.

He climbed into the car and drove away, thinking about the old doctor, trying to shake the growing dread from his mind. He and Pritchard had been friends for four years, from the time Colvin had won the election. They were, in part, drawn together by tragedy and addiction. Both men had lost their wives—in Colvin's case, his young son as well—and both men had suffered from a ruinous affinity to alcohol. Unlike Colvin, Pritchard refused to temper his drinking. The booze-induced tremors that thrummed in his hands had destroyed his surgical skills, but he could examine and diagnose well and still performed charity work, often making lengthy pro bono calls down in the pueblos. Pritchard had introduced Colvin to Carol, and because of that he'd be forever grateful.

Adjusting the radio, Colvin found the frequencies surprisingly free of static, and called Deputy Rick Lewis, who was standing watch with Tom Grove at the NRAD entrance.

"No sign of the boy, Sheriff," the deputy squawked back. "It's quiet as a tomb, and the fog's so thick you could cut out a chunk and take it home."

"Roger that. Keep calling for the kid. You'll be relieved at first light."

At home, Colvin showered and pulled on blue jeans and a black T-shirt, one that, despite its extra-large size, fit snugly around his developed arms and broad chest. He paced the room, tired but nervous-awake; thought about returning to the office to scrounge additional resources to find the missing boy; thought about Carol, how she was coping after the horror show at the hospital—

The phone rang, his fatigue evaporating as he recognized the caller.

"Carol...

"Are you busy?"

"No...that is, I just left Doc Pritchard's place. I was about to call you."

She sounded stressed. "I'm such a wimp...I know it's late, but..." Her voice became a whisper. "I could use some company—especially yours. I'm home for the night."

"I'll be there in ten minutes. Just keep a pot of coffee going."

Colvin grabbed a jacket, stuffed his gun into a side holster, and climbed into his old Jeep Cherokee. He drove onto CR 4 and headed south towards Kellsburg, pushing the vehicle as fast as he dared, cleaving a path through the thickening fog.

Carol lived in a pleasant new house just north of the downtown area. Colvin liked the place. It was an architectural mash-up: Santa Fe-style, with thick adobe walls and massive vigas, but with a pitched roof of Spanish tile. The heavy front door was of weathered pine planks reinforced with iron bands.

She opened the door a moment after he knocked and greeted him with a relieved smile. She was wearing faded jeans and an oversized red and white sweatshirt emblazoned with UNIVERSITY OF NEW MEXICO and the state's Zia sun-symbol. No bra. She reached up and laced her arms around his neck, drawing him down, and kissed him. He pulled her tight against his chest and returned the offering with interest, his hand caressing the back of her neck, fingers teasing her hair. She smelled of peaches or lilac.

Taking his hand, she guided him across a wide Navajo rug and onto a leather sofa draped with a blanket woven with American Indian designs. A few feet away, a kiva crackled with the aromatic flames of pine and piñon. Candles flickered on brass stands, the combined play of fire and shadow casting a seductive warm glow through the room.

"Great house," Colvin said, looking up at the latillas spanning the ceiling. He immediately thought the statement sounded lame.

"I spent more than I should, but it's…"

She looked nervous, was wringing her hands.

"Come talk to me."

She lifted a wineglass from the side table. "I just started. Can I get you…"

"No thanks. Just coffee."

She walked toward the kitchen, the snug jeans hugging her shapely legs and perfectly formed posterior. Colvin and she had first met at Grayson Medical, at an informal party thrown for the hospital's new director. Doc Pritchard had made the introductions, and Colvin was instantly smitten. Besides Annie, Carol was the most desirable woman he'd ever met.

Their relationship had been developing over the past several months, tentatively at first, then with gathering intensity. Colvin struggled to diminish the memory of his murdered wife and son (that's how he thought of their deaths—a truck hurtling head-on into her lane, piloted by a drunkard who knew he was guiding a killing machine and didn't give a damn). These conscious thoughts always intruded during potential romantic interludes. But his feelings for Carol were powerful and evolving, and he was beginning to feel at ease with her. Intellectually, he knew he wasn't cheating, debasing Annie's memory, but the emotion was still there, circling underneath, ready to open its jaws and destroy the moment.

Carol returned with the coffee, treading across the rug on bare feet. With the worn jeans and NMU shirt, she looked more like a college coed than a highly talented and caring physician. The only things marring her beautiful face were the recently acquired circles beneath her eyes and pinched lines of worry. She handed him the coffee as she sat beside him and drew in close.

He put his arm around her shoulders and sighed. "Isn't it time for the beepers to start beeping?"

"Hm?"

"Each time we've had some private time, gotten...uh...comfortable... with each other, the radio squawks or the beepers go off. Remember that time at the restaurant? They had just served us, and all our communications gear started buzzing at the same time.

She giggled. "And when we were going to your place—no, here— thought we'd have the evening to ourselves..."

"Yeah, both radios again. Emergencies." He sipped his coffee. "So what's on your mind?"

He watched as she poured another glass of wine.

"I've had some time to think about what happened at the hospital, when that young lineman, Jerry Martin, died." She looked up at him. "I've earned my stripes in the ER, Greg. I've seen everything. But what happened in that room was, well, so unnatural I'm"—a frown creased her forehead—"frightened, spooked." She shuddered, nursed her drink. "Also, I heard that the old woman, Catherine Klatty, was found in a similar condition this morning.

"Of course, we won't know until the autopsies. But I've studied enough science to conclude, for many reasons, that high voltage electricity couldn't possibly invade a room, jump from the wires, attack a person, and without a trace leave them devoid of muscle tissue and internal organs. The lineman was—*devoured*. There was nothing left of him but skin and skeleton. What happened defies every rule of physics. It was impossible."

Colvin watched her take another drink. "Funny you should mention 'devoured.' Danforth—the senior lineman—when he described the attack at the hospital, he said, 'It was like it got a taste of him and came back to finish its meal.' When they were at the substation tonight, when Jerry Martin was attacked, he said the electricity came from nowhere and migrated down the insulator stack, like it was chasing his partner and him. He thought it might have come from the old North Ridge power lines. But those had been disconnected years ago."

"Another thing..." Carol stared into her wineglass for a moment, then looked back up at him. "That device in the glass vial. It looked surgical."

"Yeah. I showed it to Doc Pritchard tonight and—get this—he has a human skull in his possession, one found near the river, just outside the North Ridge boundary. That skull had a hole cut in the forehead. And that device was designed to fit inside."

Carol drew a sharp breath and sat up. "It's an implant of some kind, Greg. You have to get it analyzed, find out what they were doing at North Ridge. That implant has electronic components. There's a connection between all of this. I'd bet my degree on it."

She was beginning to slur her words, and he knew she'd had more to drink than she admitted.

"I already placed a call with the FBI in Albuquerque. Maybe they'll send someone out tomorrow."

She thought for a moment, then brightened. "I know someone who could advise you. He's brilliant. I took his physics classes at NMU. He even consults on the nuclear fusion program at Los Alamos."

"Who?"

"His name's Weismann, Joseph Weismann."

Colvin locked the name into memory, deciding to locate the man tomorrow.

"I feel safe with you," Carol blurted.

Colvin's left hand found hers and squeezed. *This is the moment of truth.* He'd been dreading this moment, but it had to come. And he was prepared for the rejection. His right hand worked inside his jeans pocket and pulled out a brass coin about the size of a half dollar. On one side was the image of a triangle, with the numeral V. The opposite side carried a quote, *To thy own self be true.* His AA token.

He held his hand out, the coin centered in his palm. "Carol, there's something you need to know."

She looked into his face, an enigmatic smile playing on her lips.

"I'm a recovering...I'm—"

Her hand reached out and gently folded his fingers back over the coin. "I know what that is," she said, "and it doesn't matter. I've know about it since before we met."

"How..."

"Everyone in the county knows. And they don't care either. You're well respected, Greg, well liked." She gave a little *hmpf.* "Well, you're liked, that is, by everyone except that moronic sleaze, Donny Long."

He stuffed the token back into his pocket. "The irony, you know, is that I'm not a true alcoholic. I'm working the program so I never repeat what happened in LA. Booze ruined my career, I couldn't perform my duty, and people suffered for that. I'll never let that happen again."

She pushed up tighter against him, and his response was automatic. He twisted toward her and kissed her. This time the contact was deep and sensual. And it lingered. He pulled away, seriously aroused, feeling the heat rise into his face.

She looked up at him, her lips full, her own face flushed. Her hand traveled to his chest and her eyes fluttered as she broke into a grin. "You wouldn't take a'vantage of an indebriated lady...would you?"

"No...yes. But not tonight...I..."

This was not what he expected, or even what he wanted. Their relationship needed time to grow. Pushed too fast, it would certainly fail. He wanted this woman, but he hadn't had time to fully resolve his feelings about Annie. In his mind he was still married and still mourning. He needed time to sort out his emotions.

Her hand slipped beneath his tight T-shirt and rested warmly on his sternum.

"I can feel your heart," she said. "It's beating pretty fast."

Now he was in trouble. He wanted to do the honorable thing, leave her alone and let her sleep it off. But he'd let his defenses down, and now he'd passed a threshold beyond which there was no return.

He kissed her again hard, aggressively, sliding his own hand beneath the NMU sweatshirt, then across her taut, smooth stomach and upward, where his palm made contact with the slope of her left breast. He pushed farther, his fingers finding and stroking a hardened nipple. She was breathing rapidly now, and her hands began working at his belt (the final destruction of his good intentions, but a relief as well, as the constricting clothing had become an uncomfortable prison).

His body was flying on automatic pilot, all reserve thrown to the winds. He pulled Carol's sweatshirt up and over her head, exposing her perfect upper torso and ideally proportioned breasts. Her hands returned to work and had his belt free as he cupped a breast and teased the erect nipple with his tongue. She moaned, fought his jeans down as he kicked off his Adidas. He stretched her out on the big couch, laying her head atop a pillow, and as he struggled out of his shorts she tugged her own jeans off. He helped the panties come free and she raised her legs, looping an arm around his neck.

As he knelt, she directed him home and he paused at the threshold. Her hands slipped around his waist and pulled urgently. He plunged, feeling her tighten and buck upward, gasping. Now her hands grabbed at his shoulders and her legs locked behind him. He kissed her as he thrust, she meeting his rhythm with intense purpose. Finally she stiffened and shuddered, moaning, and he crested, his back arching in a final uncontrollable push.

"Stay," she whispered as he began to back away. And after a moment she began to move again, slowly, sensually. He found himself once more rising to the task, this time their labor stretching on for minutes until the final spasm took them.

Later, as she lay against him, he stroking her hair and offering a kiss against her cheek, she dozed. He sat up, arranged her in a comfortable position on the couch, and drew the blanket over her.

"Don' go," she said, eyes still closed, voice burdened with sleep.

"Believe me. I want to stay. But I'm going back to the office. Got too much to juggle." He dressed and pulled on his jacket. He gave Carol a final soft kiss, watched her lips form a satisfied smile, and left, locking the door behind him. For Carol, for the moment at least, all was right with the world.

His own mind was a battleground of emotions. Elation, guilt, anxiety over this possibly destructive conjoining: had things accelerated beyond his control, as had their fevered lovemaking moments ago? Well, he thought, time would reveal all. God, he loved this woman, but he and Carol Myerson were wedded to their jobs, and this is how it would always be—stealing a few moments of pleasure between duty and exigency.

He hiked his collar up and walked toward the Jeep. The night was growing colder and the fog was finally beginning to thin.

Tomorrow would be clear, good weather for searching, for finding answers.

— 11 —

Dr. Ralph Pritchard walked slowly upstairs to his bedroom and closed the door. He reached for the bottle of Crown Royal perched on the end table and filled a bar glass to the halfway point. Easing into the recliner, he lifted the tumbler and downed a third of its contents in one smooth motion. He breathed out a long sigh, pulled the old photo album onto his lap, and turned through the worn pages, searching for images of Mary and the grandkids at Tahoe.

He took another long hit from the glass and thought about Colvin, wondering how he was really holding up after having lost so much so suddenly—his wife and young son, knocked into the Great Beyond by a drunkard in a pickup truck those six years ago. But Colvin rarely exposed his feelings.

As the warm mantle of inebriation settled around Pritchard, he hummed a tune; the one Mary used to sing every Christmas. She had such a wonderful voice. Reaching again for the glass, he leaned back and began his ritualistic symphony of remembrance.

The room lights flickered, wrenching him from his immersion in the Tahoe vacation. There was a brief sparking sound, and the wall and table lamps blinked the room into darkness. *Damned old fuse box.* He sat for a moment, waiting to see if the lights would come back on, listening, thinking perhaps he'd heard something—a scratching sound—downstairs.

Rising from the chair, he felt his way across the room and opened the door. The small, battery-operated emergency light in the hallway was on, throwing enough illumination for him to see the stairwell and descend the worn oak steps. When he reached the bottom, he noticed a watery blue light brushing along the walls. Pritchard's first thought was that Colvin had returned and for some reason had switched on his cruiser's light bar, and that it was strobing through the front windows.

But as he turned the corner into the main room, he saw the windows were dark, that the strange light was emanating from his study, where he and Colvin had pored over the North Ridge maps and diagrams. Puzzled, he crossed the room and slowly pushed the study door wide. The light was coming from beyond his desk, near the floor. As he took a tentative step forward to investigate, a hissing-crackle sounded behind him, accompanied by more of the throbbing light.

He turned to look, and the arms—if you could call them arms— reached out and seized him. An electric shock blasted his nerves, and through the searing pain he felt his body violently shaking, heard his voice squeezed out in a juddering scream.

Then the thing's head nodded toward him, and the world faded to black.

12

Pain, silence, a cold, hard surface digging into his back.

Pritchard's eyes fluttered open. He found his vision partly obscured by metal bands encircling his face like the visor of a helmet. As he tried to turn his head, he felt the pinch of something sharp driven tightly against his temples. The same for his wrists, arms, legs, and torso—unyielding clamps held his body totally immobilized.

Panic galvanized him into full consciousness.

He stared between the metal bands into a dimly lit room, an operating room, from the look of it. His eyes turned upward. A gleaming stainless steel tube about six inches long was incorporated into the helmet. And it pointed to the exact middle of his forehead.

A clinking, scraping sound came from his left, accompanied by a wavering blue light that reflected from the helmet's curved surface. He could hear a soft, repetitive thudding, an electric crackle, and smell an overpowering odor of ozone. A luminescent mass crept into his field of vision, turned toward him, and drew close. Where he could see it plainly.

A long, constricted wail of absolute terror escaped his throat.

The monstrosity raised something—a surgical drill—and inserted the wide bit into the tube over his forehead.

Pritchard felt the helmet vibrate as the drill descended, heard a high-pitched whine as the motor leaped to life; a grinding pain as the pilot-bit reamed flesh, then bone. Now the spinning teeth of the larger bit plunged into his skull, bringing with it a pain so intense his bones seared and saliva spewed from his mouth as he screamed.

A snapping sound. The drill stopped and was slowly withdrawn, dragging with it a crimson disk of skull. Pritchard felt himself gasping, hyperventilating, praying for his weakened, lurching heart to simply stop beating lest he endure what was coming next.

He could see it between the gaps in the steel helmet—a device like the one Colvin had showed him, the one with the two-inch disk and the myriad, rigid needles spiking from one end. A phosphorescent human hand, through which he could see the underlying bone, slid the device into the tube centered above his violated forehead. The disk, whether pushed by hand or driven by a hidden mechanism, descended, its bristling needles traveling in a direct line to the frontal lobes of his brain.

Pritchard twisted against the restraints. His vision exploded in brilliant hues, sounds rasped and blared.

Then his muscles convulsed, goaded into hyperactivity by a searing rush of electric shock.

13

A crowd, maybe a hundred men, had assembled outside the ancient, gothic-style courthouse, flooding the small lawn, surrounding the Civil War-era cannon and some local hero's life-size likeness cast in bronze. Dozens of dirt bikes and ATVs jammed the street. Marty Berringer pulled his rented Lincoln into a metered space across from the square, hauled his briefcase from the passenger seat, and dropped a few coins into the slot. *This shouldn't take long.*

He straightened his tie and walked briskly toward the courthouse steps, where a tall official in a tan uniform, probably the sheriff, was bull-horning instructions to the attentive crowd of blue-jeans-clad men.

Marty had to give Sweeney credit. They had arrived late yesterday via KT's Learjet, and the chief attorney had pried Judge Reynolds from his dinner at the country club to sign a writ prohibiting search groups from entering the NRAD property. Now it was Marty's turn to charm the cops and local yuks this morning so no nasty feelings surfaced against Kendron Technologies.

As he pushed through the assemblage of volunteers, he noticed the CNN logo on a video camera sweeping the area. Another video team was evident, probably a regional channel. Shit. His timing couldn't have been worse. Maybe if he hadn't dawdled over the Wall Street Journal at that jerkwater café in Albuquerque…

He nudged his way through the cowboys and approached a deputy near the podium. All eyes followed him; even the TV turkeys smelled something was afoot. The custom-fitted Turnbull & Asser and suede loafers were a mistake. He should have packed rural.

The deputy leaned toward him with a wary look. Not friendly. Marty glanced at the officer's nametag and screwed on a serious, respectful countenance. "Deputy Parnell, I hate to bother you, but I must speak with someone in charge before these people begin their search."

The bullhorn was suddenly silent, the officer holding it staring back at him with a scowl that would curdle Granny's mincemeat pie. The tag identified him as Sheriff Greg Colvin.

The bullhorn went back into action. "Hold on folks. I'll be right back." The sheriff stepped up to Marty, crowding his personal space. The guy was not only tall, he was broad, and none of it was flab. Marty extended a hand, which was accepted in a crushing grip. He identified himself, and Colvin responded with a set jaw and narrowed eyes. "You here with that writ?"

"Yes sir," Marty answered. "You see, Kendron Technologies doesn't want anyone exposed…"

"There's a kid lost, possibly injured, on your land. I've got over a hundred volunteers ready to brave whatever's out there and look for him. And you want to play legal games and maybe put that boy's life in greater jeopardy?"

The TV cameras were edging closer now, maybe within microphone range. The deputy held up a warning hand and they slowed.

"Just hear me out, Sheriff. We're sending a team out here that will scour the grounds. A helicopter is on the way. If the kid's out there, we'll find him."

"What about the tunnels?"

Marty was prepared for this one. Sweeney had drilled the mantra into him as they discussed strategy: "There are no tunnels."

They both eyed the encroaching news cameras; then Colvin wiggled a finger. "Come inside." He handed off the bullhorn to the deputy, mumbled some instructions, and banged through the courthouse door. He didn't hold it open for Marty.

The courthouse décor consisted of flaking, puke-green paint, scuffed linoleum flooring, and dingy doorways. And it smelled as old as it looked. They entered the sheriff's department and walked through a central room where a fat woman dispatcher was busy filling the air with cigarette smoke and rasping away at a microphone. Colvin ushered him into his office and sat down at a gray metal desk. Marty sat in a gray metal chair.

Colvin wasted no time. "The boy who made it back off the property said there were tunnels. I believe him."

"He was injured, so I hear. It's possible he's suffering from hallucinations, or some sort of post traumatic—"

"You a doctor too?"

Mary sighed. "Nevertheless, the judge has issued a writ of mandamus." He handed over the paperwork.

Colvin took it, flicked it open with one hand, read for a moment. "What, specifically, are we dealing with? Neurotoxins, radiological contaminants, unexploded ordnance, biologicals? Where and how were they stored?"

"Well, I don't know. It's classified."

"North Ridge has been private property for forty years. It's not classified, and you're not cooperating."

"I can't..."

"Listen, if you don't find a way to get us onto that land immediately and identify the specific hazards, I will file an FOI demand and conspiracy-to-obstruct warrants, and inform the missing child's parents that they should contact their attorney and sue."

Marty's smile faltered, then regained traction. "I see you have a nodding acquaintance of the law."

"Yeah. I can also spell my name and know both of my parents." Colvin leaned forward, his elbows on the desk. "Listen, Berringer, just because Kendron Technologies throws their hot-shit, New York attorneys out here to protect their greedy interests doesn't mean us Abners are gonna' roll over and faint. You'd better serve up some damn good reasons why we can't search that property, or I will turn this into a PR nightmare for Kendron and fire a salvo of legal actions that will keep you tied up for the rest of your life."

This wasn't going quite as Marty had planned. Not only was Colvin physically intimidating, he had a smattering of gray matter between his ears. "How about you fly over the site with me. I'll show you how thoroughly we intend to search..."

Colvin was shaking his head. "I'm directing my men to start outside the fence where the boys entered. By this afternoon, unless you bring convincing evidence that the area is too dangerous, I will send my men inside. Legally. The district judge is a friend of mine. He contacted me before you arrived, and I already have the D.A. drawing up the warrant." He stood. "This meeting is finished."

Marty felt his famous charm and tact going south. "Fine. But realize that you're up against some very powerful interests. They can help you or hurt you. You've bitten off more than you can chew."

"We'll see about that."

Outside the courthouse, Marty yanked his tie loose and snatched the cellphone from his pocket. Instead of a connection, his ear was assaulted by droning static. He turned on his heel and stormed back into the building, marching toward the pay phone at the entranceway. If the sheriff wanted to play Tough Guy, OK. A lost kid was about to become the least of Sheriff Greg Colvin's worries.

14

aking the boy had been a challenge. The delicate, inchoate structure of a child's brain, the One found, required meticulous deconstruction to achieve total assimilation. A young mind possessed tentative neural pathways, relatively few algorithmic constructs, and erratic cognitive patterns.

Nevertheless, the child named Kip had been amusing; so many immature thoughts, hopes, dreams, and unfounded beliefs. Even the child's nascent sexuality had been entertaining. The worship of baseball, its players elevated to godlike status—pathetic. And there were the delicious screams for help, first directed at his escaping friend, Johnny, and then as the pain mounted, the desperate calls to Mother and Father and God. (And what was God? God was the One of highest power, was it not? An interesting thought.)

A subject's mind had to remain actively conscious during the process of capture and conversion, as replication of a mind in stasis was useless; the exchange of electric charge must be continuous, otherwise the persona would be lost. And the One wanted its subjects whole.

But always the induction of fear and terror brought pleasure to the One. It savored the invasion and ravaging of mind and body; the shrieking of the subject as its innermost being was laid bare and stripped away. Some personalities dissipated, some struggled mightily, and some simply went mad and eventually had to be neutralized.

Acting upon the central nervous system to paralyze the body, the One would penetrate deeper and deeper into the living brain, probing and excising like needle and scalpel, extracting and storing every memory and deductive process. A precise electronic copy of the mind was often quite useful; the only hazard being the constant restraint needed to prevent the individual from manifesting independently.

First the child, then Catherine Klatty—*ah, there was a win!* Even now her screaming mind refused to accept and submit. Perhaps she didn't understand, or simply felt betrayed. Other conquests had come in quick succession, including the doctor, Ralph Pritchard, whose knowledge and skills were immediately employed within the secret chambers below NRAD.

Some were brought into the fold with minds whole and intact, others were kept as mere drones, their unassimilated bodies manipulated by the radiotomes implanted within their brains.

The boy had provided the One with sufficient essence to project itself beyond the tunnels, its prison for so many, many years. The One's sensorium had migrated through the old North Ridge transmission lines into the town's electrical grid, whose power now fed its capacity to extract more mentalities and substance from the still unsuspecting populace.

The One's growth would soon become exponential, the arc of its power climbing at a logarithmic pitch, and the realization that it would have access to a virtually limitless feeding ground brought such a frisson of delight that a surge of jagged energy rippled through the power lines. If that electrical anomaly were analyzed, the One knew the waveform would produce a sound like frozen laughter.

15

Abe Murdock flipped up the visor on his welding helmet and rocked back, admiring the buttery-smooth aluminum join he had just completed. The new, pulsed MIG welder was working like a champ, allowing him to lay down a bead in half the time the old AC outfit required. The fancy trailer he was completing for his upscale Tanglewood customer would be ready for its hundred-thousand-dollar AC Cigarette boat in less than three days.

He cranked up the ghetto blaster's volume as Metallica's classic, *Sandman*, boomed from the speakers. He stood, stretched the kinks from his back, and lit up a smoke, gazing around the ragged steel shed that was home to Abe's Metal Works. Getting into trailer construction had been his best idea, and if Frieda didn't suck the life out of him with an increase in child support and cost-of-living payments, he'd enlarge the place, maybe hire an assistant.

He finished the cigarette (the hell with cancer, he'd probably get a tumor anyway from all the fumes he'd inhaled throughout his shop career), flicked the butt into the pile of scrap near the door, and picked up the torch.

The radio burst into garbled static. Muttering, he turned the stereo off and bent down to start another weld. He loved the way the plasma instantly turned the metal to a yellow-white fluid, the molten ribbon of aluminum flowing easily between the joint, leaving a bead vastly superior to the messy, jagged welds old-fashioned "cracker box" welders made.

He suddenly jerked the torch head away and lifted the visor. He had heard a sound—words—coming from the plasma itself. It had to be. The radio was off. And the words had stopped when he lifted the torch. The speech had been distinct and clear, spoken in a strange, constricted voice that sent shivers dancing along his spine.

Crazy Crazy Cathy Klatty...

Old lady Klatty's dilapidated house was only a few blocks away. He had seen on TV that she died yesterday, the body taken in for autopsy. He glanced around the shed to confirm that no one else was there. He was alone. The only sounds were the welding machine's cooling fan and the soft drone of traffic filtering in from the highway. He shook his head. Maybe he was going nuts himself.

He again bent to the trailer, positioned the torch, and closed the visor. He struck the arc, listening intently as he drew a molten bead along the seam. No voices this time, only the hiss of plasma and hum and crackle of electricity. He continued the weld, making a good ten inches, and was about to stop when it happened again.

Crazy Crazy Cathy Klatty
Husband died and she went batty...

He yanked the torch from the metal, breaking the arc. The words stopped; they were definitely coming from the plasma. He paused, then slowly brought the torch down, again striking the arc.

She says she isn't lonely, though
'Cause she hears him on the radio

A bright, quivering tube of electric fire arched from the torch head and battened onto Abe's wrist quick as a rattlesnake. He screamed and staggered backward, the electric current freezing his grip onto the torch. The current wormed into his skin, seared its way up his arm, his shoulder. His body shook as the plasma burned deep inside, as if his very skeleton were on fire. Abe thrashed, whipping the cable back and forth, pawing the torch with his free left hand, but the plasma shot up his neck and was in his brain, paralyzing, eating away even before the second scream could leave his throat.

16

The Tehuec River, about thirty feet wide where Colvin was standing, had over the millennia carved a deep, rocky canyon that now formed the eastern boundary of NRAD. In 1933, a mile down river, the Army had thrown a concrete dam across the canyon, giving birth to Lake Arrowhead, the vacation magnet that kept Kellsburg alive and fueled Tanglewood's sporadic growth.

"Hey, Sheriff," the lead volunteer called out. "That deep spot is just ahead."

Colvin picked his way through the tumble of rounded boulders and came up beside Josh Maywell, one of the five searchers combing the riverbank for any articles they could associate with the missing boy, Kip Hawkins.

They both looked down into a calm backwater where the river made a bend. Normally, the river's shallow, stone-paved bottom could be clearly seen, but at this spot the bottom dropped away like a giant funnel, forming a wide, deep hole tunneling into blackness.

"See how the surface domes up?" Colvin said. "Water's coming from below. Unless there's an artesian well down there, this could be the pipe outlet."

"Yeah, it's coming up all right, and fast."

Colvin watched as bits of flotsam jetted up from the depths and rode the strong current into the main channel. "If a kid surfaced here, he'd probably be carried close to those rocks." He started walking toward a section of beach jutting into the river. This matched the description of where the hikers had found the Helstrom boy.

The other volunteers converged on the area, heads lowered, scanning the ground for any clue the missing child might have been swept into the river along with Johnny Helstrom.

"Here's something" one of the searchers called out. He was slogging into the water at the tip of the small peninsula, stepping carefully over the treacherous river stones. He bent down and plucked a round, white object from the bottom. "It's a baseball," he said, holding it up.

Colvin strode over and examined the ball. "Hasn't been in the water very long. It's autographed. Huh—Joe DiMaggio." He patted the hardball dry and placed it into the evidence bag, then gave the finder a nod. "Good work. Let's keep at it."

He walked to the steep canyon wall and scrabbled up, dislodging rocks and sand still damp from yesterday's rainstorm. At the top, he turned and looked down at the river as it curved southward, glistening and silver in the afternoon light. The backwater pool below was perhaps ten feet wide, the dark, frowning crater at its center big enough to accommodate a large man. Johnny Helstrom could indeed have been ejected from a pipe hidden in its depths and then drift to the nearby shore.

Colvin turned again, studying the terrain. The folded land rose steeply away from the river, the woods marching up to the canyon edge. The sandy earth beneath his feet might be fill dirt from an excavation to bury the pipe, but it was impossible to tell. The installation had probably been completed fifty or sixty years ago, enough time for the land to recover most of its natural appearance.

The only real clue was a shallow ravine running straight back from the deep pool. The trees here appeared younger than those in the surrounding woods. Maybe this is where a giant backhoe had gone to work, digging a trench into which the pipe had been laid.

He walked for fifty yards along the depression, batting away pine boughs and dodging the jumble of fawn-colored boulders. One large rock had gouge marks along its side, a definite indication that machinery had been at work. He parted the branches of two young trees and stopped. The metallic glint of razor wire winked from the dense foliage a hundred feet ahead: the North Ridge perimeter fence. A concrete wall bridged the low areas beneath the chain link, sealing off the underside of the barrier and allowing the fence to remain level. Tubes a foot in diameter ran through the concrete, big enough to permit drainage, small enough to keep anyone from crawling through.

Satisfied he had found the pipe's likely pathway, Colvin turned and headed back toward the river. The distant thump of a helicopter drifted in from the north, and he paused, listening. Maybe Kendron Company was sending its promised search team. He doubled his stride, eager to find if he had been granted legal clearance to reenter the base. Radio communications were totally screwed, and he'd have to drive halfway back to the station before he could get a clear transmission.

Absently, he teased the baseball from the evidence bag and rotated the autograph into the light. This was the second day of the Hawkins boy's disappearance, and if Kendron Technologies continued to deny him access to the NRAD property, and if the search efforts they promised were insufficient, sparks would fly indeed.

***

Colvin slammed the door to his office, sat down heavily in the creaky chair, and punched in the number for the D.A. The call connected.

Colvin posited his question. The sparks were ignited.

"Hell, Greg," District Attorney Allen Rhoades said. "You're fighting the governor here. By the time you get another warrant to search that property—if you get a warrant—that kid'll be dead. Back off. Make sure Kendron does a proper search."

Colvin scowled. Another Kendron attorney had unloaded a pack of bullshit on the governor; something about NRAD being so dangerous that only the company's HAZMAT-trained specialists could enter the property. Result: another writ barring all outside personnel from Kendron's land.

Colvin's grip tightened on the phone. "I'm not through yet." He hung up, thinking about the pipe in the river.

Deputy Parnell poked his head through the door. "Some guys from the University of New Mexico to see you. It's about the kid's camera."

Colvin dragged another chair from the corner as the two men entered. The eldest, a tall, slender man with a full beard and a shock of unruly white hair extended his hand. "Professor Joseph Weismann," he said, smiling.

"I appreciate your coming all the way out here, Professor."

Weismann turned to the punkish wraith standing beside him. "This is Kerry Shaner." The younger man was wearing a pair of ragged jeans, sandals, and a black T-shirt bearing the logo of some death-metal rock band. Avoiding direct eye contact, Shaner gave Colvin's hand a limpid grasp.

"As you know," Weismann continued, "I'm head of the physics department. Kerry is an assistant professor in computer science. And we're very grateful you contacted us"

Colvin glanced again at Shaner. His androgynous figure and smooth, oval face made his age impossible to guess. *Geek.*

Weismann opened a briefcase and extracted a manila folder. "Water had damaged the electronics in the Helstrom boy's camera, but Kerry performed some miracles and extracted enough data from the memory chip to reproduce these." He pulled six eight-by-ten photographs from the folder and held them out.

Colvin spread the photos across his desk. "They're grainy," Weismann said, "and some were grossly underexposed. But Kerry performed some additional magic and coaxed a complete image from them."

Colvin studied the prints, each of which revealed dark, cavernous rooms filled with complex-looking machinery looming from the shadows. "These should help. You guys are amazing...really."

"Piece of cake," Shaner chirped. His gaze was drifting around the room, his foot tapping impatiently against the floor.

"Sheriff," Weismann said, his voice taking on a hesitant tone. "The reason we came here is to, well...I know your current focus is finding the lost boy, but these photos, and the apparatus they show are of extreme interest to us. There are some very strange anomalies we'd like to investigate."

"Finding Kip Hawkins is definitely my greatest priority, gentlemen. But we have a mutual problem. They, meaning Kendron Technologies, won't let us search the property. They insist it's too dangerous. They also say there're no underground structures, and that's where I think the boy is."

"I've been holding out on you, Sheriff," Weismann said, withdrawing more photos from the envelope and handing them over with a flourish. "I wanted you to appreciate the effort we've made, hoping you'll take us further into your confidence."

Colvin gave him a quizzical look and took the photos. He audibly gasped as he saw the first one. There, in an image so soft and grainy as to be nearly indistinguishable was a logo—NRAD. Below the lettering,

Colvin could make out a triangular shield and stylized skull with lightning bolts radiating from the eye sockets and mouth, all encircled with the words, PROJECT MESMER.

"That's an enlarged and enhanced image from one of the other photos," Weismann said. "We can again thank Kerry for his expertise." His face clouded. "And this last one, well, it's quite disturbing, really." He came around to Colvin's side and, using his pen as a pointer, indicated areas of the ghostly-faint image. Shaner stopped tapping his foot and watched with genuine interest.

At first, Colvin could make no sense of the picture. He could see angles, a gray mass like a dingy sheet, and a rounded contraption with rods radiating into its center, converging on something that, as the shape finally took form, sent an electric shock coursing along his spine. It was a human skull.

"This is an operating table," Weismann said. "Beneath the sheet is a person. An apparatus is securing the skull with clamps and pins."

Colvin's heart began to pound. The photos corroborated Johnny Helstrom's story. The two boys had, indeed, stumbled upon an underground facility...and more.

"It appears," Weismann continued, "that they were performing some sort of surgery when this man died." He paused and straightened. "Why he was abandoned, of course, is a mystery."

"If they were performing...um...clandestine surgical procedures, maybe this room is underneath the hospital complex."

"Considering the destruction said to have been wrought upon the surface of North Ridge, and the comparatively pristine condition of everything shown in the photographs, I'd say the boy may be telling the truth—that they were underground."

Colvin rose to his feet. "Follow me."

Inside the conference room, he unrolled the NRAD site plan across the table. Sure enough, the hospital and mental ward complexes were about a quarter of a mile from the river and the drainage-pipe outlet. The boy could have been sucked into the pipe somewhere beneath the hospital and ejected into the river.

Now he had tangible evidence with which to confront Kendron's legal thugs. Now it was time to pay Marty Berringer a visit.

"Gentlemen," Colvin said, turning to his two guests, "you have just made my day."

17

Marty was seated in a dark booth inside the Eagle Lounge, the screen of a laptop throwing a bluish haze against his boyish features. Only one other patron occupied the room—a man in a leisure suit slumped at the bar, well into his cups. Carrying a file folder, Colvin crossed the floor and dropped onto the bench opposite the attorney.

Marty looked up with a frown and shut the laptop. "Now what?"

Colvin withdrew Weismann's photos from the folder and fanned them across the table. He clicked a penlight on and highlighted them in sequence. Marty looked at the photos for a moment, then sat back, raising a glass to his lips. "Okay, I give up. You gonna' tell me what the hell this is about?"

Colvin switched the light off. "The tunnels."

Marty sighed. "Bullshit! So you have some old photographs of God-knows-what. That proves nothing."

"These photos were taken yesterday by one of the kids who entered North Ridge. His buddy is the one who's missing"—Colvin tapped the photos—"down there."

The attorney threw up his hands. "I can't believe you're still trying to prove the damned tunnels exist. The governor…"

"Screw the governor."

Marty grabbed his laptop and slid from the booth. "Fine."

"How are you gonna' feel if that kid dies?"

"I can't do anything about it. It's out of my hands now."

"You care about your company? The press will annihilate Kendron Technologies if I'm right about this."

"You know who I am?"

"Thomas Kendron's grandson. About to inherit more money than God."

"And what if you're wrong about those tunnels, Sheriff? What if you're pushing too hard, wasting everyone's time, accusing my company of lying? And trying to bring a bunch of amateurs onto some really dangerous property?"

"You need more convincing?"

Marty turned away.

"Do the right thing, Marty."

The attorney stopped and cocked his head. Colvin noticed he had ditched the expensive lawyer's suit for a pair of jeans and a denim shirt. He'd even combed out the Mr. Power-Executive hairstyle. The new look reduced his asshole quotient several points.

Colvin stood up. "Come with me."

Marty heaved a long sigh. "Yeah, sure, okay. Whatever blows your skirt up.

***

Marty stepped from the Sheriff's car and eyed the big Helstrom house, which was surrounded by a wide green lawn, the lake beyond glittering through a pine woods that swept down to the beach. Upstate New York, the place would fetch five million, easy; here in the sticks it was probably worth a mil. Regardless, the Helstroms were obviously very well off. He followed Colvin to the front door, where the kid's parents waited for them.

Joan Helstrom was a looker, her jeans and sweater showing off a trim, athletic figure. Marty tore his gaze away from the seductive form to shake John Helstrom Sr.'s hand. He was a good match for his wife, with a tanned, handsome face and a body that suggested hours spent in the gym.

The parents led Marty and Colvin across the main room to the foot of a curving staircase, where John Sr. stopped and turned to his guests. "We were a little reticent about this interview," he said. "Johnny's been having nightmares…"

"But then," his wife added, "we thought it might be good for him to talk about his…experience…and to help find Kip."

"We won't be long," Colvin said. He cocked an eye toward Marty. "I believe what he tells us will be quite useful."

They climbed the stairs, walked down a hallway, and with a knock entered Johnny's room.

A big German shepherd confronted them just inside the room, a low rumble escaping his throat. Marty took a step back.

Joan Helstrom brushed the dog's head with her fingertips. "Max, *einstellen. Sitz.*"

The dog slunk a few paces into the room and sat, quietly facing the two strangers, a Don't Fuck With Us expression on its otherwise handsome face.

The Helstrom boy was propped up in bed, a Gameboy cradled in his lap, looking his guests over with a neutral expression. A bandage spiraled around his left forearm, and Marty guessed, from the bulges beneath his T-shirt, that more bandages covered his torso. Introductions made, Marty and Colvin sat in chairs beside the bed, while the parents took a nearby couch.

Colvin silently held the photos out to Johnny, who stared at them with widened eyes. "These are from my camera, right?" he asked. "This is that big room I told you about, the one that had all the monitors and stuff and was set up like Mission Control." He lifted another photo, his face contorting with a shock of recollection. "This one...this one is where Kip fell, where those glowing things were..."

Marty glanced at the parents, who had leaned forward on the couch, watching their son with obvious concern.

Colvin collected the photos and looked at the boy. "You say something glowed. What color?"

"Blue, and, well, sorta purple. And they made sort of a hissing sound, like electricity." Marty saw Colvin react to this statement as if he himself had been goaded by a tiny electric shock.

"Well," Colvin said after a moment "that's interesting." He fished something from the bag he was carrying and held it out to the boy. A baseball.

Johnny turned it over in his hand. Marty saw tears well up in the kid's eyes as recognition and confusion hit him. The eyes flashed to Colvin. "It's Kip's!" he said. "He had it with him. Where did you get it?"

"We found it in the river this morning, close to where they found you."

"I don't understand. Maybe he fell in too...maybe..." He stared off into space.

Colvin stood and patted the boy's knee. "You've been a great help, Johnny. We'll keep looking for him, don't you worry." The boy was staring at the baseball again, rolling Joe DiMaggio's signature over and over in his hand, his brow furrowed in concern. "Why don't you keep that?" Colvin said.

Marty followed Colvin toward the door, then turned back. "Johnny?" he said. The boy looked up at him. "Are you sure you went underground...inside some tunnels?"

"Yeah. I'm sure." His gaze flicked back to the baseball.

***

Colvin strode purposely across the driveway, head bowed, Marty hustling to keep up. They climbed into the cruiser and Colvin paused, staring through the windshield, seemingly lost in thought.

After a moment, Marty turned toward him. "That kid was telling the truth." Colvin merely glanced at him and nodded. "Look," Marty added. "I'm not promising anything, but give me some time. I'll see what I can find out."

Colvin started the engine. "Hurry. Because there was something that boy said that has me very worried."

As they drove away, Marty tried the cellphone and was pleased to find the static had fallen enough to allow conversation. Sweeney answered. "Charles," Marty said, surprised at the strength in his own voice. "I need the helicopter. I'm flying out to the North Ridge base."

18

P ull over here," Charles Sweeney barked into the intercom, and the big limousine swerved into a small parking area bowing out from the side of the mountain road. Tires crunching over gravel, the car rolled to a stop beside an outcrop of massive sandstone boulders. The driver and bodyguard got out and walked several yards away, ensuring the attorney's privacy. They were just south of Kellsburg, and a safe distance from the infuriating radio interference that plagued the area.

Sweeney settled back into the limo's plush leather seating and keyed the satphone. There was an electronic beep, and the encrypted connection was made.

"This is Dodgsen." The voice was clipped, cold, intimidating. And Sweeney respected that. Philip Dodgsen was god, the real power behind Kendron Technologies, and for the past two years, as Thomas Kendron slipped ever closer toward the grave, Dodgsen had gradually closed his iron fist around the entire corporation. Old Man Kendron was still president, and mentally sharp; but he was immobile, physically removed from the company. And he was dying.

"Phillip, there's been a development."

Silence at the other end. Sweeney continued. "It's Marty. He insists on visiting the facility, and he knows about the tunnels."

"I see."

"What do you want me to do?"

"Exposure is not an option."

"I know, but…"

"What's the project status?"

"We're still in the sub-basement. And we've lost a second man."

"What the hell's going on, Sweeney? Why have you lost a second man?"

"Apparently, there's something down there—"

"Sweeney, two twelve-year-old kids got into those tunnels. This operation is costing me a quarter of a million per fucking *day*."

A bead of cold sweat tickled its way down Sweeney's back. He loosened his tie. "Yes sir, I under—"

"So you push, Sweeney. *Push*. Think what's riding on this. You deliver, and you become a very rich man. You fuck up; you get fitted for a prison uniform. I've paid people off, called in favors, and broken a dozen laws. Certain military figures are frothing at the mouth for this. It shouldn't be that difficult. We need the *device* and as much ancillary electronics as you can salvage. Then you blow the works up. Without the device, we have nothing."

Sweeney pictured Dodgsen seated behind the ornate CEO's desk, his panther's mane of black hair slicked back, his unsmiling, arrogant face that both threatened and commanded. Dodgsen was ruthless, cunning, and effective—the perfect corporate leader. He was Sweeney's ideal, and a man he both loathed and wished to emulate.

"But there's something else at work down there," Sweeney said. "We have no idea what it is. The men are spooked."

"You go there in person, and you tell the Captain and his pussy black-market thugs that I want action—now. If it's too tough for them,

I'll find another team. Clear?"

"Very clear, sir. But, there's still the matter of Marty Berringer..."

"He's a weak link. Fly him out there. Let him see. Read him. If he plays, he's in. If he's a Boy Scout...well...he's going to have an accident down there. Take Nick and Carmen with you. They're discreet. Get it?"

Sweeney's hand tightened on the armrest. "Yes sir."

"And one more thing. Next time you call, I want to hear that Marty's been dealt with and you've made serious progress inside those tunnels."

Dodgsen broke the connection.

Bastard. Sweeney snapped the phone shut and puffed out a lungful of air. He was too old for this shit—diverting corporate funds, lying, running around in the goddamned woods in the middle of frigging nowhere. And now he'd been roped into possibly committing murder. Dodgsen had essentially ordered the hit as easily as he'd order pastrami on rye. But Sweeney was in too deep to pull out now. He rolled the window down and signaled for the driver

This is a pass-fail test, Marty, and you'd better have the right answers.

Colvin dropped Marty off at the hotel and was headed out to find the search teams at NRAD when Margie's voice broke through the static. "You got another strange one," Margie said. "They found Abe Murdock dead at his metal shop in Kellsburg…"

Colvin pulled a U-turn and sped off southward. Ten minutes later, he slammed to a stop beside two police cruisers parked on the worn asphalt drive at Abe's Metal Works. Large patches of rust had eaten through much of the decrepit building's corrugated steel facade, and in places the roof sagged at an alarming angle. The only indication that anyone gave a damn about appearances was manifest in the professionally lettered sign at the edge of the parking area.

Colvin walked up to the entrance, where the tape had already been stretched across the open sliding door. The police chief was inside, scratching at his bald scalp. "You're late," he quipped.

"This," Colvin said with a sweep of his hand, "is getting to be a habit." He surveyed the scene: a boat trailer on blocks, welding machine nearby, and a body slumped at the end of a taut electric cable, a charred hand still clutching the welding tip. The same nauseating smell from Klatty's house and the lineman's death-room hovered in the air. The coroner fired his last camera shot and backed away as Colvin approached Abe's crumpled form.

The body was in a contorted position, appearing to have fallen while convulsing or twisting. The welding helmet, visor still closed, remained fixed to Abe's head. Colvin bent down and reached out to touch the helmet, then stopped, eyeing the amber fluid oozing from beneath its lower edge and pooling below the neck, where the vertebrae were visible beneath a shroud of loose and sagging skin. He held his hand up and wiggled his fingers. "Jim, got any...?"

The coroner tossed him a pair of latex gloves, and as Colvin tugged them on, the two other men crowded in behind him, expectantly watching. The silence grew, the only sounds coming from the creaking and popping of the metal shed as the sun began to fade.

Colvin seized the welding helmet in both hands and gave it a gentle tug, producing a thick sucking sound, but it remained firmly attached. He sighed, afraid to pull harder lest he separate the head from the body. He began gingerly lifting the black visor, hoping it would give him a view of the forehead—and any charred tendrils that might have found entry to the brain.

"I just want to see—" The visor snapped open on its spring-loaded hinges. Instead of the empty sockets exhibited by Klatty's and the lineman's skulls, Abe's eyes were still intact, the glistening, white orbs tethered by ragged strands of pinkish muscle. They stared lidless through the visor's rectangular frame, floating within darkened, gelatinous flesh. The irises contracted as the light hit them, and Colvin gasped—*Impossible!*

He jumped when the eyes suddenly darted to him.

A croaking voice rose from somewhere inside the sunken chest: "Col-vinn."

Leinway stumbled back, thrusting his hands out as if warding off an attacking dog. "Jesus!"

A breathless moment passed in the silent shed; then Colvin cautiously bent down to look again into the goggling eyes. "Abe?"

Abe's hand shot up, the bony fingers making a popping noise as they snatched at his windpipe. Colvin lurched backward and collided with the two men behind him. "Get away!"

They bolted for the shed's entrance, and Colvin paused and looked back as an intense electric buzzing rattled the welding machine. A crackling, blue-violet glow engulfed Abe's twitching body, expanding and contracting like the beating of a heart.

***

The Mesa Electric crew laconically disconnected power from Abe's welding shed and attached measuring equipment across the feed coming from the transformer in the alley. A skinny electrician in a blue jumpsuit left the building and ambled up to Colvin. "There's normal, three-phase, two-forty coming in. Ground connections are intact. The circuit breaker tripped from that short circuit inside, like it's supposed to. There's no problem, far as I can see."

Colvin nodded, and both men turned to watch the coroner's crew loading Abe Murdock's remains, an irregular mass within a black body bag, into the waiting van. The electrician shook his head. "Poor bastard," he said quietly, and walked off toward his truck.

The radio squawked, and Colvin climbed into the car and responded. Margie's voice was loud and clear, interrupted only by tiny bursts of static. "Morgue says they're ready, Sheriff. Also, Doctor Myerson will be there, like you requested."

"Have Jimmy contact Professor Weismann and Kerry Shaner. Tell them I've got a big job for them, if they're interested."

"Ten-four."

"Oh, yeah. Next time you hear loud static, write it down. What time, what it sounds like."

"Sounds like?"

"You know, screeches, grunts, buzzing, whatever."

"Ten-four, if that's what you want. Search party is breaking up for the day. They're pretty discouraged."

"Right."

"Commissioner Long was on TV. Says he's putting together his own search party, since you can't find that boy."

Colvin gave an exasperated sigh. "Great."

The coroner's van pulled away, and Colvin cranked the engine and followed, frowning, his mind replaying the ghastly scene inside Abe Murdock's shop. He glanced westward, toward a red sun suffocating behind a mass of heavy clouds, apprehension building like an August thunderstorm.

***

Beneath the glare of the overhead lights, Catherine Klatty and lineman Jerry Martin lay side by side on gleaming, stainless steel tables. Against the white-tiled purity of the autopsy suite, the dark cadavers, with their yawning mouths, eyeless stares, and claw-like hands, seemed even more horrifying than when Colvin had first seen them at their death sites. Doctor Carol Myerson, standing beside him, gave a brief shudder.

He knew she was still recovering from last night, when she had witnessed Martin being eaten alive by what Colvin now viewed as a rogue electrical force. He had called her this morning and apologized for having left her alone, and for having taken advantage of her less-than-sober state. "Oh, Greg, she had breathed, you have nothing to apologize about. It was wonderful." That statement lifted him off the ground; maybe he hadn't rushed things too much after all.

Now she pressed close to him—enough for him to feel the warmth from her body—seeming to draw comfort from his presence. He stifled the urge to put his arm around her and draw her in closer...

On Colvin's left stood Detective John Rios, from the Kellsburg Police, and Lieutenant Robert Breckley, from his own department.

Pathologist Roger Thornton, his plump, normally jovial face now clouded and somber, shoved his hands into a pair of latex gloves and walked to the table holding Klatty's remains. He took a deep breath and looked up, his gaze finding each of his visitors in turn. "I have never, in my fifteen years as a pathologist, learned of anything that would cause such a peculiar and severe degradation of the human body.

"You might be tempted to consider a ridiculous phenomenon such as spontaneous human combustion as the agent, but something even stranger happened here. The degradation appears to have been exogenous. These two cadavers exhibit evidence suggesting electrocution, but as for the rest of the...uh...injuries, I am at a loss to explain what happened."

He moved to Klatty's head and lifted free the top section of the old woman's skull, revealing an empty cavity. "When I cut away the skull, in order to remove the brain for examination, I found that something else had beaten me to the task. The entire brain is missing."

He paused for a moment, again sweeping each of his guests with a dark gaze. He held the skull section up before the light and pointed to a small dark spot in the forehead. "The frontal bone has been penetrated. This hole, which is three millimeters in diameter, is surrounded by black striations similar, I believe, to the current tracks produced by lightning. The cranial vault and both orbits have the same marks." He placed the section on the table and looked up. "The spinal cord is also gone."

Colvin's feeling of apprehension ramped up to full-blown alarm. "What about Martin?"

"Injuries in both bodies are the same." He frowned at Colvin. "Bear with me, Greg. I'm not finished." He turned to Klatty's shriveled chest, where thin, loose skin sagged between the ribs like a grimy yellow sheet.

The Y incision had been made and the ribs severed, but instead of the body cavity being left open, the coroner had folded the sections back together. "Every internal organ is missing. The body is exsanguine. I haven't been able to collect enough blood for an analysis."

"What about marrow?" asked Breckley.

Thornton picked up a six-inch section of bone from the table, turning it so Colvin and the others could see it was completely hollowed out. "From each bone I examined—tibia, femur, rib, scapula—all the marrow has been removed."

He motioned to the observers, and they shuffled forward in a reluctant line to peer closely at Klatty's chest. "Here is another puncture, one centimeter in diameter, similar to the one in her skull, just below the xiphoid process.

"I could assume that these holes might be the points of extraction or expulsion, where organs, vaporized by an intense electrical current, might have been ejected. But I found no ejecta, no evidence to support this. The holes, in fact, seem to tunnel inward. There was no residue on or near the bodies, other than a small amount of the thick fluid Greg first noticed."

Doors banged open as two dieners wheeled in another cadaver, still zipped inside its black bag, on a rattling gurney. They parked the body beside Klatty and began peeling away the plastic. It was Abe Murdock. Even with the powerful exhaust fans, the room soon filled with a foul odor.

Colvin stared at Abe's head. The helmet had fallen free when the paramedics removed his body from the shed, but now the gruesome, animated eyes were gone, leaving Abe with a blackened, leathery skull locked into a grimace of agony and terror.

Thornton slid his gloved fingers beneath Murdock's head, testing its weight, then pressed gently against the sunken sternum, his hand meeting little resistance. "Identical to Klatty and Martin," he murmured. "That's three people in two days, and these injuries are, well, impossible."

Colvin folded his arms, his eyes scanning the three ghastly remains. He cocked his head at Carol. "'Impossible' is a word I've been hearing a lot lately."

20

Going local?" Sweeney said, eyeing Marty's blue jeans and open-collar shirt. Despite the warm environment, the KT attorney was still wearing an expensive three-piece.

Marty felt defensive about having switched from necktie to denim, but the change had somehow been liberating. "Yeah," he replied. "Let's me merge with the enemy. Besides, they're comfortable."

The Bell 430 helicopter lurched and he grabbed the armrest, trying to steady his roiling guts by staring at the seat in front of him. This would be a short trip, and he was determined to manage the acrophobia without Dramamine. He forced himself to look at the ground and was amazed at how sparsely settled the area looked from the air. When the military had searched for an isolated spot back in the forties, they got it when they found the North Ridge site.

After a moment, he glanced at Sweeney, who was watching him with an inscrutable expression—or perhaps one of disdain. "Tell me what's going on," Marty said.

"I'm glad you're doing this, coming out to see. We've got this thing really well organized..."

"Have they found anything about the kid?"

"We've got fifty men on the ground, plus two very well-equipped helicopters."

"Just to find the kid, huh?"

Sweeney shot him another look. What was it: arrogant, supercilious, smug?

"Ah," Sweeney said, peering through the window, "here we are."

Marty took a deep breath and looked down again. Below was a vast stretch of forest, its green canopy broken here and there by the browns and tans of wrecked buildings. From the air, the demolished, overgrown roads and parking areas could be plainly distinguished. The view reminded Marty of aerial photos he had seen of ancient Mayan or Incan ruins. Off to his right, he glimpsed the silver thread of a river running in a deep gorge, feeding into the shining blue expanse of Lake Arrowhead.

The chopper slowed, and as it turned he saw a cluster of ruined buildings and a wide clearing occupied by two enormous black helicopters. The Bell descended and settled onto the freshly cleared ground, kicking up a swirl of damp pine needles and decayed vegetation. Marty stepped from the chopper and picked his way over the rough earth, bending low beneath the spinning blades.

He followed Sweeney toward a portable contractor's shed, about twenty feet square, erected in the shadow of a three-story gray building. The big building's roof was partly gone, and a portion of the wall had been blasted outward, leaving a deep mound of cinderblocks and bricks long claimed by vines and dense undergrowth. Marty noticed windows set into the somber walls were narrow and barred. Like a prison, he thought.

Nearby, men in fatigues were unloading metal containers of Semtex plastic explosive from one of the helicopters and stacking them on pallets near the edge of the clearing. A generator big enough to light a small village grumbled beside the portable building, its exhaust emitting a dark plume of diesel smoke.

Marty was surprised to see two fully armed guards in combat uniforms flanking the small building's door. Pausing before the entrance, Sweeney said, "This is the nerve center for the operation. Come in, I'll introduce you to the captain."

"Captain?"

Sweeney opened the door and they stepped into a windowless room that smelled of sweat and hot wiring. Against the far wall, three men wearing headsets sat before a row of electronic gear and computers. Marty could just make out garbled speech fighting through static that crashed and hummed from a nest of speakers. On an easel near the center of the room stood a diagram of some kind—probably a building elevation—but he could make no sense of it.

From behind a desk on his left stepped a rugged-looking man of about forty, dressed in green, tan, and gray ACU fatigues. His hair was cropped so close to his skull that pink, shining skin dominated his appearance. He was not smiling. As he approached, Marty noticed the captain's bars pinned to his lapel and an unidentifiable insignia on his chest. Then he noticed the pistol strapped to his belt.

"This is Captain Robert Torsen," Sweeney said.

Marty introduced himself and returned the brief handshake.

"What branch of the military?"

"We're a security division," returned the gruff, clipped voice.

Sweeney broke in: "They handle special situations, such as toxic substances, bombs, unusual threats, that sort of thing."

Marty again directed a question to Captain Torsen. "What's so dangerous that a federal unit would be called in?"

Torsen's gaze traveled to Sweeney. "We're investigating several potential threats."

"Like what?"

Sweeney interrupted before Torsen could answer. "I'm taking him below."

The captain frowned. "This isn't a good time…"

"It's all right. I want Marty to see everything. We have nothing to hide." With that, Sweeney took Marty by the arm and began pulling him toward the door. "I'll explain more, but let's let this man do his job…"

Marty broke Sweeney's grasp and turned back, feeling the blood rush to his face. "Any progress finding that kid?"

Torsen shot Sweeney another look. "Not yet." An intercom bleated, and without another word Torsen turned on his heels and strode back to his desk.

Marty glanced again at the diagram on the easel. Now he thought the drawing might represent tunnels and rooms, and if this were true, there was an entire complex below ground. Sweeney tugged him again toward the door.

Outside, the dying sun had thrown a brilliant, red-orange wash across the sky that highlighted the greens and earthen tones of the surrounding woods and hills. *Christ*, he thought, *I'm actually beginning to like it here*. The perimeter lights snapped on, filling the clearing with amber light.

Marty turned to Sweeney. "Now tell me what's really going on."

The attorney gave him a sideways look. After a long pause, he answered. "Your grandfather wanted you to accompany me, wanted you to know what it takes to protect a company as large and diversified as Kendron Technologies. This property is a serious liability.

"There are things that we can never allow to become public, things we must protect against prying eyes." He looked aside for a moment, then spoke slowly. "And things from which we might derive a great deal of profit." He paused again. "But it all has to be handled with... discretion."

"What has this got to do with finding a lost child?"

Sweeney gave a long sigh and hiked up his pinstriped trousers. "That boy is dead."

"How do you know that?"

Sweeney's voice sharpened, became oddly condescending. "Because there is something terribly, terribly *bad* inside those tunnels. We know it kills. It has already killed two of our men."

Marty froze for a moment, then took a step toward Sweeney. "What the hell are you telling me? First you lied about the tunnels, and now you're saying we've not only got tunnels, but that something inside them is killing people."

"It's moot. After we learn more about this...thing...we're going to destroy the tunnels."

"This is insane! How would that protect the company? Why not tell the truth?"

"That's an asinine question, and you know it. Why do you think? Because of the company's history, Marty. We would be ostracized—demonized. We would be ruined."

"But when people learn about this..."

"No one will." Sweeney's eyes locked onto Marty. "Unless someone talks."

"Damn you, Sweeney! What about all these men? How are you gonna' keep them quiet?"

"They're a covert team. The government has a stake in this too."

"Jeez!"

Sweeney's gaze traveled out toward the woods. When he finally spoke, his voice had turned hard and low, the words forced. "You'll see it...see for yourself what's hiding down there, and what we've got to gain—or lose."

He whirled around and began striding along a dirt path that wound through a copse of trees, toward the destroyed building. Seething, Marty watched him for a moment, then followed.

Light from construction lamps illuminated the building's entrance, which was relatively intact despite the explosions that had ripped through three floors and taken out part of the south wall and roof. Electric cables from the generator snaked along the path and disappeared into the fractured entranceway, providing power for a string of bright, tripod-mounted floodlamps.

Inside, leaves and pine needles suffocated the floor, and an odor of dampness and decay hung heavy in the air. Dark, hollow offices with shattered windows brooded to the left. Ahead, a concrete countertop that must have served as a reception desk supported an ancient, mold-encrusted telephone and a wire-mesh basket choked with rotted papers.

The cracked wall to their right held a rusted steel door inset with a window hatched with steel bars. Above the arch, faded lettering read WARD-A.

Sweeney snapped on a flashlight and pushed the door open on protesting hinges. "This way." They walked through a long hallway, feet crunching over fallen plaster and fractured glass. Gaping cracks in the ceiling and walls crawled with shadows as they passed, and in some places the overhanging masonry looked so precariously suspended that an entire section could collapse with no more than a whisper of encouragement.

Numbered rooms with steel doors and shuttered observation windows appeared at intervals along the hallway, like the quarters of a primitive mental institution. Marty shivered.

They turned left at an intersection and passed what appeared to be a nurses' station. Gurneys covered with black and tattered bedding lined the narrow space, and moldering, dust-covered clipboards, medicines, IVs, and other paraphernalia crammed the storage shelves. It looked as if no one had visited the place since its abandonment in the sixties.

Sweeney ducked into a dark stairwell and Marty followed him down, hearing only his own heavy breathing and the echoes of their footsteps on the gritty stair. The air in the lower floor was as still as death, laced with a fetid odor that constricted his throat.

In the wavering beam of Sweeney's flashlight, Marty could make out DIAGNOSTICS-3 lettered above a door. Inside the room, a small utility lamp faintly illuminated a rusted X-ray machine hulking in the shadows, its curved armature arching down like the head of a predatory beast.

A window on the right wall, glowing with a pale yellow light, silhouetted a man in a white lab coat. Marty instantly recognized Dr. Carl Heim, the dour scientist he had met on the company's helicopter the day before. Without uttering a word of greeting, Heim glanced up, then resumed studying a small electronic gadget he was carrying, evidently taking readings of some sort. Two somber men in combat dress stood close to the window, rifles ready, staring at something in the space beyond.

Waved on by Sweeney, Marty edged close to the window and peered through the thick glass into the adjoining chamber. It was set up like an interrogation room, with a long, heavy table and two straight-back chairs bolted to the floor. His eye was next drawn to a slash of graffiti on the far wall—GHOST MACHINE—scrawled in heavy, hesitant strokes the color of dried blood. Beside the lettering was a crude drawing that reminded him of a Grateful Dead poster: a skull whose empty cranium hosted a stylized bolt of lightning.

Then he noticed two military uniforms splayed across the shadowy floor like rags. He looked closer. Something was inside the clothing, giving them bulk, and there, above the shirt collar, deeper in the shadows, a head—eyeless, with a film of wrinkled flesh hugging the skull. Marty jumped back. "What..."

"They were killed five hours ago." Sweeney's voice was close to his ear, low in tone, strangely modulated.

Marty stared at the attorney, his mouth open, stunned, his eyes begging the question.

"They were part of the advance search team," Sweeny said. "They found this room, and something attacked them...left them...like that." His body tensed as he spat the next words. "And that's why this place is so *fucking dangerous!*" He edged closer. "Don't you see? This cannot be revealed—"

"Will you *shut up!*" Dr. Heim hissed. "Keep your voices down."

The scientist stood four feet away, scowling, his face taut with anger and fear. As he lifted a handkerchief to mop sweat from his forehead, Marty could see his hand was shaking.

Footsteps scraped softly across the floor, and Marty turned to see two men in business suits enter the examination room—the same heavyweights he had met aboard the helicopter in New York. With only a brief glance around the room, they took up positions immediately behind him, their attention drifting to Sweeney.

"Stinks down here," one of the thugs said, a bemused expression playing around his shark's eyes.

"Yeah," said the other. "Stinks"

Marty stepped away from them, new concerns creeping into his thoughts.

The instrument Heim was carrying beeped, and he studied the readout. "The level has dropped." He turned to one of the uniformed men. "Rickland, you can go in now. For the extraction. I think...it's safe enough."

Rickland was about thirty, muscular, with short brown hair and a pug nose. He looked tough, seasoned, his movements swift and confident. But his eyes betrayed a deep apprehension. He slung his rifle so its muzzle pointed forward, took a deep breath, and put his shoulder to the steel door connecting the two rooms. The door grated and scraped as he pushed, alarmingly loud in the suffocating quiet. A strong odor crawled through the widening gap—more of the acid stench that permeated the lower floor.

Rickland eased into the interrogation room and slowly approached the two fallen men, his right hand curled around the rifle, his free hand twitching nervously at his side. With a glance back at the window, he bent down, grasped the nearest body by the ankles, and dragged it quickly to the open door. The remaining soldier rushed to assist and pulled the corpse across the threshold.

Marty brushed a hand over his eyes as a sudden lightheadedness threatened to buckle his knees. Maybe it was the stale, rotten air combined with the sight of the grotesque bodies, but the urge to turn and race for the surface was almost overwhelming.

He glanced at Sweeney: he was staring intently through the window at Rickland as he cautiously approached the second corpse. The attorney's mouth twitched, his expression one of fascination—or was it more like that of a Roman emperor anticipating the final torture of a slave?

Beyond the window, the second collapsed soldier lay face-down, partly obscured by the steel table, and as Rickland bent down to seize the dead man's legs, something reared up from the body—ripped out of it—like a great, segmented insect. In the blink of an eye, it fell upon Rickland, its crackling, lightning-bolt appendages stabbing and squirming into his flesh like neon fangs. Rickland let out an ululating scream and staggered backward, the clinging monstrosity enfolding him in a lover's embrace from Hell.

Rough hands suddenly seized Marty beneath the arms and shoved him headlong into the interrogation room. Simultaneously, Rickland's M-16 jerked up and spat an arc of automatic gunfire that raked the walls and disintegrated the window.

Shielding his face against the slash and sting of exploding glass, Marty regained his footing and launched himself at the door. He grabbed the handle and pulled with strength born of total panic. Rickland twisted and bellowed, dancing closer and closer, atomized blood misting the air as he jerked against the thing writhing into his body.

The door yielded and Marty burst into the examination room, slid across a floor slick with blood and spiked with shattered glass, stumbled over a body and slammed into the wall. A light strobed on his right, screams penetrated the ringing in his ears, and he saw what his mind refused to acknowledge: the X-ray machine had moved into the center of the room, and impaled upon the beak-like radiation terminal was Sweeney, his body and arms jerking like a berserk marionette, his head spastically vibrating right and left, blue fire spewing madly from every orifice in his skull. It was like the electrodes of an immensely powerful arc welder had been shoved up his neck and the switch thrown to maximum.

Through the haze of smoke and blood, Marty saw ribbons of electricity burning, crackling, zigzagging over the splintered windowsill, down the wall, across the floor, sizzling in the pooled blood, worming straight toward him.

The generator cables exploded in a succession of loud, hissing pops and spewed bright fans of molten copper across the room. The incandescent bulb flickered out, the darkness now pierced only by the fitful glare of invading energy.

Marty bolted from the room and raced headlong into the jet-black hallway, his throat belting out a stark cry of terror.

21

arty groped forward in total darkness, his trembling hands crawling across the rough concrete wall, desperately feeling for the entrance to the stairwell. The screams emanating from the diagnostics room had ceased minutes ago. Now the only sounds were his heart hammering wildly in his ears and his breath sobbing in and out in a ragged cadence.

He found an opening and stepped through, arms sweeping the black void, probing for the stairs. Something scraped along the floor close behind him, and the air suddenly swelled with a ghostly blue radiance. He whirled around and dropped into a protective crouch.

The thing before him had a man's shape, an old man's head, with long thin hair waving wildly from the skull. It wore an unbuttoned coat, no shirt. And where the chest was exposed, there was no flesh, just the hint of spine and ribs, all entombed within a shimmering gelatinous mass.

The lips parted in a grim parody of a smile and an arm rose, extending a skeletal hand. The thing spoke, the slow, protracted words vibrating from its mouth infinitely pained and sad: "Hello. I'm Doctor Jack Pritchard."

Marty jerked away from the apparition and slammed backwards into the concrete wall. He looked to his right; the feeble light exposed steps, a handrail. He turned and fled, his legs powering him in a panicked dash up the stairs.

At the top he saw lights lancing through the dark, heard shouted voices and the pounding of boots on concrete. The soldiers rushed past him and knocked him aside without heeding his screamed warning. Then they were gone, six or eight of them, thundering down to the floor below.

Automatic gunfire echoed up the stairwell and poured into the hallway, and Marty stumbled in the direction from which the soldiers had come. A faint rectangle of yellow light: a door. Marty burst through it and into the building's reception hall. Flickering construction floods blinded him. More soldiers racing by. He saw the front entrance and staggered through the shattered door and down the steps.

In the fading twilight, he found the trail leading to the command hut and the helicopters. More men had gathered in the clearing, readying weapons and gear, Captain Torsen shouting orders. Beyond the soldiers, rotors of one of the black helicopters were spinning up, its twin engines emitting a rushing whine.

The Kendron Technologies Bell 430 was a hundred feet away. He raced to it, flung the door open, and vaulted in. The pilot turned to stare. "What the hell's going on? They've been—"

"Fly this sonofabitch out of here."

"What about Mr. Sweeney?"

"I said *get us out!*"

The pilot cast a worried glance at the dark staging area, then tugged on the headphones and flipped switches on the console. A low, rising moan escaped the turbine, and in a minute they were riding a cloud of debris, climbing above the ruined gray building, the black helicopters, the now silent generator, and Captain Torsen's electronic command center.

As the chopper's nose dropped and they accelerated southward, Marty thought he could hear, rising above the whining engine and whirling blades, the chatter of machine guns and the agonized screams of men.

22

Nurse Betty Aldrich left her VW Beetle in the driveway and walked toward the rear of the house, her white hospital sneakers treading silently along the uneven brick path. As she approached the back door, the security lighting clicked on and revealed her handsome Siamese cat, Casper, who watched expectantly from the kitchen window. The last two days at Grayson Medical had been harrowing and exhausting, and she was eager to spend a little quality time with her pet and settle in early with a good book.

She glanced up at the hill that began its rocky ascent just beyond the garage, her gaze coming to rest on the old mining-tunnel entrance. She could usually glimpse the locked steel doors that prevented the foolhardy from venturing inside. But now, in the feeble glow of a shrouded quarter moon, there was nothing but darkness at the mine's entrance, as if the doors had been opened. Strange.

When she had rented the old house in Cielo, she thought it was interesting to have a historic mining shaft within a stone's throw of the backyard, but over time the sealed opening had acquired more of a sinister feel. Tonight its ovoid shape seemed to resemble a great alien vagina, some horrific sculpture artist Richard Giger might have carved using bulldozers and dynamite. She shuddered at the concept.

Pausing at the back door, she looked once more at the tunnel entrance. In the wan light, the doors definitely looked as if they were open. If the county had been working on them, they would have barricaded the doors to keep people out.

Aldrich entered the house quickly, locked the door, and began turning on the lights. After witnessing that poor lineman being electrocuted right there in the OR, she had been feeling a bit jumpy, and had almost asked for the day off. But Dr. Myerson, and even that wuss Dr. Floran, had toughed it out, so instead she decided to work. This afternoon, though, she had gotten the shakes just riding the elevator to the second floor, and told the staff she hated approaching the room where the lineman had died.

Inside the kitchen, she popped the lid off a can of Tuna Especiale (Casper's favorite), emptied it onto a clean dish, and placed it in his feeding nook beside the refrigerator. But Casper ignored the proffered dinner and began making nervous figure eights around her legs, mewling, hanging on her every move.

"What's the matter Caz?" she asked. "You feeling spooky too?" Dogs and cats, with their hyper-acute senses, could detect abnormal phenomena that a human might miss entirely. Now, with Casper acting skittish, Aldrich was feeling more than a little apprehensive, and she'd never been afraid in her own home.

She grabbed a flashlight from the kitchen drawer and walked into the den, which offered the best view of the mining tunnel, and turned off the room lights. She switched the flashlight on and poked it up flat against the window, aiming the beam toward the mineshaft's dark mouth. But the glass and screen attenuated the beam, and the tunnel doors remained hidden in shadow. "Well," she said to the cat, "I'm certainly not going outside to check them."

She turned the house lights back on and picked up the phone. "I'll call the Sheriff, see if they'll send someone around. Can't have that cave open—"

The line was dead. Aldrich slowly hung up the receiver, tracing the cord with her eyes. It was still plugged solidly into the wall jack. Cordless units weren't reliable in Grayson County, any more than radios or televisions. Everything had to be hardwired because the local interference would often scramble a wireless signal.

Casper made that low, moaning-growl cats did when frightened, and she looked down at him. He was standing stiffly on the arm of the couch, looking straight out the window; then he arched his back. The lights flickered, and from the utility pole in the side yard came a loud hum followed by a *crack* like a rifle shot.

The lights went out.

Casper hissed as if he'd been struck in the face, and bolted from the couch. Aldrich could hear him scrabbling down the hallway toward the bedroom, where she knew he'd zoom under the bed, his primary hiding place, and ball himself up in the corner.

She looked again toward the tunnel.

And froze.

An ethereal blue light was sifting from the borehole's mouth— the same aura that had throbbed from the OR when lineman Jerry Martin was being electrocuted—and silhouetted against that nimbus were two dark figures shambling across the rocky terrain toward her own backyard. Perhaps it was a trick of the light, but pinpoints of blue seemed to race along their limbs and flicker where their eyes should be.

Aldrich backed away from the window. *Think, think.* Nurses were trained to react calmly and rationally during emergencies, but this terrified her almost to the point of paralysis.

The car was just outside, but what if more of the strange men were lurking beside the doors?

She didn't have a gun. But there were other weapons.

Leaving the flashlight off, Aldrich felt her way down the hallway and into the kitchen. The house was totally silent now, and she could hear her own breath surging in and out, the blood pounding in her ears. *Calm down!*

She reached the countertop, found the wooden knife caddy, and slid out the Henkel carving blade. If anyone came after her, they'd feel the bite of eight inches of finely honed German steel.

Knife grasped tightly in one shaking hand, the flashlight in the other, Aldrich reentered the den, where she could monitor both backyard and tunnel. *They know I'm here. They saw my car, saw me come inside, saw the lights...*

She moved cautiously toward the window and peered outside. A flickering will-o'-the-wisp still bled from the tunnel's maw, raising tongues of spirit-fire from the strata of fog creeping low across the ground. Phantasms of moonlight shape-shifted over the landscape, insufficient to illuminate any dark form or anomalous shadow.

Standing in the yard was a man, incredibly thin, little more than a ragged scarecrow. And he turned to stare at her with two baleful blue orbs

Then a closer mass reared up and cast its ghost-gaze through the glass. Aldrich involuntarily raised the knife high and clicked the flashlight on, pointing it straight at the creature standing just outside. Then she bent forward and screamed.

Red and black folds of flesh sagged from the figure's skeleton. Its chest cavity, outlined by the white of severed ribs, gaped wide and hollow. The skullcap and brain were absent, leaving only a truncated, empty vessel above the radiant eyes. Betty knew what stood before her, recognized it in an instant. It was the autopsied corpse of lineman Jerry Martin.

This cannot be!

A bony hand shattered the window and groped inside for the latch. Betty ran.

She charged to the front door, threw off the lock, and reached for the handle. Two luminous points floated past the bay window on her right—*eyes*—approaching the porch. *No! No! No!* She held her breath. From the den came a thump, then a crunching of glass as something lurched across the floor. In moments Martin's horrid form would come heaving into the living room.

She raced into the kitchen and stumbled to a halt: dazzling electric bolts sizzled from the light sockets and appliances and zigzagged across the floor, buzzing and popping, forming little blue fireballs that skittered toward her—*rising up on legs.*

A shock ripped through her body like a hot blade and she collapsed onto her back, the flashlight and knife flying from her hands. As she lay gasping, trying to regain control of her limbs, she saw Martin shamble into the room. Electricity snaked and flamed across his body, his cadaverous form pulsating with a blue-white corona. Martin's truncated head tilted down and he bent toward her. His fractured jaw gaped wide on its broken hinges, his claw-like hand opened, reaching...

Betty's eyes rolled back, and as consciousness fled she thought of Casper: *Who will feed you now?*

~~ 23 ~~

Colvin opened the basement door and stepped into the sterile confines of the Grayson Medical Center pathology department. Electronic equipment, computers, glassware, and cold-storage units nested on crowded countertops and lined the walls of the big room. He walked along a row of humming test instruments and nodded at two lab technicians as they looked up from the eyepieces of stereo microscopes.

Another door on his right, marked TEM, admitted him into an adjoining room filled with more electronics and rows of lab tables. Professor Joseph Weismann sat at a black table in the room's center, arms thrust into a pair of heavy latex gloves, manipulating something inside a plastic isolation chamber. Illuminated by a small overhead spotlight, the Plexiglas box seemed to glow independently in the room's darkened atmosphere. Against the far wall, in deep shadow, a human skeleton dangled from its metal stand like a grim marionette.

"Greg," Weismann said, an enthusiastic grin breaking across his face. "You have to see this."

Dr. Carol Myerson, standing several feet behind Weismann, looked up with a frown. Kerry Shaner was hunched over a countertop at her right, furiously working the keyboard of a laptop computer. There was a whir as a tiny printer curled out a sheet of paper.

"I acted on a hunch," Weismann said. "I took a sample of the fluid you collected at the scene of the lineman's death and, well, watch…"

Colvin peered into the chamber. Under the dome of a bell jar was a glass beaker holding about twelve ounces of an amber fluid. Two wires from an electronic box connected with terminals on the bell jar's base and entered the substance.

Weismann tapped the jar with a latex-gloved finger. "This is from the sample you gave me yesterday."

Colvin cocked his head. "That's a lot more than I collected. Where did the extra come from?"

"I'll get to that. First, watch *this*." He snapped a switch on the electronic box, then moved his fingers slowly toward the bell jar. A mass of faintly glowing tendrils instantly rose from the fluid, reached toward his hand, and tapped against the jar's thin glass wall with an audible pinging sound. As Weismann moved his hand over the jar's surface, the tentacles became agitated and stretched upward in a groping movement.

Colvin straightened. "Christ!"

"Now…" Weismann removed his hand and the tendrils melded into a phosphorescent trunk that twisted aimlessly inside the jar, as if searching. "It behaves somewhat like the pseudopodium of an amoeba, although far more aggressively." He turned a knob on the electronic box, and the trunk retracted back into the beaker, the substance settling again into a motionless amber pool.

Now this," Weismann said, lifting the lid of a small plastic container, "is the truly frightening part."

Carol ran a hand nervously along her arm, as if warding off a chill. "Careful, Dr. Weismann."

The lid came away, revealing a small cube of flesh-colored substance. Weismann fished the cube out with a pair of tongs. "It's a bit of chicken from the deli. I didn't have time to procure a dead rodent." He lifted the bell jar's domed top from its metal base and placed the meat inside, next to the beaker. "You asked how I increased the volume of the fluid..."

Colvin anticipated the next event, and the contemplation sent another cold finger squirming up his spine.

When Weismann turned the control knob, the fluid animated again, but this time the pseudopod lanced up from the beaker, arched over the side, and attached itself to the cube of flesh. In the subdued lighting, Colvin could see a faint blue light scintillating at the area of contact. If he pressed his ear against the enclosure, he was certain he'd hear a faint electric crackle.

"Hungry," came Shaner's voice. He was standing beside the professor now, peering into the box.

Weismann clicked the electronics off. "It's already assimilated half the meat."

The pseudopod slowly retreated into the main body of liquid inside the beaker, slinking away like a sated predator.

"I know what I saw," Colvin said, staring into the bell jar. "But what the hell just happened here?"

Weismann pulled his hands from the heavy gloves, leaving them dangling inside the chamber like shed skin. "Quite miraculous, really. The substance...perhaps we should name it something..."

"Something ghoulish," Carol said. She was now standing against a row of shelving, her arms hugging her chest.

"Ghoul-lash," suggested Shaner with a straight face.

"I'll name it Elektrum. That's what the ancients called static electricity. It was a complete mystery to them."

"I don't give a damn what we call it," snapped Colvin. "Tell me what it is—what it does."

"Well," Weismann said, sitting back, "you've seen what it does. It consumes flesh and grows. It remains inert until it receives an electrical jolt, accompanied by a command."

"A command?"

"You know," Shaner offered. "Sit, stay..."

Weismann turned to him irritably. "Do you *mind*, Kerry?" He looked back at Colvin. "The command is a modulated voltage. In this case, I mixed a signal with the DC feed from the power supply, the output of which goes through those two wires into the beaker. You saw what happened."

"Now I'm really confused."

"We can assume that the Elektrum is activated by some outside agent, and that it is quiescent until it receives enough current at a certain frequency." Weismann turned to Shaner. "Show him the trace."

Shaner rotated the laptop's screen into view and hit a key. "Already on it."

The screen crawled with a jagged green line that reminded Colvin of a heart monitor, or an oscilloscope representation of music or human speech.

"Kerry and I attached two digital storage oscilloscopes across the AC lines here in the hospital. This is one of the recordings. It shows a series of complex frequencies superimposed over the sixty-Hertz line current. The amplitude varied throughout the last twelve hours, ranging from nearly zero to a little more than five volts. These frequencies are the ones I duplicated for our experiment and constitute, I think, the command signal I was referring to."

"And, yeah," Shaner said, holding out the glass vial containing the circular implant. "I checked this scary baby out. It's made of old silicon-based semiconductors...really basic...but really smart. It's got FM oscillators and amplifiers plus a broadband low-frequency antenna system. All packed in epoxy resin and attached to the plastic disk. The output goes to these stainless-steel spikes." He tapped the vial with a forefinger. "And yeah, catch this. It's also got a passive radiator..."

Colvin folded his arms. "Now tell me what you just said."

Shaner gingerly placed the implant on the counter. "It's a transceiver, see, and it gets its power through low-frequency radio waves."

Weismann broke in. "Kerry was speculating that maybe that's why the radio interference is so high in this area."

"Bottom line," Shaner continued, "is that, if you stick this thing in somebody's head, it's sending and receiving right into their brain."

Colvin sighed and raked his fingers through his hair. "For what purpose?"

Shaner's pierced eyebrows lifted. "Ever see that fifties movie, Creature With the Atom Brain?"

"No."

"They cut off the tops of people's skulls and stuck electronics inside." He shrugged. "Radio-controlled people."

Colvin frowned, his own brain trying to grasp the implications. "If that's the case, then who's got the joystick?"

Carol stepped quickly forward and stared into the isolation chamber. "Dr. Weismann!"

Colvin's attention snapped to the bell jar. At first, he saw nothing.

"The power supply," she said, pointing.

Now he could see a thin wisp of smoke licking from the power supply's metal cabinet. Glistening amber fluid oozed from the instrument's cooling vents, massing into a thick glob beneath.

"Damn!" Weismann jumped to his feet and yanked the power cord from its socket.

The smoke dwindled, and the slime ceased its crawl from the vents.

"That's never happened before," Weismann said, his complexion pale. "How? The bell jar is sealed airtight..." He started to place his hands inside the gloves again, then stopped, clearly having second thoughts. "It would appear that this material, this Elektrum, is potentially far more dangerous than I had anticipated."

"You sure it can't get out of that box?" Colvin asked.

"I'm not sure of anything anymore."

"Then we destroy it..."

Weismann nervously rubbed his hands together. "No. Give me a little more time to...analyze it." He paused. "This is an astounding discovery. We cannot let something this important slip away from us. I'll take precautions for safety."

Shaner leaned forward. "Hate to interrupt," he said, "but you're missing the big question."

The professor turned to him with an impatient frown. "Well, what?"

"How did it get from the bell jar to the power supply?"

Weismann glanced back at the isolation chamber, and with only a brief hesitation shoved his hands into the gloves. He lifted the unplugged power supply and rotated it, carefully avoiding the trace amounts of slime that drooled from its chassis. "There is no visible trail connecting the power supply and the Elektrum inside the bell jar." He rotated the instrument and examined its sides. "It's almost as if it traveled through the copper wires themselves, which, of course, is impossible..."

"There's that word again," Colvin said.

Carol stepped forward. "I want to run a DNA sequence. I'll also need a sample for topology and morphology." She nodded at the apparatus behind her. "We have a good low-voltage electron microscope."

"DNA? Of course," Weismann said. "It's undoubtedly a protein of some sort. Perhaps it has a cellular structure." He set the power supply down and extracted his hands from the gloves. He inspected each finger, as if looking for traces of foreign material. "Obviously, this substance must be handled with extreme caution."

Carol nodded, glanced at her watch. "I have rounds to make, then I'll get started."

Weismann stood. "I'll have more equipment brought up from the university. I'm beginning to form an idea about the Elektrum, and while I admit I'm excited by the science behind it, I must say that I find this quite disturbing."

Colvin looked into the plastic chamber, then at the skeleton grinning from its stand against the wall. "Put the pedal to the metal," he said. "We've had three victims involving this...this stuff within twenty-four hours, and I have a queasy feeling things are getting out of hand."

— 24 —

Carol watched as Professor Weismann carefully inserted a frozen, 50-nanometer slice of Elektrum into the LVEM5 electron microscope, sealed the specimen chamber, and started the vacuum pump. Handling the mysterious substance, she thought, was potentially more perilous than wrangling rattlesnakes.

They were working late, and at this hour the pathology department was vacant, the only sounds their own movements and the faint hum of the electron microscope. There was no time for CDC protocol in isolating and handling the Elektrum—too much was at stake. They needed answers now, and Weismann, with doctorates in both physics and biology, was one of the preeminent few qualified to analyze the dangerous substance.

The LVEM5 monitor lit and he twisted the controls, manipulating the focus. "I'm in STEM mode," he said. "That way we'll have the most complete image, using both transmission and scanning methods simultaneously. "I'll start with two-thousand magnification."

The powerful microscope would, they hoped, reveal enough of the Elektrum's anatomy to understand how it functioned, and suggest ways to neutralize or destroy it.

She leaned in close to the monitor as the shadowy image took form. Sharpening on screen was a remarkably complex structure comprised of myriad branching veins that seemed to radiate outward from a central point.

"They resemble an electrical discharge, or the dendrites of a nerve cell," Carol said.

"I'll shift the axis, follow the branches." Weismann manipulated the joystick, moving the focus along one of the long channels until he found the source—a single dendritic cell hovering like a fireball in a thunderstorm, shooting frozen lightning bolts from its villous membrane through the surrounding plasma.

"It's really large," Carol said. "Possibly two hundred microns. Maybe it's some kind of motor neuron."

Weismann's voice rose in excitement "I'll go deeper, see if we can find the nucleus."

He increased magnification, refocused, and the cell's internal structure came into sharp relief.

The professor was silent for a moment; then he stiffened. "My God! This can't be real!"

"What?" Carol could see only a tangle of strange geometric shapes and angular, interconnecting lines nesting within the cell's body. "Some of it vaguely resembles crystals, or plasmids and amyloid strands."

Weismann's hand was trembling as he pointed. "The...the components, connections. Don't you see?" He took a deep breath. "There—the separated plates of a capacitor. And here, the emitter, base, and collector of a semiconductor. There's even an inductor, and electrocytes for building an electric charge. It's as if the cell were part of an integrated circuit."

He jerked his hand away from the screen and straightened, shaking his head. "I would never have thought this possible. The Elektrum is an inconceivable synthesis of electronic circuits and living matter—some sort of bioelectronic life form."

He reduced the magnification, and a dozen intertwining cells now filled the monitor. "They're a strange form of neuron," he said. "And yet I'm seeing mitosis—replication—with incredibly long DNA strands."

Carol looked at the professor, her heart racing. "Nothing like this exists in the natural world."

There was a faint whir as Weismann twisted the joystick. "I'll drop magnification to its minimum level."

Suspended in the Elektrum's amber plasma was a galaxy of bioelectronic cells, all wired together and communicating with one other—and possibly with something outside.

Carol shuddered. If not for the fact that the sample was frozen, she was certain the cells would be moving, searching. And if they received a command through the wires, or from radio waves or some other source, those cells would be reaching out, stabbing their lightning-like dendrites toward her, attempting to kill with an electric charge and assimilate...

But even as she considered this, the image suddenly jumped, the dendrites flaring outward in a snatching movement. Carol jerked away from the microscope as Weismann punched the switch, killing the instrument's high voltage accelerating current.

"I should have anticipated this," Weismann said, his voice taught with alarm. "The signal riding the AC line must have followed the electron beam, and the Elektrum was beginning to warm, allowing motility." He worked the power cord from its socket, wrapped it around the microscope, and stared down at the instrument. "Let's leave this for now. The Elektrum can't get out of the specimen chamber, and I have another experiment to perform immediately. If my fears are confirmed, we will have to deal with an emergency of extreme proportions."

With that, he wheeled around, sat beside the plastic isolation box, and thrust his hands into the latex gloves affixed to the side panel. Grabbing a pair of copper wires inside the box, he clipped them to electrodes rising from the container of Elektrum.

"These wires lead through sealed holes in this Plexiglas wall and terminate at a battery-powered converter supplying 120 volts. You'll also notice that I've placed a cube of protein an inch below the wires, next to the converter. This way, the Elektrum is totally isolated from the protein and the AC line—no Elektrum can escape, and it cannot pass the wall. The attached modulator introduces a signal that should activate the substance. Now, Dr. Myerson, if you'll please dim the lights."

Weismann pressed a button on the converter and removed his hands from the gloves. There was a faint hum as the device began delivering current through the wires and into the sample of Elektrum.

Carol turned off the overhead fluorescent lights and moved in close to watch. At first, she saw nothing. After a few seconds had passed, she noticed a faint glow forming on one of the wires passing above the cube of meat. A ghostly thread of electricity wriggled from the conductor and rapidly lengthened until it touched the cube; then it flared brighter, reflecting from the sides of the box, smaller threads of electricity crackling faintly across the morsel of protein. The flickering striations were identical to the horrid electrical discharges that had killed Jerry Martin a day earlier.

Carol stepped back. "That...that's what attacked the lineman. Oh, shut it off, shut..."

Weismann shot his hand back inside the glove and stabbed the power button into the OFF position. He removed his hand and slowly rose, backing away from the isolation chamber, shoulders hunched, faint light from the box reflecting from his eyes and throwing the hollows of his face into deep shadow. "Carol," he said, his voice barely a whisper, then gaining strength. "The room where the lineman was killed...we must sterilize it immediately. This room—locked. No one to enter without our approval." He turned to face her. "We're in very deep trouble."

— 25 —

It was ten PM when Colvin finally stepped into his house. He ripped off his tie and gun belt, dropped them onto the coffee table, and lowered himself with an exhausted sigh onto the leather recliner. Even memories of last night's intimacy with Carol couldn't rejuvenate his flagging energy.

His eyes roamed to the liter of Jim Beam in its glass-fronted case on the mantle (The plaque read: Break in case of emergency!), thinking how good it would be to feel that burn again, de-burring the senses. Some wag had given him the bottle as a joke, not knowing, in a twist of irony, that six years ago he'd started getting regularly swacked, and that the booze had cost him his job with LAPD. Working with a hangover didn't sharpen one's skills as a detective.

If he hadn't moved to New Mexico, and if the opening for Sheriff hadn't been waiting for him like a gift from God, he'd be...well, he didn't know what he'd be. He sighed. The difference between Doc Pritchard and himself was that the good doctor was still self-medicating his way down memory lane.

Grabbing the remote, he switched on the television and surfed to Channel 12. He had been up and running since before dawn—seventeen hours nonstop. He needed sleep, but the events of the last two days kept churning in his mind, depriving him, it seemed, of even the capacity to relax.

The mental images played in a constant loop: electricity crawling from a common electrical outlet and attacking a person, penetrating the head, somehow burning out the brain and internal organs...the stuff of lurching nightmares.

The skull Doc Pritchard had shown him—one of two that apparently came from NRAD—exhibited evidence of radical brain surgery. To what purpose? Was there a connection with the preternatural events that started with Klatty's death? Colvin had been lied to and stiff-armed by hotshot corporate attorneys determined to prevent access to the property.

Regardless of how he manipulated the data, all roads eventually led to Kendron Technologies, and to dark underground chambers hiding something so horribly dangerous and incriminating that, to protect the secret, a young boy's life was forfeit.

Tomorrow he'd again call the FBI resident office, insist they send a team of experts immediately. If that failed, Judge Reynolds would hear about it, as well as Senator Wellbourne—hell, even the governor. Marty Kendron was still incommunicado, and if no report were forthcoming by morning, Colvin would call a press conference and dump all over the state, the Feds, and Kendron's fat corporation.

He ground his palms into his eyes, exhaustion pinning him down like nails in a coffin. The TV droned on, repeating the local stories: a short bit about the missing boy, and another infuriating appearance by Commissioner Donny Long, vilifying Colvin and touting his own redneck offspring, Billy, Colvin's soon-to-be opponent in the next election. The news broke for a commercial, and he leaned back in the chair, thought about Carol. Her eyes—green, with a hint of gold. Beautiful...

A strange voice, distant, almost beyond the range of hearing, whispered his name. Colvin's eyes blinked open. The television was delivering a constant, soft hiss, its screen a mass of raging ghosts. He glanced at his watch: after midnight. The station was off the air; the voice had been a dream, sleep having taken him more than two hours ago. He grasped the recliner's handle and levered himself into a sitting position, determined this time to rise and make it into his bedroom.

The ethereal voice soughed again: "Grregg."

Colvin froze. The anguished words had come from the television, riding the hissing static like a wraith. An instant memory flashed into his mind: Abe Murdock's jellied, pop-eyed face staring up at him as Colvin peeled open the welding helmet; the beyond-the-grave snarl that rattled from the man's chest; the claw-like hand that struck at his throat...

"Hurrrry."

Colvin stared at the television, tensing to leap from the chair and run, fearing that effulgent blue threads of electric force might lance from the wiring and engulf him as it had Abe, and Klatty, and...

"*Hurry*," the voice groaned. Not threatening—tortured. He somehow recognized that voice.

"*Danger.*"

It was Doc Pritchard, sounding as if he were trying, with some final desperate breath, to deliver a warning.

"Comminng..."

The static ramped up to a full-blown roar. Colvin shot to his feet, snatched up his gun belt, and bolted through the front door, slamming the screen aside with his shoulder. In the front yard, he turned and watched the house, his breath exploding in quick bursts. The pale light from the television, which he could see through the side window, flickered brightly and snapped out, plunging the house into total darkness.

"Doc," Colvin whispered. He ran to the cruiser and tried the radio. Massive static blared back at him. "Shit!" He grabbed the cellphone and keyed Pritchard's number. "Shit again!" He threw himself into the car, cranked the engine, and smoked the tires onto the county road, light bar ignited. As the cruiser gained speed, he toggled the siren.

***

Colvin kicked the front door open with a crash and stepped quickly inside, sweeping his flashlight in a searching arc. He prayed the old doctor was upstairs asleep and had not responded to Colvin's shouts because of his diminished hearing. But he knew otherwise; the house was too dark, too silent. The light switches by the door, he noted, were in the ON position. He started to reach for a nearby lamp, then snatched his hand back. *Avoid the electricity*, the voice in the back of his mind commanded.

Then he detected the sickly-sweet odor of ozone.

"Doc!" Colvin raced upstairs to the bedroom. On a table was an open bottle of whiskey and a half-filled glass. A scrapbook lay open on the nearby chair. Pritchard had been amplifying his past with booze and had left the room, his reminiscence interrupted by—what? He checked the other rooms and flew back downstairs.

The smell of ozone thickened as he approached the den. He entered cautiously and licked the flashlight's beam across the desk, the side table, chairs, floor. Nothing. Then his eyes picked out a faint, blackened trail branching from the electrical outlet on his right. He let out a long sigh: Pritchard had probably come downstairs to investigate sounds or lights coming from this room. And then...

He searched the remaining rooms, then rushed through the back door and trotted to the garage. The doctor's old Lincoln was still there, doors unlocked, empty. He walked the grounds until the flashlight's beam began to weaken. Frustrated, he climbed into the cruiser and tried the radio. This time, his signal punched through gaps in the buzzing static. Peter Sanchez, working night dispatch, picked up.

"Lots of calls been comin' in about missing persons, Sheriff."

"Since when?"

"Since about twenty-one hundred."

"Why didn't anyone tell me?"

"Deputies are on it. Thought we'd let you rest—"

"Hell with that..." Colvin caught himself. "Sorry, Pete. Got another missing person for you. I want an ATL on Doctor Ralph Pritchard."

"Old Doc?"

"The same."

"And get some coffee brewing. I'm coming in."

"Ten-four, Sheriff."

Colvin started the car and sped away, calls cracking through the speaker as deputies checked in. Screw being tired. He'd amp-up on caffeine at the office and lay out a plan.

He could feel it in his bones like the approach of an electrical storm. Something monstrous was barreling their way, and it was gaining momentum by the second.

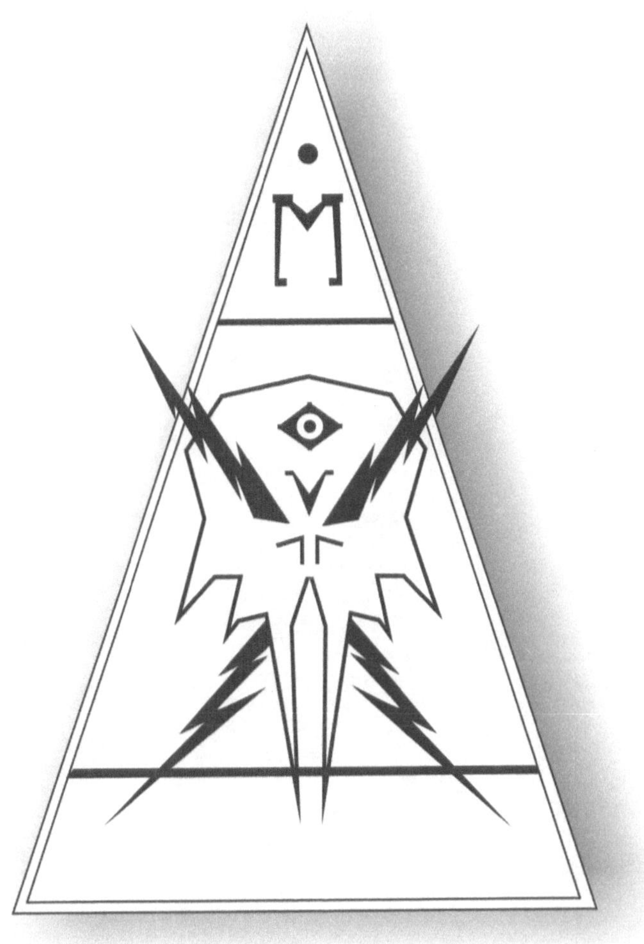

Part Two

The Electricity Is The Life

26

ey, Sheriff!" Sanchez looked up from the mike as scratchy blasts of communication zapped through the radio's speaker. He held out a sheet of paper. "Here's the update. The last missing person was almost at midnight. Lady called about her son, a high-school kid."

Colvin took the log sheet and coffee into his office, sat down and scanned the list. Eight people had vanished since nightfall: an electronics-store clerk who failed to return home; three power-company technicians checking out the old substation; two Kellsburg cops sent to look for the technicians; a nurse, and a teenage kid.

He swiveled around and faced the windows. Black against the grimy, bone-white walls of the office, they bore an uncanny resemblance to the eye sockets of a great skull. They blinked an ominous electric blue: a thunderstorm was cruising the horizon, its powerful discharges igniting the lowering bellies of massive clouds.

His telephone shrilled. It was Weismann, his voice strained and urgent. "Kerry and I have some extremely important information for you."

"Yes?"

"Can we meet at your office?"

I'll be here for an hour…"

"We'll be there in ten minutes."

Weismann was true to his word, and in fifteen minutes he and Shaner were seated across from Colvin's desk. They were tired and rumpled, but their eyes sparked with excitement. Weismann leaned forward, gesturing as he spoke.

"Dr. Myerson and I ran more tests and made some of the most astounding discoveries. At first, I didn't believe it. I thought there must be an alternative explanation. But it seems that the fluid, the Elektrum, is indeed a protein. It contains an incredibly strange DNA matrix that has, among other things, replicated numerous functions of electronic components, and…well…I'll spare you the details and get to the point." He paused, gathering a breath, then straightened and fixed Colvin with his eyes. "It travels through wires."

"What?"

"The Elektrum apparently converts itself into an energy form that can travel through an energized conductor, like power lines or house wiring. It can project itself from the conductor for a short distance as an electric charge, then change itself back into its physical form. This is inter-conversion of matter and energy. It's…unbelievable…utterly astounding!"

"Why does it do this? For what purpose?"

"To *feed*. You saw that. It absorbs protein, grows, travels through the wiring to find another…victim."

"Carnivorous electricity," Shaner said.

Colvin was silent for a moment, trying to sort this bombshell. "You're telling me the stuff—the Elektrum—I saw in that isolation chamber, is what killed Klatty and the other two?"

"I think so, yes."

"Colvin's voice became a whisper. "Good God."

"There's more."

Shaner unrolled a large map across Colvin's desk and pointed to an area bordered in red marker. "All of your weird deaths occurred in Cielo and Kellsburg, which get their electricity from the old Mesa generating plant upriver. They're on a separate grid from the rest of the county."

"I don't understand the significance."

"There's a power line running through the base that was disconnected from the substation around 1964."

"So?"

Shaner sighed impatiently. "The Elektrum can travel for a distance without needing a conductor. So even if the power line had been disconnected, the stuff might get into the substation and, you know, hitch a ride on the new line into Kellsburg."

Colvin shook his head, trying to clear out the cobwebs.

The Professor began again. "When the Elektrum is active, that is, feeding or converting from one form to another, it generates radio interference."

"So that's why our frequencies are knocked out…"

"Not entirely. It would require a great deal of power to obliterate reception over such a wide area."

"How does it manage to speak?"

"Speak?"

"Two hours ago a voice came out of my TV—called out to me. It sounded like Doc Pritchard's voice."

Weismann looked at him incredulously, frowning, but remained silent.

"And at the welding shop. Abe's body was lying there on the floor. He'd been attacked. He was dead, but he spoke my name. The sound came from inside his chest—not his throat. The others heard it too."

The Professor sat back in his chair and swiped a hand across his mouth. "It's possible for an electrical plasma to reproduce sound quite faithfully. But this...this opens an entirely new set of questions. It would presuppose an observing intelligence, something able to modulate the current to create specific sounds. Words." He shook his head. "I don't know."

"It's like ghosts," Shaner offered. "Maybe you should change its name to Ectoplasm, or maybe Electroplasm..."

Colvin sighed. "How do we stop this thing?"

Weismann thought for a moment, then replied with a tired voice. "I think we've only seen the tail of the beast. I'm afraid it will be necessary to go there, to North Ridge, and find out how it was created, for what purpose, and how they controlled it."

"Maybe that's the problem."

The Professor was silent, his brow lifted in question.

"Maybe they couldn't control it. Maybe that's why NRAD was destroyed, and the truth hidden."

"Something's got to be controlling it," Shaner said, "and I bet it's inside those tunnels."

Colvin glanced at his watch: 1:45. "I'm calling a press conference tomorrow—today—and I'm going to lay out everything, the full story. Before that, I'm calling the mayor and Commissioner Long and demand we organize an evacuation of Kellsburg and Cielo."

"What about NRAD?"

"There's a place Kerry and I need to visit first."

— 27 —

The tangle of vines hanging low across the entrance arch swayed uneasily in the fitful breeze, leaves fluttering like the wings of frenetic insects. Colvin stepped onto the porch, his flashlight beam centered on the yellow police tape stretched across the front door. He pulled the tape free, rattled the key into the lock, and stepped into Catherine Klatty's moldering house. The foul odor still soured the air.

Kerry Shaner entered the room behind him. "Stinks," he said, flicking his light around the cluttered space.

"Don't touch anything. And listen for anything...odd."

"You don't have to tell me."

They walked silently down the hallway and paused before the door opening into the den. Colvin entered, motioning Shaner to stay back. His flashlight beam touched the patched recliner, then traveled to the floor, lingering where fluids from Klatty's crumpled body had pooled and stained the threadbare carpet; then it found the ancient radio and its wooden face, veined by the mysterious charred tracks that had bled from the old woman's outstretched hand.

Colvin jumped as Shaner came up beside him. "So that's the famous radio?" he asked.

"Listen," Colvin said sharply. "This is not a game. I told you to wait."

Shaner shrugged. "Sorry."

Giving the radio a wide berth, Colvin walked to the attic door and tugged it open. Stairs led steeply up. "Forensics said there were boxes of old documents up here." Shaner followed as he slowly ascended the creaking steps and stepped into the attic. Junk, uniformly cloaked with dust and cobwebs, choked almost every square inch of the plank flooring. Colvin sighed—this was going to take forever.

Looking down, he noticed tracks left by the forensics team. They had evidently performed a cursory search, tossed a few things aside, and then left. Colvin hunched beneath the low rafters and followed the footprints to a corner and a stack of cardboard boxes. Tucking the flashlight under his arm, he dug into a box and lifted out a thick binder. It was dark blue and bore an embossed emblem: PROJECT MESMER.

He replaced the binder, lifted the box, and handed it to Shaner, coughing as a cloud of dust boiled up. Taking out a pocketknife, he cut away the cord securing the box beneath and opened it. It was packed with more of the blue binders.

Shaner breathed an awed whisper. "This is some gnarly shit, man." He was flipping through a binder, its pages fanning particles of glittering dust through the beam of his flashlight.

Colvin looked as Shaner held the binder out: a series of color photographs of a man's shaved head clamped in a shiny metal contrivance; a cylinder sliding into place; the cylinder being removed; another device being inserted—a steel jellyfish like the one Johnny Helstrom had found inside the North Ridge tunnels.

Colvin's radio suddenly hissed with static. He clicked it off and glanced at Shaner, who was staring at him with alarm. Just as Colvin hefted the second box, the stairwell's throat resonated with a thin, distant voice:

Crazy Cathy Klatty

Shaner's binder hit the floor with a thud. "Oh God!"

Colvin gave him an urgent nudge. "Get moving!"

Shaner snatched up the fallen binder, grabbed a box, and with Colvin behind shuffled to the stairwell.

"Wait," Colvin whispered, stepping around the younger man. He killed the flashlight and stared down into the black void, hearing only his and Shaner's rapid breathing. Flicking the light back on, he crept down the steps and peered into the silent den.

At first, he saw nothing. Then, across the room: two faintly luminous globes hovering about three feet above the floor, tethered by ghostly cords rising like smoke from the back of Klatty's radio. He pulled back inside the stairwell. "Shit!"

Behind him, Shaner squeaked. "*What?*"

"Some kind of...things above the radio."

Shaner's reedy voice almost cracked "What're we gonna' do?"

"We'll be trapped if we go back up."

Husband died...

A buzzing sound issued from the darkness, and Colvin again looked into the room. A blue-white light sparked from the back of the radio, casting scintillating, abstract patterns against the walls and ceiling.

"It's changing."

Panic rose in Shaner's voice. "We have to get out of here!"

"There's a window on the left."

A new sound: a pulsating hum, rising and falling, droning from the attic. Colvin looked up. A pale light appeared, and through the black stairwell opening above crawled a phosphorescent mass shaped like a five-fingered claw. Pulling itself forward on long, spindly fingers, it crept steadily down the steps toward them.

Colvin burst into Klatty's den and threw aside the cardboard box. He grabbed a wooden chair and swung it against the window, smashing a ragged hole to the side yard. Something behind him sputtered and flashed. He turned: a swarm of spidery shapes erupted from the radio and thrashed across the floor toward him, their forms crawling with pinpricks of light.

Shaner lurched from the attic doorway. The heavy box spilled from his hands. "*Damn!*"

Colvin gestured frantically. "Get out—*now!*"

But the other man had frozen where he stood, staring at the onrushing shapes. Colvin grabbed Shaner by the collar and belt and in one fluid motion hurled him headfirst through the shattered window.

He looked back. The phosphorescent things were ticking across the floor and walls, now less than eight feet away.

Colvin snatched up a box, tossed it after Shaner, and grasped the next one when he saw one of the spiders crawling onto the cardboard lid. A pair of luminescent jaws snapped at his hand. He heaved the box and its glowing passenger through the window, then swung his legs over the sill. A violent electrical shock ripped through his body and he felt himself falling back into the room, saw the hand creeping on its witch-fingers toward him, the spider-things converging like a glowing tide.

Another shock seared his system, and his thoughts dissolved before an onslaught of amplified screams.

***

Splinters of light flashed behind his tightly shuttered lids. He was on his back, being dragged, each jerking motion firing shards of pain through his body. He forced his eyes open, heart hammering from his last memory—spidery monstrosities swarming…"Stop!" he croaked.

A face appeared. "Greg. You okay?" The voice belonged to Deputy Frank Parnell.

Colvin rose on an elbow and wrestled himself into a sitting position. He felt as if he'd been thrown from a moving car. Light played across his eyes, and he looked out to see a house engulfed in flames, smoke boiling into a sullen sky. Approaching sirens whooped and shrieked. "Where the hell am I?"

Parnell nodded toward the fire. "That's Catherine Klatty's house. You're across the street."

"Kerry?"

"Right over there."

Shaner was sitting five feet away, flashlight in hand, head bent toward one of the binders they had salvaged from Klatty's attic. Two cardboard boxes with the remaining documents rested on the lawn beside him. He looked up, gave an indifferent wave, and resumed reading. Clusters of people stood in nearby yards, goggling at the conflagration.

Colvin rubbed the back of his neck. "How did I get out?" His tongue felt thick.

The lead fire truck, a foam unit, stopped with a squeal of brakes. Its crew hit the ground and began pulling hose.

"I had just arrived, so I ran over and helped," Parnell shouted over the rising noise. "Kerry had you halfway through the window."

More sirens and the blatting of air horns sounded as another fire truck roared up, an ambulance and patrol unit following in its wake. Parnell pulled Colvin to his feet and pointed him toward the ambulance.

Colvin squared his shoulders and winced as pain spiked from his back. "Don't need the medical."

Parnell nudged him forward. "Come on, just to be sure."

Inside the ambulance, he sat down on a gurney, then saw the blood weeping from lacerations on his arms and legs. A few on his back and butt, too. He had undoubtedly gotten them from broken glass when he was dragged through the busted window.

He shucked off his bloodstained trousers and eyed the swollen, red-purple blotches circling his right calf. He gingerly probed the tender area. "That's where that damned thing got me," he mumbled. The paramedics exchanged questioning glances, but Colvin decided not to explain. He looked over at Shaner, who was seated on the opposite gurney, his scrawny torso exposed to the bright light. A paramedic was applying a gauze bandage to a glistening slash on his chest. "I see you took a few hits too," Colvin said.

The computer geek gave him a sour look. "You didn't have to throw me through the window."

"You froze up…"

"I was studying the things."

Colvin sighed. "Well, thanks for saving my life."

Shaner shrugged.

Colvin winced as the medic applied something to a cut on his back. He looked at Shaner again. "How did you get me off the floor? I weigh two ten."

A smile cracked Shaner's face. "Wasn't easy."

"And those spider things..."

"They faded out. I think they ran out of charge, because they weren't connected to anything. But that claw-shaped thing was still coming. If that had gotten you..." He shook his head.

Beyond the ambulance, the pump unit's motor roared, a white swath of liquid foam arching up from the fire hose, jetting into the orange fireball that had been Catherine Klatty's house.

28

Legions of dark clouds rolled across the sky, suffocating the early morning sunlight, reflecting leaden gray from the lake's unquiet surface. Along the shoreline, the woods still held the night's shadow.

Johnny Helstrom turned from the window and looked down at the toy soldiers arrayed in assault positions on the table: tanks, mortars, artillery, rifle platoons. A phalanx of alien monsters crept over the sandy ridge, ready to ignite the battle for planet Earth.

He plucked the figures from their carefully arranged positions and dropped them into a shoebox. Toy soldiers were for play. Life was actual. And the aliens with skull faces were too…real.

He was sliding the box onto the closet shelf when his father came into the room. "Hey, Tiger. You're up early."

"I couldn't sleep."

His father sat on the bed and motioned Johnny beside him. "Let's have a look at those bruises." He lifted Johnny's T-shirt and examined the purple welt that had blossomed on his left side. "Looks better."

"Looks awful."

"At least nothing is broken."

"Feels like it."

His mother walked in, suited up in her pink and black jogging outfit, ready for morning exercise, and frowned at the monster bruise. "You're to get plenty of rest. Doctor's orders, remember?" She sat down beside him, brushed his hair back, kissed his forehead. He hated being babied, but this time he secretly appreciated the attention.

His parents went downstairs, and even with Max's comforting presence, the room suddenly seemed colder. Pulling the backpack onto his lap, he unzipped it and fished Kip's most prized possession from the inside pocket. He turned the baseball over in his hand so the autograph showed—Joltin' Joe DiMaggio—dated 1937.

Kip could quote Yankees stats until you went comatose, and DiMaggio was his favorite player of all time. Baseball had been Kip's life. Even though he was small, his skinny arms could wallop a ball farther than anyone else on the team, including Johnny, who was an inch taller and outweighed him by ten pounds.

Johnny remembered the day Kip first showed the autographed ball to him. He'd worked and saved for an entire year to buy it. And when his family visited New York last summer, his dad took him to a Yankees game, and then to Grandstand Sports on Mad Avenue, where he paid over twelve hundred bucks for it.

Instead of putting it in a glass case, or a box or something practical, Kip carried it wherever he went. If he had a pocket big enough, that ball would be in it. And woes betide anyone who tried to take it from him. Two assholes at school had tried to steal it—older and bigger kids who had once beaten Kip up, calling him a pussy and teasing him for his "girly hair." They knocked Kip down and tried to take the ball from his pocket. Those kids limped home after that encounter, one guy with a broken nose and the other with a shiner that lasted for three weeks.

It had been wrong to tell Kip he was stupid to carry the ball around, or that it wouldn't bring him good luck (although *that* was certainly true). The ball was special. It had absorbed the roar of the crowd, felt the impact of DiMaggio's powerful bat, been held by Joe himself and signed by him. And just maybe that homerun jolt had hammered some of the game's magic past the stitched leather into the core of the ball itself...

Johnny felt a curious comfort as he cradled the ball against his chest, shielding it from the tears that burned their way down his cheeks.

It was he, Johnny, who was stupid.

And guilty.

29

The wipers chopped rain from the windshield as Marty carved the final turn to the mansion. The frantic rush from NRAD to Hyde Park had taken over four hours, and he was bone tired, disheveled, filthy, smelling of smoke and God-knows-what. He had called his grandfather's personal number from the Learjet and the old man, to Marty's astonishment, had granted him the privilege of a visit.

He braked the rented car before the steel gate, and the guard stepped from his cubbyhole and scrutinized him through the side window. After a minute, the gate swung silently open, and Marty drove through.

The great house, a gargoyle-festooned monstrosity, crouched from the side of a small mountain rising from a dozen acres of security-fenced granite in upstate New York. Despite the abundance of exterior lighting, it radiated as much warmth as a mausoleum.

He parked, walked up the broad steps, and paused before arched doors large enough to accommodate a double-decker bus. A bruiser in a dark suit, radio mike curling up to his mouth, appeared in the doorway. Another brief scrutiny. "Mr. Berringer?"

"That's me."

The gorilla stepped aside and gestured to a thin man gloved in a formal butler's outfit. "Please come in, Mr. Berringer. Hascombe will show you up."

Marty stepped inside and fell under Hascombe's cold stare. The white-haired butler stood for a moment, hands clasped behind his back, his narrowed eyes weighing Marty's appearance. He finally turned and started off across the ballroom-sized entrance hall. "This way, sir."

Marty glanced up at a twenty-foot frescoed ceiling heavily framed with ornate molding. Gilded furniture sat in formal clusters, mirrored by the polished marble floor. Gray walls hosted enormous portraits that glowed softly under the rays of hidden lighting.

They rounded several corners, traversed a maze-like hallway, and stopped before hardwood-encrusted elevator doors, which slid quietly open at Hascombe's touch.

As they stepped inside, Marty glanced back down the broad hallway: he was already lost, and a small shiver squirmed up his back as the space reminded him of the North Ridge tunnels, albeit with more expensive appointments and better lighting.

Hascombe pressed a button and they ascended. The elevator opened across from a sliding glass door, which parted as a severe-looking nurse in a crisp white uniform approached from the other side. "I'm Julia Kress," she said, her face emotionless. She nodded toward a bed centered in the big room beyond, where a slight figure lay with its upper body slightly raised. Tubes and wires coiled down to the figure from racks of blinking instruments and IV bags dangling from metal stands. From a paneled wall on the right, muted televisions strobed disco colors into the dimly lit space. Despite the floral arrangements and conspicuous air freshener, the place stank of hospital.

"Mr. Kendron has consented to see you," Kress said, "but I caution you, he is gravely ill, very weak. Please make your visit brief."

Marty walked up to the bed and stared into the wizened face. Translucent skin sagged against the skull and cheekbones; liquid eyes wallowed within bruised sockets. Marty shuddered: The president of Kendron Technologies bore an uncanny resemblance to the ghastly bodies crumpled on the X-ray room floor at NRAD.

He managed a smile. "Hello, Grandfather."

The eyes fixed on him. "Marty...tell me what happened." The desiccated words were exhaled between the mechanical pumping of a breathing apparatus jacked into his windpipe by a translucent plastic tube. "I must know—"

"Something monstrous is loose, Grandfather. And it's killing people."

The beep of the heart monitor stumbled.

"Where?" came the sharp reply.

"Inside the tunnels."

The rheumy eyes widened. "What was its appearance?"

"Blue. Wriggling. Sounding...like electricity."

The old man's face became agitated. His eyes focused inward. "After all these years." He looked at Marty again. His voice became urgent. "They...they'll have to blast the tunnels...*hsssp*...seal it inside. Prevent it getting out."

"It? What is *It*?"

"The parchment hand wavered up from the sheets. "You were always my favorite—don't go back there."

Marty was shocked—his favorite? He hadn't seen the old man since he was twelve.

"I have to help them."

Kendron shook his head. "Too late. If it gets out..."

"There may be a kid lost inside the tunnels."

"Can't help...no way to stop it."

Marty's voice rose. "You have to tell me what *IT* is, what they were doing." He paused, waiting for a reply, then said with emphasis: "It may already be inside the town."

The old man's eyes gaped wider. The heart monitor faltered again.

The nurse edged in. "Sir..."

"They can't bomb a whole town."

"I tried to stop it long ago. I sent you so you could keep people away. "The company...I haven't been in charge for twenty years. They've been waiting for this!"

A beefy orderly joined the nurse. "Time to leave, sir."

But Thomas Kendron beckoned, and Marty bent down, placing his ear next to the grim mouth. He could hear oxygen hissing through the tube angling into the old man's throat. A wheeze as his lungs inflated. Kendron's pale hand crawled onto Marty's shirt and grasped his collar with surprising strength, drawing him closer. The parched voice began in a crackling whisper: "In the wine cellar," —Another cycle of breathing— "a locked door." As his breath constricted, he squeezed out the lock's combination and said: "The black briefcase."

Marty tried to pull away, but the old man held him back. Close enough to bite. "Careful. *Careful.* They're watching. They'll try to take it, use it." The hand released him, but the rheumy eyes implored, the whisper acquiring urgent strength: "You are in mortal danger!"

A firm hand curled around Marty's arm. "Sir? Time to leave."

As Marty straightened up, the old man's expression suddenly changed. His eyebrows rose, his mouth stretching into a grimace. There was a laugh, a sound like sandpaper chuffing across a pine plank. "Marty," he said, "take the Rolls." Another rasp of laughter: "Take the Roller." Then his eyes glazed over, his head fell back into the pillow, the emaciated face now resembling a death mask.

Marty patted the old man's hand. "Goodbye, Grandfather." He turned and left.

Hascombe was waiting for him outside the glass door, hands again folded behind his back.

"Look," Marty said, "I've had a really, really bad day. Think you can let me sit down for a minute, have a drink and a bite to eat?"

"Of course, sir. I'm sure Mr. Kendron would extend that courtesy to his grandson. Let me accompany you to a dining area."

Two floors down and through another maze, they arrived at a small room Marty thought must be used by the servants. He sat at a marble-topped table, and Hascombe left him alone. A few minutes later a smiling young woman in a black, short-skirted outfit appeared. "Hello, Mr. Berringer," she said, her hands clasped primly across the white apron. "My name is Sally. May I get anything for you?"

"Can you rustle me a fat club sandwich and bring some coffee? Make it black."

"Certainly, sir."

She turned and left. Beyond the swinging door, he glimpsed a bustling kitchen. Cooking aromas elicited a growl from his stomach. He leaned wearily back in the chair. The mansion's layout was slowly coming back to him. He had last been on the property some fifteen years ago, when he and his young cousin explored the huge estate, wandering from basement to attic, eluding the watchful staff. The dungeon-like wine cellar, he remembered, was close to the garage, just beyond the kitchen and service entrance. But his grandfather's words haunted him: *Careful. Careful. They're watching. They've been waiting for this. They'll try to take it...use it.* The old man was sick, but he wasn't senile.

The door swung open as Sally glided through, balancing a tray loaded with sandwiches and coffee. She leaned forward and set the meal before him, displaying an alluring cleavage.

Marty reached for a plump, neatly trimmed sandwich. "That was fast."

She poured coffee. "The chefs are excellent."

He took a bite. "I'll second that."

"Is there anything else I can get you, sir?"

Their eyes met, and Sally looked away, reading his thoughts. A blush flamed on her cheeks. Marty suppressed a smile. Not only was Old Tom of sound mind, but his libido must still be in gear if he was hiring staff like Sally. Marty's answer was muffled through a second mouthful of club sandwich: "I'd like to get cleaned up a bit..."

She darted him another glance. "Of course, sir," she said, gesturing. "There's a washroom beyond the kitchen."

Marty watched her leave. If only life hadn't taken a turn toward the dark side... He polished off the sandwich and coffee, feeling a welcome jolt of energy return to his depleted system, and rose from the table. He received deferential nods from the cooks as he passed through the kitchen and entered the hallway.

On his right was the service entrance. The door to the washroom was next, then—the wine cellar. Looking around to see that no one was watching, he opened the cellar's metal door, flicked on the lights, and descended the stairs.

The floor was cement, the walls brick, the ceiling arched. The atmosphere was surprisingly cool and dry. He walked past row after row of wine racks, each shelf carrying a premium vintage. Once upon a time, Thomas Kendron's parties must have been spectacular.

He finally spotted the heavy steel door. It was set into the brick wall and had a handle and single-dial combination lock on its left side. He entered the numbers Thomas had whispered and pressed the handle down. The door opened silently to reveal a large space rimmed with filing cabinets. On a table in the room's center rested a black aluminum briefcase. It was locked. "Christ," he mumbled. "I don't even know what I've got."

He leaned against the table and puffed out an angry sigh. Within a 24-hour period, he'd been bruised, badgered, scared shitless, and almost killed because of the greed and ineptitude of a giant corporation with more skeletons in its closet than Jeffrey Dahmer's bedroom. He should just get the hell away from it, leave Podunk and Kendron Technologies to their own devices.

But he thought about the missing kid and his buddy—two twelve-year olds who had more guts than he did—and the malignant evil his grandfather and his cronies had spawned over forty years ago. He could see one hell of a class-action lawsuit in gestation, one that would annihilate Kendron Technologies and crucify his family name. The company wanted him out of the picture: roll over and beg like a good dog, Junior. Maybe we'll throw you a bone—or to the wolves.

He had to go back, and wondered again at his compulsion. Part of him didn't even care about vindicating the family name. But he, God help him, wanted to Do The Right Thing. He hefted the briefcase and headed for the stairs.

At the top landing, he cracked the door and paused, searching the hallway. A birdlike chirp of a voice echoed from around a nearby corner. It was Sally, the servant who had brought his meal. She sounded close to tears as a low, gruff voice bore down on her: "...where he went. You're supposed to watch him!" There was a pause, then the voice took on a more threatening tone. "Find him *now*!" The hall became quiet.

Marty waited a moment, then darted into the hallway, turned left, and rushed for the back of the house. They would be watching his car and covering the exits: he needed to steal a ride. As he sprinted past the kitchen, he stumbled to a halt as a figure stepped in front of him—Sally. She let out a squeak, looked up at him, and froze. Her eyes were red-rimmed, her hand grasping a tissue in mid-dab. Urgent voices rose from the kitchen, accompanied by the squawk of a two-way radio. Sally looked toward the sounds, then back at Marty: she was wrestling with a decision. He screwed up a pleading expression and held a finger to his lips. "Please," he whispered.

Sally gave him a slight smile and cocked her head. "I'd better see you again."

He returned a grateful nod. "Where's the garage?"

She pointed toward a door some twenty paces away. The voices from the kitchen were louder now, the footsteps rapid. Without thinking, he slid his arm around her waist and kissed her full on the mouth.

Then he ran.

30

arty threw the door open and stared. Row upon row of exotic cars stretched out before him, their liquid-smooth skins sparkling in the overhead lights. A mechanic's bay was to his left, the cars parked in precise columns on his right. Beyond the bank of wooden garage doors, he could hear the rain pelting down with renewed fury.

From the hallway, footsteps pounded, voices shouted.

The keys—*where are the keys?* He spun around and saw them, stuffed into the cubbyholes of a shelf fastened to the wall. Take the Rolls... Marty ran his finger along the labeled slots, found the correct set, snatched them, and turned, scanning the line of spit-shined autos. He spotted the immaculate gunmetal beauty—a vintage Silver Shadow—just inside one of the garage doors, five cars away. He leapt down the steps and hit the floor running. He heard the hallway door bang open as he jammed the key into the lock.

Pulling the car door open, he slung the briefcase into the passenger seat and jumped in. Soft gray leather enfolded him. He tugged the door, noticing that it rode with enormous weight on its silent hinges. It closed with a definitive *chunk*. Through the side window, he saw two men in dark suits pounding down the steps—clones of the thugs who had thrown him into the interrogation room at North Ridge. Their hands disappeared inside their coats and returned, grasping seriously large handguns. *Jesus!*

He fumbled the key into the ignition and twisted, expecting to hear the sedate purr of a civilized motor built for quiet touring and polite conversation. Instead there leapt from the engine compartment a throaty, southern California drag-strip rumble that reverberated threateningly from the brick walls, vibrated the steering wheel, and shook the thick leather upholstery of the driver's seat. The two men were less than ten feet away, drawing a bead on him.

Marty jammed the console-mounted shift lever into reverse and hammered the gas, praying the antique Rolls could withstand an impact with the heavy garage door. The engine roared, the tires bellowed, and the big car rocketed rearward, throwing Marty against the seatbelt as it sledge hammered through the door in a blast of ruptured wood. He fishtailed onto the wide brick driveway and screeched to a halt.

The headlights switched on automatically, slashing twin cones of light through the slanting rain. With a more ginger approach to the throttle, Marty roared through the arched porte-cochere and onto the long, sinuous drive leading to the front entrance. As he accelerated past the house, lights flared in his rearview—cars racing up behind him. Through the downpour he could see the heavy iron gate, some 200 feet ahead, was fully closed. Low stone walls lining the driveway deleted any chance of going off-road. Bracing himself, he aimed for the gate's center. He shut his eyes reflexively as the front bumper met wrought iron at sixty miles an hour.

A metallic crash resounded through the car, and Marty felt a shudder as the vehicle sheared the gate from its hinges and threw the twisted metal aside. He hit the brakes and careered onto the twisting mountain road, steering right, barreling for the first downhill turn.

Pursuing vehicles poured through the mangled entrance and swerved in behind him, the glare of their headlights growing steadily in his rearview mirror.

He had expected the impact to yield a crumpled hood ready to rip free and a cab draped with shattered glass. But the hood remained unscathed. Wrought iron had indeed struck the windshield, but had left only a souvenir of smudged black paint.

As Marty wrestled the heavy car through a tight, reverse-angle curve, a wan smile lightened his face. *Tom, you sly old son of a bitch...* His grandfather had reaped dedicated enemies as well as massive dividends during his climb to the top, and that explained why, he realized with a shock, that the ancient Rolls-Royce was armored—a rolling fortress—and with enough horsepower to challenge a dragster.

Yellow dots sparked in the mirror as guns discharged. Bullets walloped the car's body and rear window. Marty hunched his shoulders and fought the wheel, concentrating on keeping the brute machine on the road. Another screeching drift through a looping curve and the Albany Post Road intersection rushed into view.

Marty vaulted the Rolls into the southbound lane and punched the accelerator. The speedometer showed a hundred miles an hour and climbing, but the chase cars were gaining. Christ, there must be six of them! Despite the armor protection, they'd have the advantage.

A sign flicked by: Airport 10 Miles. Headlights swerved close to his rear—gunmen pulling the PIT maneuver, trying to cartwheel him off the road. *Faster*! The speedometer vibrated at 130; the engine was maxed out.

Then he saw the garish red lever on his right poking up incongruously from the burled walnut dashboard. The white letters said BOOST.

Marty's heart froze as a car lurched onto the road ahead and stopped, blocking both lanes. The driver bailed, heading for the protection of the encroaching woods. The chase cars dropped back. Trapped was a good as dead.

He yanked the red lever.

From under the hood came a whine like a jet fighter winding up for takeoff, and Marty felt a potent surge as the rear tires bellowed and smoked and spun the big car into the realm of Indianapolis 500.

31

olvin climbed through a mental fog to a throbbing headache and tiny sparks of pain flashing through every nerve in his body. *Thirsty.* With a groan, he reached out for the cup on the bedside table. He remembered little of the ambulance ride from Klatty's burning house, only a fatigue so sudden and deep that he had almost passed out.

He glanced at the clock: a little past 4 am. They had stuck him in a private room on the second floor of Grayson Medical. Given a choice, he would have returned to the office and stretched out on the couch for an hour or two. He sat up, peering through the dimly lit room for his clothes. Leaving was a priority; he not only had to find what the hell was going on, but also his memory of lineman Jerry Martin's gruesome death on this floor was far too vivid—*It was like it got a taste of him... then it came through the electric lines to find him...to finish its meal.* He should have shut the place down.

As he struggled to extricate himself from the cocoon of sheets, there was a shuffling as someone entered the room and quietly closed the door, shutting off sounds from the hallway and nurses' station beyond. He heard slow, sliding footsteps as a white uniform materialized from the shadowed entrance. The nurse was taking small, deliberate steps, her forehead obscured beneath dark hair combed oddly across her brow. Her lips had drawn back, exposing teeth in a snarling grin. The silent television mounted on the wall suddenly broke into a dazzling flurry of static.

Colvin's pulse hammered. "Nurse..."

As the face rotated toward him, the eyes locked onto his own, and he thought a faint luminescence pulsed from their depths. She drew closer and stretched out a hand, and Colvin could see tiny electric sparks wriggling from her extended fingers like tethered worms.

The hand stabbed toward his chest, and he twisted away, struggling against the grasping sheets. He crashed to the floor, upending the service cart and its plastic cups and leftover food. The nurse zombie-walked around the bed, arms raised before her, outstretched fingers charged with crackling light.

Colvin jumped to his feet, and with his remaining strength lifted the heavy cart and swung at her. The impact threw her against the wall, and when the tangle of dark hair peeled back from her face, Colvin saw that it was Betty Aldrich, the nurse who had been present when Jerry Martin died. Then he saw the circular wound and its weeping stitches embedded in her forehead like a crude third eye. She locked a feral gaze on him and rose to her feet.

The door burst open and the senior nurse rushed through. She took in the room with a horrified look and gasped. "What have you done?"

"Don't touch her," Colvin croaked. The words seemed stuck in his throat.

But the nurse stepped forward to assist Aldrich, whose arms began to reach out. Colvin grabbed up the table and swung again, feeling the sharp impact as its edge crunched into Aldrich's skull. She staggered against the vanity and collapsed into a sitting position, head nodding against her chest.

A pulsing rope of electricity shot from her hand, burned across the floor, and stabbed into the electrical outlet on the wall behind her. The discharge crackled for several seconds and stopped, leaving a stench of ozone and seared flesh. The senior nurse screamed and backed away, blinking in terror.

Two orderlies tumbled through the door. "What the...*hell*..."

"He hit her," the nurse said, pointing at Colvin.

One of the men bent over Aldrich, and Colvin again yelled: "*Don't touch her.*"

"Stay back, sir," the other man warned, stepping between Colvin and Aldrich.

"Jesus, I think she's dead," the first orderly said, and gave Colvin a hard look.

Colvin slumped onto the bed, his head spinning. This was the fourth attempt on his life in two days. Too much, too fast. After a moment, he stood up. "Get Dr. Myerson," he said, staring down at Aldrich's body, "And don't let anyone in this room." He gave the body a wide berth, opened the door, and rammed through the chattering crowd gathered outside the room.

At the front desk he dialed his office. Sergeant Robert Bradeley had the con.

"Set up a press conference," Colvin said. "Call the mayor and tell him I'm calling for an emergency evacuation."

"Evacuation? Like, the whole *town*?"

"Do it now."

"Okay, Sheriff, uh, but you should know..."

"What?"

"Commissioner Long convinced the mayor to have you temporarily suspended."

"*What?*"

"Yeah. I just found out about it. Constable's got the papers."

Heat burned into Colvin's face. On one level, it felt good, fired him up, displaced some of the pain gnawing at his nerves. "That's not even legal."

"I know, Sheriff. But you'll have to tell Mayor…"

"I need my car."

"It's already there. Front parking lot. And something else, Sheriff. More people are turning up missing, and weird stuff has been happening."

"Well?"

"They've been seeing things…like…"

"Like what?"

"Ghosts."

Normally, Colvin would have laughed. Now the information caused his jaw to tighten and the hammer pounding his brain to strike a heavier blow. He hung up and steamed back toward his room; he'd get his clothes, confront the mayor and Constable Swint, and start getting people the hell out of Dodge.

— 32 —

The small neighborhood was a hundred years old, and Doc's house was probably a quarter of a mile from the nearest dwelling, sitting alone on two hundred acres of undeveloped land. Secluded, just the way Doc like it.

Deputy Frank Parnell parked the cruiser, walked up to the front door, and slowly pushed it open. He waited, listening to the silence, then called out. No answer. Colvin had warned him about entering the place, but he decided to check the rooms anyway. In the study he found the strange, carbonaceous tracks Colvin had told him about, the ones spreading from the wall socket near the door, and smelled the chemical odor that permeated the downstairs.

Finding no one inside, he retraced Colvin's steps and searched the immediate grounds up to the fence. The formal yard occupied about an acre, and it took Parnell the better part of an hour to cover the property. He was about to return to his car when he noticed a footprint in the damp sand. He bent down for a closer look: the morning sun highlighted the fresh ridges of a jogging shoe that pointed away from the house, toward the western gate. *Shit!* Pritchard could be anywhere on those two hundred acres. Parnell needed another search party, plus

Kaleb's dogs, but the radio was so screwed up he couldn't even call in to report his find.

He pushed through the wooden gate and walked into the field. A wide swath of muddy soil painted the picture: at least two people had crossed the ground, one walking erratically, stumbling, and another treading evenly alongside.

The tracks vanished at a granite outcrop. If the two walkers had continued in a straight line, they would have entered a copse of spruce just ahead. Parnell walked beneath the rain-drenched trees, an occasional drop of water pattering onto his hat from the overarching limbs. A hundred feet farther, he emerged at a hillside roughened by a massive tumble of gray rock piled along its southern slope. *Of course,* he thought. This was an entrance to one of the old copper mines. The county was peppered with them. Contractors had to be careful they didn't build over an old shaft and cave it in.

He picked his way across the rubble and stood before the mine entrance. A railroad track—one of those weird, three-rail types, like on a subway—ran from a black cleft in the hillside and stopped at his feet. All the old entrances had been sealed long ago by dynamite or the installation of steel doors. This one had a huge set of riveted metal doors, pocked and bleeding with rust. Judging by the footprints in the damp, sandy earth beneath, they had been recently entered.

Parnell jammed his fingers into the wide crack where the doors met and tugged. The right-hand door swung outward with a metallic growl. Stepping through the opening, he pulled the aluminum flashlight from his belt and thumbed the retaining strap from his Glock.

The rough, narrow tunnel ran straight ahead, rapidly disappearing into gloom. With a start, Parnell realized that the shaft, if it maintained its course, would be heading for the river. By road, the Tehuec River was a ten-mile journey from Pritchard's. In a direct line, it was probably less than a mile. And the river formed the southeastern border of NRAD.

Flashlight probing the darkness ahead, he began following the ancient steel rails, his feet crunching over the decomposed granite of the tunnel floor.

33

Margie Pruett shook her head as another blast of static erupted from the radio. "Dammit! It's just gettin' worse and worse. It's almost useless!"

Colvin nodded. "Just stay at it."

He ducked into the conference room, where Deputy Grove was spreading the county evacuation plan across the table. "Jeez, Sheriff. I didn't know this was so complicated. I don't see how we can pull this off."

Colvin stared down at the disordered pile of maps and manuals. "Plan" was a misnomer. What should have been streamlined and straightforward was instead a procedural nightmare. With the budget cuts, orchestrated in part by Donny Long, he had lacked the time and manpower to assemble a coherent evacuation scenario.

"We'll deputize as many as possible, have them work the neighborhoods. When the mayor signs off, we call the governor, the National Guard..."

"Sheriff." A voice sounded behind him.

Colvin turned around as Professor Joseph Weismann walked into the room, Kerry Shaner fidgeting beside him. The fastidious professor looked disheveled, eyes sagging and red-rimmed. Colvin wondered if he had been up all night. His voice was laden with weariness. "We have to talk."

They sat down in Colvin's office, where Weismann opened a fat black briefcase and lifted out a manila envelope and a stack of blue-clad manuals—the ones Colvin and Shaner had found in Catherine Klatty's attic. The professor looked up solemnly at Colvin. Gone was the enthusiastic glimmer, the ebullience over scientific discovery he had shown earlier. He now exuded an umbra of profound dread. He withdrew a large transparency from the envelope and slid it across Colvin's desk.

It was an X-ray. Colvin held it up so it would be backlit by the overhead fluorescent light. He could see the ghostly white form of a human skull, with its eerie shadowed eye sockets and dim glow of grinning teeth. In bright, glaring contrast was the rigid silhouette of an object penetrating the forehead, a series of sharp lines intruding deep within the soft, faintly visible tissue of the brain.

"That is a lateral X-ray of nurse Betty Aldrich," Weismann said. "It was taken shortly after she attacked you. As you can see, the implant in her brain looks identical to the one the two boys found on the North Ridge property. The longest electrodes extend all the way through the cerebral cortex to the corpus callosum. I'm not a neural specialist, but I can tell you those needles penetrate regions of the brain responsible for personality, intelligence, and rational thought. I'd say it's nothing short of a massive lobotomy."

He leaned forward, his hand stroking at his beard. "This may seem irrelevant, but bear with me." He paused for a moment. "In the 1930s, a Dr. Antonio Moniz performed a number of lobotomies with an instrument he called a leukotome, or 'white matter knife', which he used to destroy certain areas of his patients' brains." Weismann pointed to the blue Project Mesmer journals resting on the briefcase. "There are references in these manuals to a *radiotome*—the implant Johnny Helstrom found inside the North Ridge tunnels.

"Dr. Moniz performed his abominable operations to attempt a cure for various mental conditions. He found that if he destroyed enough brain matter in certain regions, he could render a violent person quiescent, or reduce obsessive-compulsive behavior. But this was accomplished at great expense to the patient, whose ruined mind was now devoid of personality, intelligence, self-will, motivation. In short, he created zombies."

Colvin glanced toward the windows. Outside, masses of black cumulus clouds obliterated the sun, punching into the stratosphere like great iron fists. The windows blinked with another faint pulse of lightning

"And, yeah," Shaner said, "I did a ton of research. They had this scientist working out there at NRAD—I know 'cause it's in the manuals, and I Googled the Simon Wiesenthal Center—his name was Dr. Wilhelm Fechter, and he worked under that Nazi concentration-camp doctor, Josef Mengele.

"And he experimented on prisoners at Auschwitz, and they brought him here after World War Two, like Wernher von Braun. And he did some really nasty shit like putting probes into people's brains, and lobotomies, electroshock, neurostimulation—shit like that. And guess what? He worked on Project Mesmer at North Ridge, under that guy, William Klatty, who had a Ph.D. in electronics. Klatty, he was a neurosurgeon too."

Shaner stood up and opened one of the manuals. "Look at this." He tapped a forefinger on a page bearing a color photograph. It took a moment for Colvin to decipher what he was seeing: a young man's shaved head clamped inside a complex metal device. The face was thin but healthy in appearance. The eyes were closed. Rods extended from a ring encircling the man's head and touched or penetrated the skull. A caption: Subject C-468. Date 17-11-60.

Colvin turned the pages. More photos: latex-gloved hands clasping a round instrument with an electric cord snaking out one end and a wide cutting bit at the other; the hands inserting the instrument into a guide centered over the man's forehead and driving it downward with a geared knob. Then it was removed to reveal, nestled between the bit's finely serrated teeth, a bleeding disk of skull.

The man's forehead now possessed a neat round hole about two inches in diameter, rimmed by a layer of pale skin and white bone. An expanse of folded and convoluted gray-pink flesh spanned the bottom of the hole: the brain neatly exposed to the next device being inserted into the cylinder—an implant. The radiotome.

The last photograph displayed the result: the disk of skin neatly stitched back into place, leaving a puckered red ring in the center of the man's forehead. The eye sockets had acquired the tones of a fresh bruise.

Colvin felt an icy coldness spreading from his solar plexus.

Shaner opened another book. "There's more."

The series of photographs tested sanity. The same man, whose brain now harbored an implant, performed various tasks. Terse captions described command and response. The man shot, stabbed, and garroted what appeared to be living people—prisoners? He carved his own flesh with a razor; held his blackened hand above the spear-point flame of a welding torch; endured, without apparent pain or reaction, various acts of torture. The photos went on and on, with different subjects, minds overridden by implants, enduring injury like enervated automatons.

Weismann's voice was low. "It's quite obvious. They were

engineering the ultimate soldier—a creature impervious to pain, without conscience, totally and selflessly obedient to its masters."

Colvin's voice was almost a whisper. "How could they control a person's entire mind?"

"Possibly you wouldn't have to override every nerve. Remember, they called it the Mesmer Project. Maybe all that's necessary is to electronically induce a deep hypnotic state, transmit the commands, and let the rest of the brain perform the required task."

"Like Al Qaeda makes suicide bombers."

"Um, perhaps, but with infinitely more flexibility. And they could probably create a subject in a matter of hours. According to Dr. Myerson, the operation performed on Nurse Aldrich happened less than a day before she, ah, came into your room."

Shaner broke in. "And yeah, guess who supplied the tools back in the fifties, like, that ice pick instrument they used for transorbital lobotomies, you know, where they punched a hole through the eye socket and swished it around inside a person's brain—"

Colvin silenced Shaner with a loud sigh. "I want to thank you guys for these insights, but what I need are..."

Weismann interrupted. "Kendron Company started out in the eighteen-hundreds in the patent medicine business, then graduated to medical instruments, making some of the phony electrical healing devices popular at the turn of the century. Later on, they started building electroshock-therapy machines and stereotactic instruments used in radical brain surgery. They branched out, producing mind-altering pharmaceuticals. From what we can infer, in the fifties and sixties they were working hand in glove with the military to develop advanced interrogation methods, among other things."

Colvin tried again: "Look, my main problem now—"

Weismann's voice became strident. "This information is relevant because it supports our belief that the implants were developed by Kendron Technologies and are part of a system designed for controlling humans, and that there must be a central transmitter and processing site—at North Ridge."

He paused, his face drawn and angry. "I must also say that this has turned into a nightmare. I have never in my life encountered such vile technology, such evil intent, and such horrifying disregard for humanity." His words roughened. "What they were doing to people—whether they were soldiers, prisoners, or the insane, or whatever—was beyond inhuman. Like the Nazi death camps and their perverted experiments..." Weismann's voice faded to a whisper, and he blinked and looked aside. "Sorry. I didn't mean to sound so...to digress."

A long silence ensued, during which not even Kerry Shaner intruded with a rudely shaped comment. Weismann passed a hand over his eyes and finally spoke again. "There is no mention in the manuals of the strange electrical protoplasm, the Elektrum. I have no idea what it really is. But the electronic signal that accompanies its movements has been increasing in intensity and duration." He looked at Colvin. "The answers lie at North Ridge, in those tunnels. Someone, or some thing, is at work there."

Colvin looked at the report lying on his desk: Deputy Brennan's precisely typed note saying that Nurse Betty Aldrich had left the hospital at 8:30 pm, her usual hour. No one noticed her return in the wee hours of this morning—not until Colvin slammed her against the wall in his room and a glowing slug of Elektrum slithered from her body and wriggled into the nearby electrical outlet.

"Hey!"

A figure stood in the doorway. His left arm was tucked inside a black sling, and several small, flesh-colored bandages dotted his face.

Colvin stood up. "Marty!"

The attorney stepped forward with a limp. "Hope this helps," he said, dropping a heavy briefcase on the floor with a thud. "I went through hell to get it." He sank wearily into a chair, then reached forward, unsnapped the briefcase, and retrieved several leather bound manuals.

"Gentlemen," Colvin said, turning to the other men. "This is Marty Kendron."

Weismann's voice went cold. "Kendron?"

Uh oh. Colvin came around the desk. "He's Thomas Kendron's grandson, and—"

Weismann glared at the new arrival. "What is he doing here?"

Colvin held up a placating hand. "Give him a chance. He's trying to help us." He picked up the manuals: the embossed covers revealed the skull and lightning bolt logo of the Mesmer Project. He handed them off to Weismann, who was still frowning. Nodding at Marty's left arm, he asked, "What happened?"

The attorney pulled his injured limb from the sling and flexed it, grimacing. "It's not broken, just bruised." He looked up at Colvin. "I saw Thomas Kendron."

"What...you went to New York?"

"Upstate New York, actually. If encouraged, The Company Learjet can be exceptionally quick. Tom gave me those manuals, and KT's thugs wanted them back. I escaped...well, I had Tom's car, see. It was armored. They had a roadblock and I plowed into it—sliced through it, you could say. The car had a supercharger, and you wouldn't believe the speed that tank could muster..."

"Greg!" Weismann interrupted. He was leaning forward in his chair, his finger stabbing at a manual. "The answers are here—the control frequencies, power levels, and modulation for the radiotomes."

"How does that help us?"

"If we can duplicate the signals, theoretically we can control the implants. Maybe it will stop these abhorrent abductions and surgeries—perhaps even neutralize the Elektrum itself."

"Can you do it?"

Weismann sank back into the chair. "Unfortunately, we have to compile and fully decipher all this."

"Uh, yeah," Shaner said, reaching for the last manual. "But you can always jump to the bottom line." He flipped through the pages. "Yeah, here—right here. The results are summarized. There's about a dozen..."

"Let me see." The Professor snatched the manual away with uncharacteristic abruptness. He read for a moment. "He's right. There seems to be a universal control frequency that can activate or shut down all the radiotomes simultaneously. Perhaps we could improvise a transmitter that would override their signal."

"We're virtually out of time," Colvin said. "How long...?"

"Weismann shook his head. "The frequencies are in the VLF to ELF range—exceptionally low frequencies. A transmitter with any power would take days, and that's assuming I could acquire parts quickly." He paused and sighed. "Otherwise, the shutdown codes must be transmitted from the originating source."

Colvin glanced away, steeling himself for the unavoidable conclusion. "Well," he said. "It seems our best hope lies in a visit to those tunnels."

"You must take Kerry and me as well. We could identify the relevant technology and advise how to deal with it."

"This is not a field trip to a college science lab. You know how dangerous..."

"He's right," came Marty's terse voice. "I've been there."

Colvin was aghast. "When?"

Marty shut his eyes for a moment. "Last night."

This time, the attorney was silent for a long period. The windows blinked again with the glint of distant lightning, and Colvin thought he heard a faint boom of thunder roll in from the west.

"We went down into the tunnels, into a room," Marty finally said. "And…I saw…a thing rise out of a dead man's body and attach itself to another man, and kill him." At the memory, his face twisted with horror. "The thing was huge." He paused, slowly shaking his head. "It somewhat resembled electricity. But it had form and substance."

He looked up, his gaze sweeping each individual in turn. "Kendron Technologies, and our own military, created whatever is down there. Some very powerful corporate types want it. And they want to develop it further and exploit it. I don't know what frightens me the most—that, or the hideous thing itself."

There was another long silence. "I'll get a couple of deputies and assemble some equipment," Colvin said at last, "and we'll go in, try to shut it down." He looked at Weismann. "Do you and Kerry still insist on coming?"

A look comprised of both fear and anticipation clouded the professor's face. "Yes," he said. "I'm afraid so."

34

Colvin looked out at the faces peering back at him from the jury box and gallery: more than 200 people jammed Courtroom Four. Not a bad turnout for 8 PM, he thought, especially considering the short notice. Reporters from the Sentinel and the Gazette were there, plus KREL radio and TV 10 and 12. The only absence was CNN, which had a team en route.

His attitude darkened: true to form, here came Donny Long, squirming through the crowd like a lamprey eel, sucking free publicity from the lifeblood of the media, hoping to leave Colvin drained and flopping like a beached carp before the cameras and microphones and raised pencils of the press.

Colvin tapped the mike and cleared his throat. "Everybody," he began. All eyes focused on him. "We have a growing crisis in this town." A murmur rose up. "All of you know about the young boy missing on the North Ridge property. You've probably heard about the mysterious deaths at the hospital and at Abe's Metal Works, and at Catherine Klatty's. People have been calling my office reporting missing persons. People have also been calling in about seeing...strange things. (He didn't want to say *ghosts*.)

"I brought in some experts. We've looked over the evidence. And I'm convinced there's a connection between the deaths, disappearances, strange sightings—and the old facilities at North Ridge. Something is going on that represents a danger to our community, and I think it would be best to evacuate Kellsburg, Cielo, and Tanglewood until this question is resolved."

Another murmur, loud this time, rose from the crowd. The cameras and microphones thrust closer; they didn't want to miss a single word as Colvin began his journey as insightful hero or village idiot.

He watched as Commissioner Long slithered his way beside the podium. A worried Constable George Swint trotted close behind, a sheaf of papers clenched tightly in his fist. Long stopped a few feet away, arms folded over his chest, a smug look embedded in his fat jowls, and allowed the sweating constable to approach. Swint had been a deputy for ten years, finally realized a promotion to captain would never materialize, and opted for the position of constable—the only county officer with the authority to arrest a sheriff.

Swint stepped up to Colvin and held out the papers. "I have a warrant from the mayor."

Colvin ignored the interruption: "I have ordered my office to implement an evacuation plan effective immediately. Automatic telephone messages will be sent—"

"Sheriff, what's going on? What's really happening?" a reporter from the Sentinel shouted.

Microphones bobbed, camera operators tweaked their lenses, flashes exploded, questions avalanched: "Is something coming out of North Ridge...? Is it radioactive...? Poison gas...?"

Constable Swint slapped the warrant against Colvin's chest. "You are to step down immediately—"

Colvin snatched the papers, wadded them in his fist, and hurled them back at the constable. He threw a hand up, waiting as silence slowly filtered back into the room. "Something apparently is coming out of North Ridge. We don't know what it is, other than it seems to be electrical in nature."

"Electricity?" someone shouted out. "What do you mean?"

Colvin calmed the group again. "I've seen what it can do. I've been attacked myself. Until we learn what we're up against, I think the entire town is in danger. So I'm calling for an evacuation."

The man from the Sentinel again: "Isn't that far-fetched, Sheriff? Surely—" A TV reporter cut him off: "What kind of evidence—"

"I don't want to cause a panic, but if you need a graphic description to get you motivated, I'll give it to you." Colvin saw the constable draw aside and begin an animated discussion with two deputies, who kept glancing his way. "There's a strange type of electricity—or something like electricity—that's getting into the power lines and into our homes. There have been at least three deaths, apparently from this anomalous stuff, or force, or whatever..."

The press machine-gunned their questions: "How...? What happens...? Does it electrocute people...? Is it safe to turn on the lights? What do you call it, the Light Bulb Monster, the Toaster Roaster?" There was a scattering of derisive laughter.

Colvin's fuse was beginning to burn short. He stared the crowd down, waiting as silence again descended. He began softly, his voice slowly rising: "I've seen the bodies, seen the autopsies. It strips the blood, and meat and organs right out of people. Leaves them a sack of bones."

"An electric *vampire*, Sheriff?" Another voice boomed over the P.A.—Commissioner Donny Long. He had jacked a microphone into the amplifier and cranked the volume up. "Our sheriff is seeing things, folks. First he says he wants to get inside NRAD, then he can't get inside

NRAD, can't find that lost boy. Next, he doesn't want anyone inside NRAD. Now he sees electric vampires and monsters in the power lines. He wants us to leave our town." He made a "drinking" motion with his hand. "He's seeing spirits all right. We know about your past, Sheriff, and it's *you* who should leave."

Colvin shouted a response, but his words were swallowed by the noise: Someone had yanked Colvin's mike cable from the amplifier. He nodded to the two deputies, who were already closing on the commissioner.

"The mayor has stripped Greg Colvin of his authority," Long went on. "High time. And time for a new sheriff." The commissioner stepped away from the microphone, throwing his hands up at the approaching deputies and backing away with a triumphant grin.

Colvin stormed across the courtroom floor, onlookers, reporters, cameras, and microphones swarming him like hornets. He drew up beside Long. "You try that again and I'll throw your ass in jail."

"But you're under arrest," Swint stammered, clutching the wadded papers. "The mayor said—"

Colvin spun around and strode off toward the judge's chamber. "Follow me."

They filed into the small, wood-paneled office and Colvin slammed the door shut behind him, cutting off the crowd.

Swint smoothed the crumpled papers and thrust them out to Colvin, who snatched them up and briefly scanned the terse paragraphs. "That's a bench warrant. It isn't legal."

"But the mayor said—"

"Where is the mayor?"

"What? I don't know."

Colvin jerked the telephone from its cradle. In twenty seconds he had his answer. He turned back to Swint. "He hasn't been in his office, and his home phone doesn't answer."

The constable puffed out his chest. "Sheriff Colvin, I'm placing you under..."

But Colvin was already headed for the door. "You," he said without looking back, "are coming with me."

35

The house was old, a two-story Victorian sequestered on a tree-shrouded lot off York Street, close to the center of town. The windows were dark, the house silent. The mayor's Mercedes sat in the driveway, its polished black surface draped with brown leaves fluttering down from the huge oak overarching the yard. Colvin brushed his hand across the car's hood: the engine was cold.

To the west, lightning wormed and rumbled through the rising thunderhead as the approaching storm gathered force. A breeze hissed through the oak's branches, carrying the scent of rain-dampened earth. Followed closely by Constable Swint, Colvin walked up the steps and onto the broad front porch. He pressed the doorbell, heard it chime through the quiet house. He knocked hard, waited. No one came. "Door's locked," he said, rattling the handle. He turned to Swint. "It's your call."

The constable swiped a hand across his mouth. "I don't know, Greg. Something's not right. What with him missing all day and..."

There was a shattering sound as Colvin's flashlight punched through the adjacent window. He hooked his arm through the opening, unlatched the door, and stepped through.

"Mayor Bennett," he shouted out. "Hello. Anybody?"

Swint came up behind him. "What's that *smell*?"

The pungent odor of ozone drifted down the dark tongue of the staircase, its ornate mass curling upward from the room's center. Colvin loosened his pistol and they began to climb, the old steps creaking beneath their feet.

He paused at the top of the stairs and peered down the long hallway. Except for a slice of yellow weeping beneath a single closed door, all lights were off. Colvin walked to the door, grasped the knob and, motioning Constable Swint to one side, threw it open.

The room beyond had pinkish tinges. Frilled, baby blue drapes covered the windows, and cuddly stuffed animals peeked out from rows of shelving. Movie posters and images of male heartthrobs adorned the walls.

Illuminated in the soft glow of a table lamp, Mayor Bennett sat motionless beside the queen-size bed. The bedsheets were thrown back in a white gash, and his left arm was extended toward the person lying there. From the bed there rose a hissing sound, and Colvin's breath caught in his throat.

Beneath the mayor's splayed fingers lay the naked form of a young girl. Colvin knew whom it must be—Bennett's daughter, Suzie: high school beauty queen, cheerleader, A-plus student. But her body had lost its healthful glow, its peach-colored tones and youthful curves: her skin shivered and crawled, collapsing inward, folding against the bone.

Bennett's hand, limned in pulsing blue light, hovered above the girl's shrinking flesh. Filaments of electrical plasma wormed between his palm and her body. The veins in his forearm bulged—engorged. Colvin felt himself go rigid, his mind shrieking: *Bennett is drawing the substance of his daughter into himself, feeding the thing that inhabits his body and eats his mind...*

He barely registered Constable Swint's mewling words: "What... what is..."

A trail of red threaded its way down Mayor Bennett's face, weeping from the circular gash in the center of his forehead. His lips drew back to expose clenched teeth, and a word rasped from his throat: "Colvin." The eyes flashed blue. The hissing of electricity intensified. He began to rise.

An explosion hammered the room as Colvin fired the 9 mm automatic. Bennett fell back into the chair. There was a heartbeat of silence; then Bennett's form began to sink into itself like a deflating balloon, the skeleton expanding through its sagging sheath of skin. Electricity buzzed from Bennett's feet where they touched the floor, and burned across the carpet. Colvin wheeled around and pushed Swint toward the door.

The constable fell back, screeching. "What is that...what is that?"

"*Move!*" Colvin shoved him through.

With Swint breathing down his neck, Colvin turned left and raced down the hallway to the next door. He threw it open and licked the flashlight beam inside, revealing an empty bedroom. Looking back toward Suzie's room, he saw a horde of arachnoid shapes erupt through the door and charge toward him, their spindly legs a luminescent blur as they scurried down the hall in a neon tide. He tried the next room— also empty.

"*Jesus...God!*" Swint screamed. "We have to get out of here!"

Colvin looked back again. The glow spiders were fading, snuffing out, running out of energy or battery power or whatever the hell kept them going.

Swint snatched at Colvin's arm. "Have to leave *now*!"

Colvin grasped the doorknob of the final room and twisted. "He has a wife..."

He opened the door.

Just inside, in chiaroscuro with the darkness, stood a figure. Colvin gasped and staggered back, the flashlight almost tumbling from his grasp. The figure was motionless and naked, and like a tinted X-ray its skeleton showed pale white through the phosphorescent blue substance that cloaked its bones. The skull throbbed yellow-red, the sockets bulging with gelatinous orbs that simulated living eyes. Jagged threads of electricity danced through the body like lightning in a frenetic thunderstorm.

The ghastly figure started forward, arms slowly extending, hands clenching, unclenching...

Colvin's gun bucked again. The thing fell backward and crashed to the floor, then without a pause sat up and began to rise, inhuman eyes glaring malevolently from the electric skull. The head tilted up; the mouth grinned wide. But if it intended to speak, Colvin didn't stay to hear.

He turned and ran.

Colvin burst through the front door and stumbled onto the lawn, panting. Constable Swint was already in the yard, doubled over, hands on his knees, vomit drooling from his open mouth. He turned toward Colvin, his voice quivering and panicked "What the hell happened to them? What was that?"

Above the house, sheet lightning clawed the sky, and Colvin for an instant felt as if the atmospheric discharges were an extension of the monstrous shape inside the house, as if he were himself suddenly engulfed by the alien force pumping out of NRAD.

"It's getting in through the power lines," he said, looking at the wires leading to the house from the utility pole.

"What?" The constable's voice sounded as if he thought Colvin had gone mad.

Colvin rounded on him. "How many times do I have to say this? This...thing...is getting to people through the power lines. It gets into the house wiring and..." He paused, noting the constriction in his throat and that his hands were shaking. With an effort, he calmed himself. "You understand? We have to evacuate this town."

Constable Swint looked up at the house, and Colvin followed his gaze. Against a backdrop of lightning, he could make out a faint blue glow rising and fading in the darkened upstairs windows. He turned and rushed back toward the car, the constable staggering behind.

— 36 —

Colvin tried a second time to feed a quarter into the slot. *Big, tough sheriff.* His hands were still shaking. See something a little scary and get rattled... The quarter found its home, and he punched his office number into the pay phone. Margie Pruett patched him through to Captain Dave Finlay.

"Yeah, Sheriff."

"Call everyone in. There will be a briefing"—Colvin glanced at his watch—"at twenty three hundred. And call Kellsburg Police. We're starting the evacuation."

"Sheriff, there's no sign of Deitz or Garrent, and Parnell is still missing."

"Christ!"

"And Mesa Electric called, said they were missing a bunch of men they sent to repair the Kellsburg substation."

"Yeah?"

"I sent Grove and Reiser out there an hour ago. Haven't heard back. The radio's still crapped out, and now you can hear that noise over the phones."

Colvin pinched the bridge of his nose. "Any word from the Guard?"

"Yeah, they're waiting for the governor."

Colvin's shoulders slumped. Of course the mayor hadn't called the governor; he was busy getting his brain drilled and sucking the life from his once-beautiful daughter… "Right. Swint and I will check the substation. Listen, Captain. Call the governor. Tell him the mayor's been killed—"

"What—"

"Tell them we've got an emergency." He paused. "Captain…"

"Yes sir?"

"With or without me, or the Guard, or the cops, just get that evacuation started."

"Roger that, Sheriff," Finlay breathed. "We'll do the best we can."

Colvin trudged across the parking lot at Joe's Gas N' Go and climbed back into the car. The constable was leaning forward, hugging his chest. He cast Colvin a doleful look. "Where are we going?"

"Checking the electrics."

***

The transformers, insulators, and sundry components of the Kellsburg substation glowed from work lights beaming up from tripods spaced around its perimeter. Ten vehicles were parked within the fenced area, two of them Mesa Electric trucks that had raised their hydraulic lifts beside a ribbed insulator that jutted up beside a transmission tower. Men moved back and forth in a silent cadence, carrying tools, wheeling equipment, pulling heavy cable from groaning steel spools mounted on the rear of a flatbed truck.

Arc welders sparked fitfully from dark areas of the substation, throwing a quivering nimbus of light and shadow across the ground. With the lightning-veined thunderhead as a backdrop, the scene looked like a public-works project from Hell.

"What are they doing?" Swint hiccupped.

Colvin cut the cruiser's lights and pulled through the gate, rolling slowly over the crunching gravel. He knew the moment he shut the engine off that he should have simply turned around and driven off. But another car was parked a few yards ahead—Deputy Reiser's vehicle. It was empty.

He opened his cruiser's door and stepped out. The air hummed and crackled with electricity, and Colvin noticed most of the sound seemed to be coming from his left, from the old crooked towers leading from North Ridge. The once-dead lines flickered with a blue radiance, and heavy cables now connected those towers with the substation. Weismann was right: corrupted energy was being fed from NRAD into the town's electric lines—now in mass quantities. Swint crept tentatively from the car and stood beside the open door.

Two of the Mesa linemen suddenly dropped the instruments they were carrying, turned in unison, and began walking toward the cruiser. Their hard hats were pulled low, faces veiled in shadow.

Colvin held out a hand. "That's close enough." The men stopped, and Colvin's flashlight beam flicked into a lineman's face. "Mr. Danforth? That you?"

The man's head rotated toward Swint, then back to Colvin. He started forward again.

"Talk to me," Colvin said. Danforth was close now, and beneath the low brim of his hat, Colvin saw what he expected—the red line of a circular incision, the skin crudely stitched together in the center of his forehead. Somehow, just like Doc Pritchard and the others, he had been immobilized and dragged off to NRAD for a quick little operation.

As Colvin backed toward the cruiser, he heard the door slam. He swiveled around and saw Swint inside, squirming into the driver's seat. Colvin yanked the handle. "Unlock it!"

Swint's hand was frantically scrabbling at the ignition switch, feeling for the keys that now resided in Colvin's pocket.

Two men came from the shadows on Colvin's left. One, a teenager, wore baggy pants and an oversized T-shirt. The other was a paunchy, middle-aged man in a grimed and ripped business suit.

"*Unlock the fucking car!*"

Danforth accelerated his pace, arms rising, eyes keenly focused on Colvin. Blue fire crawled from his outstretched fingers.

Colvin drew his pistol and fired directly into Danforth's chest. The lineman twisted to one side, made a final lurch, and collapsed onto his back. His head turned to face the sheriff. Through gnashed teeth came the guttural chant: "*Crazy Cathy Clatty…*"

The implant burst from the lineman's head and a fountain of red sparks popped and sizzled from the breached opening. As Colvin edged toward the rear of the car, a legion of glow spiders erupted from the man's rent head, rose up on their spindly legs, and ticked across the ground toward him.

He ran for the passenger door. Swint was staring out the driver's window, his balled fists tucked rigidly beneath his chin. Colvin jammed his key into the lock, knowing that Swint could defeat this effort with the push of a button. "Unlock it!"

The teenager and paunchy businessman reached the driver's side and slapped their open palms against the windshield. Electric sparks darted from their splayed fingertips and fanned outward, jagged bolts roaring across the glass in a fiery mass.

A gunshot popped from Colvin's right, and he spun around to see the two missing deputies walking toward him, weapons raised. Another shot cracked and the bullet thwacked into the door beside Colvin's hand. He bolted for Reiser's empty cruiser. Behind him, through the closed windows of his own car, he heard Swint's voice raised in a harsh, wavering scream.

He reached the deputy's car and jerked the door open: the keys were still in the ignition. As bullets pocked the passenger side, he cranked the engine and gunned the machine into a tire-burning U-turn. He flew past his own cruiser, saw its interior flaring with light, and through the dazzle saw the violent thrashings of Constable George Swint as electric arcs punched through the windshield and raked his body. More zombies from the substation were lurching toward the vehicle with outstretched arms, threads of electricity spewing from their clawed fingers.

Colvin roared through the gate, rear wheels spinning up a raucous tail of loose gravel. Bullets slammed the cruiser's body. "Shit!" The tires bit asphalt and he accelerated southward over the two-lane road. On his left, the utility poles leading from the substation marched through the darkness, their glowing copper lines pumping electricity—and something else—into Tanglewood and Kellsburg.

Colvin punched the throttle, fighting to keep the car on the uneven road. He had to get people out—*Now*—any way he could.

$$=\!\!=\!-37-\!=\!\!=$$

A hideous funneling sound fills the air as water twists and swirls into a transparent tube, a thundering sound throbbing up inside, echoing liquid screams from its glassy walls...

The vortex pulls Johnny from his bed, through the door, along the darkened hallway strobed by lightning slashing through distant windows.

He claws frantically at the carpeted floor, tries to stand, to crawl, to slow his movement. But the relentless suction drags him on and on, gliding him smoothly down the staircase, around the corner, down into the basement, where he sees the maelstrom's eye. And as he slides into the cold black water and is sucked toward the whirling funnel, he feels liquid hands seize his legs, fights with every fiber of his being.

A white mass bobs up beside him. It rides the swirling current and turns—the pleading face of Kip Hawkins, whose arms reach out to him. "Here...come here..."

Johnny's own screams jerked him awake and into a sitting position. Lightning stabbed its blue-white rays into the room, the posters on the wall jumping out and back as the shadows played their tricks.

He sat still, heart lunging against his ribs, drenched in sweat, and darted his gaze about the room, too frightened to move. Then he heard Max—a short bark followed by a brief, cutoff cry.

The sound had come from down the hallway.

"M...Max?" His voice sounded more like a croak. He called Max again, this time louder, and was met with the sound of wind keening beneath the eaves.

He pushed down the covers and stepped from bed. He was wearing only a T-shirt and shorts, and the sheen of sweat on his arms and chest chilled him. He tried the light switch, but the storm had knocked out the power; his flashlight was downstairs, in his old backpack.

A familiar voice, oddly distorted, called his name. The sound sent more shivers crawling up his spine. He paused at the bedroom door, then walked softly down the hallway toward the source. "Kip?"

A flickering blue light played across the floor, emanating from the game room on his right. Maybe it was lightning. Maybe it was something else. Maybe it was the same blue spark inside the tunnels at North Ridge, the same glow that had skittered across the floor on spider legs and pulled Kip down...

His heart was laboring, his mind screaming for him to *run...run!* But he approached the door and walked inside the room. The light came from beyond the pool table, from a naked figure standing there—a ghost the color of lightning. It was Kip—or something that looked like Kip—and it smiled an awful smile, its mouth and eyes a brighter glow than the rest of the body. "Johnny," it said. "Come here. I need your help. Please, Johnny." Kip held out his hand, beckoning. "If you'll just take my hand..." The voice sounded strange and mechanical, as if it were reproduced through the cheap, tinny speaker of a toy robot.

Then he saw Max. He lay there next to the Kip-thing, his eyes closed, chest moving as if he were sleeping, breathing slowly and deeply...up and down. A glowing tube crossed the floor and connected the two like an umbilical cord. But instead of giving life, Johnny realized, it was taking. Max's bones had begun to show, his fur slowly collapsing through the ribs.

Johnny staggered backward through the door and held up his hands in a pushing motion. "*You get out of here!*"

Max suddenly reared up, his eyes shedding fire, blue rays pouring through his sagging skin and ribs—a rotted dog corpse with swamp-light beaming from within. Johnny could see teeth and skull, a skeleton thrown into dark relief against the blue light glaring deep inside its body. Max grinned wide, all fangs and chopping jaws, rose to his feet and stumble-charged after Johnny.

A scream tore from Johnny's throat and he bolted down the hallway, found the stairs, sprinted frantically down in darkness, hit the floor, shot across the wide space toward his parents' bedroom. Chest heaving, he paused and looked back.

Max crept down the stairs like a stalking panther, his glow-light reflecting from the polished banisters and white stucco wall of the staircase. He reached the floor and turned to Johnny, his Jack-O-Lantern face lit and ready for business.

Johnny burst into his parent's bedroom and belted out a ragged cry. "Mom—Dad—Help—Get Up!" Lightning lit the windows and he could see his parents sleeping side by side, his mother on the left, his father nearest the door opening onto the deck. He rushed to the foot of the bed and screamed for them: "*Get up!*"

And they did.

They rose together into a sitting position, bedsheets falling away, and opened their eyes. Ghost eyes. Blue—like lightning. Their heads throbbed reddish-amber from within, as if their brains were burning embers.

"Johnny..." they said in unison, their voices strange, rough, and distant, like their speech had been filtered through some special-effects audio console at Universal Studios.

He froze, not breathing, feeling the blood leach from his face and limbs, a blackness wanting to steal away his conscious mind.

The forms of his mother and father crawled forward, moving closer. "Johnny...Johnny..." Hungry voices. *Vampire* voices. Johnny could see veins shimmering beneath the transparent skin, hear a crackling sound like electricity. They exhaled a foul, chemical odor. In the space of an instant, he thought he would faint, would vomit.

Hands reached out. "Johnny..."

Then something clicked inside his brain and he was running, his parents' synthetic voices shouting after him. Through the screaming panic, part of his mind was calmly giving orders: avoid the dog; avoid Kip; find your backpack—*run!*

He flew across the main room. There was no sign of Max or Kip, only a darkened house fitfully brightened by strokes of approaching lightning. He saw the dark bulk of his backpack lying in the foyer, snatched it up, and slammed through the front door into the night and rising storm.

Jagged fingers of lightning raked the sky and strobed the ground. He charged into the driveway, heedless of the rocks and gravel biting at his bare feet.

He stopped short.

Along the U-shaped driveway stood columns of quivering blue flame. Will-o'-the-wisps. People. They shambled toward him, grotesque zombies with outstretched arms and incandescent bodies. And beneath the glow, skeletons shining a brighter blue-white; eye sockets brighter yet; skulls a pulsating amber-red. Moans rose and fell in unison—the speech of the living dead.

Johnny yelped and dodged past their closing ranks, his churning legs driving him toward the road. More lights. A car gliding slowly toward him. He could see "Sheriff" in bold, black letters on the door, and the light bar clamped to the roof.

He ran toward it, his backpack slamming up and down against his body. The car stopped and the window slid down. "Get in, Johnny."

In a glare of lightning, he saw the officer's face. He was real, all right, with skin, and hair, and a uniform. And he smiled and beckoned. But his smile was all wrong, and blood was oozing from a round gash in his head that had been sewn up with big, clumsy Frankenstein sutures…

The officer was leaning toward him now, extending a hand. "Let me help you."

Johnny backed from the car. "No!"

Around him, the glowing horrors were converging, closing the circle.

Sibilant voices spoke in unison: "Come with me!"

Johnny bolted for the woods, tearing across the lawn, racing for the black tangle of trees and branches beyond. Limbs and rocks and vines ripped his feet, slashed his skin, sent him sprawling. He got up and ran on and on until, finally, somewhere between his own house and Kip's, near the crashing storm-waters of the lake, he collapsed; curled beneath the swaying limbs of a broken pine, insane moans escaping his throat. He pulled his tormented feet against his body, hugged his torso, shivered as rain drove the tears from his eyes.

Then he saw a light sweeping through the branches.

His spent body refused to move. The light found him, and his mind rushed into a swirling darkness.

Commissioner Donny Long punched the remote door opener and, minding the tight clearance, carefully steered the H2 Hummer into the garage. He noted with pleasure that his wife's car was already there. Annette was home early. Sometimes her job at Steelman & Drake kept her slaving into the late hours, even though she didn't have to work— not with the dough Long was making—but it kept her busy.

He let himself into the house, walked unsteadily into the den, and stopped at the built-in bar. He poured a generous shot of 30-year-old single-malt into the bar glass. Just one more nip as he caught the local news and viewed his masterful performance at the courthouse. Channel 12 had assured him the segment would air promptly at ten.

He settled into the recliner, switched on the wide-screen TV, and brought the scotch to his lips. He smiled. He'd nailed Greg Colvin in public and on camera, setting the stage for Billy's run for Sheriff come November.

Yep, Colvin would be out, Billy would be in, and Long himself would campaign for Mayor. "Mayor Long" had a sweet ring to it, he thought. Senator Long sounded better. But Governor Long was best.

The greatest perks of holding public office were the generous offerings of especially appreciative constituents (in return for those back-door favors), and insider knowledge. As commissioner, he was the first to know where the Highway 4 extension would go, because he helped plan it. So, naturally, it behooved him to have purchased a critical parcel squarely in its route. He'd made a killing on that deal. As sheriff, Billy could also provide him with additional early tidings, like who was being foreclosed, who was getting sued, or who was getting their ass served for whatever.

"Hey," he shouted toward the stairs. "Come see me on the TV!"

The windows blinked pale blue and thunder rolled over the house. "Fuckin' storms will never end," he mumbled. As he spoke, the television hissed and the power snapped off, leaving the house in dark silence. *Well, if that doesn't beat shit.*

Long slammed back the drink, pried himself from the recliner, and felt his way down the hallway toward the cabinet that held flashlights and spare batteries. He found a light, clicked it on, and started up the stairs.

Annette's voice floated down from the landing. "I already seen you on the TV."

Tonight, his wife's voice was sultry, seductive, like he hadn't heard in years. It turned her on, too, he thought, seeing her husband mind-fuck an erstwhile tough-guy sheriff on TV. He pointed the flashlight upstairs and saw Annette's ample buttocks swishing toward the bedroom. She was wearing the frilly pink nightgown. It no longer fit so well since the weight gain, but what the hell; he'd added a few pounds himself. Plus, he was drunk, and horny enough to fuck a bullet wound. And the lights would be off.

He walked into the bedroom and undressed by flashlight. Bountiful Beefettes, that's what the jerkoff mags called them. Girls with more-than-abundant curves, and lots to hold onto. All good looking women, but carrying more adipose than the anorexic starlets that usually graced the foldouts.

The flashlight was no longer required, so he turned it off and climbed into bed. Besides, he could see more than he needed from the coming storm.

"Annette, hey." She must be in the bathroom, although what she was doing in total darkness was anybody's guess.

"I'm here."

The voice startled him, coming from the foot of the bed. He hadn't seen her enter. But there she was, and her voice still had that low, silky, sexy quality. A distant flicker through the windows painted her form; the pink nightie was wide open, dangling enough bulging mammary to impress the Beefettes.

"Come on, baby," he said. "Me and my stand-up buddy are waitin' for ya'."

She knelt on the bed and crawled forward, shedding her flimsy nightgown in the process, and slowly straddled him. Long strands of blond hair spilled down to caress his torso, sending shivers of anticipation through his body. She grasped his erect member and raised up, directed it home, and settled down, taking him full inside.

Long's hands stroked her thighs. "Oh, yeah, Baby, oh yeah…"

A tingling began in his groin and radiated outward. "Jesus, Baby, that's amazing, that's—"

Something warm and wet pattered onto his chest. He swiped the substance up and brought it close to his face, rubbing it between thumb and forefinger. He didn't need a light to discern blood.

"Hey…"

Annette grasped him, squeezing, pressing downward, her pubis heaving painfully into his groin.

Son of a bitch!"

Her pelvic bones spread, hinged open, engulfed his hips, and began to close, crushing him as if he were caught between the piston-driven jaws of a vice.

"Oh Ghaaad!"

He bucked and twisted sideways, but she pinned him rigidly in place, thrusting, grinding away with rising force. Her arms had locked against his biceps, and at those points of contact he could feel the bones of her fingers press through yielding flesh. Multiple strobes of lightning shocked her image from the darkness: she was riding him, her back upright, her distended breasts melting toward his chest like wax from a burning candle. Her skull split through the skin itself; teeth bulged through retracting lips, the nose and its cartilage flattened and pulled aside, eyes sloughed from their sockets, tethered by tenuous cords of muscle and nerve.

Long bellowed, and through stars of blinding pain saw a red-yellow candescence throb from within his wife's morphing head. With a click and chatter of bones, Annette sank farther, her torso pressing against his own, her mass rolling slowly forward like the tread of an army tank. The grinning death's head drew closer, and with a wet sucking sound her rib cage opened and expanded. Yawned to engulf him.

He felt their spines merge. And he heard her voice. Her voice—and another—and fell screaming into the electric chasm.

39

ightning cracked so close Colvin almost twisted off the road. The blast was instantaneous, popping loud inside the car despite the roar of engine and wind. Colvin barely took notice, but feathered the throttle, steering reflexively, suppressing the unreal horrors of the last 48 hours.

Through a windshield wrinkling with the first heavy drops of rain, he could see the town fanning out below the ridge, lights winking through the storm-haze. Something was not right: there were fewer lights. Areas of the town were splotched with darkness. Entire blocks had lost power.

He rolled the window down and slowed, hearing the wail of storm sirens. What was it? Tornado, high winds, or—? He flicked on the wipers, listened to the steady thump, thump, thump, so much slower than the racing pulse of his heart.

He tried the radio, received a gush of static, threw the mike in anger and frustration. The road curved, revealing part of County Road 4 and a red chain of taillights headed southward. The evacuation, he noted with a glimmer of satisfaction, had started. One problem: the taillights weren't moving. There was a jam.

It was as he had feared; with insufficient organization and zero communications, the evacuation was a fiasco. But if he could at least get people out of buildings and homes, away from electricity and power lines, maybe some of them would be safe.

Punching the accelerator again, he swerved left and rolled through the landscaped entrance into Tanglewood. All lights were off, the development as black as the night-clad hills. As he rounded the curve, he noticed a pale luminescence shivering in the air like an aurora.

He turned into the Helstrom's long driveway, dreading what he might find inside the home. Taillights flicked on and off ahead: Deputy Garrick's cruiser. As he slowed, a barefooted boy darted around the rear of Garrick's car and dashed for the woods. In the same instant, the deputy climbed out, flashlight in hand, and shambled after him.

Moving zombie-slow, about ten figures issued from the rain-slashed darkness beyond the cruiser and began shuffling toward Colvin's own car. Some of the figures were fully clothed, shredded rags barely clung to others. Some were naked. Each was a human skeleton shrouded in Radium-X Jell-O.

Colvin grabbed the riot gun and flashlight, kicked the cruiser's door open, and charged across the lawn after Garrick and the boy.

A hundred yards into the tangle of brush and woods, he saw Garrick walking slowly, sweeping his flashlight back and forth in a searching pattern. There was no sign of the kid. Lightning flared flashbulb-bright, and when the dazzle faded from his eyes, Deputy Garrick had turned and was facing him.

Colvin squinted. "Get the damn light out of my face."

In the beam of his own flashlight, he saw a pistol rising in Garrick's right hand and the bloody, stitched circle in the center of his forehead. His voice croaked the word: "Colvin."

The blast from the riot gun sent the deputy backward, the report joining a sudden boom of thunder rolling across Lake Arrowhead.

Garrick lay still, eyes staring indifferently into the pouring rain.

"Sorry," Colvin whispered, staring at the dead man, his own emotions too overloaded for a proper response. He sidestepped the body and jogged into the woods, following the faint cleft of an overgrown trail, the presumed path the boy would have followed.

Close to the lake, where storm-driven waves crashed against the beach, he saw the kid, huddled up and shivering, staring into the flashlight's beam, absolute terror etched into his young face.

"Johnny!" Colvin said. "It's me. Sheriff Colvin. I'm here to help."

The boy rallied for an instant, then fell back, the fear never leaving his eyes. His unprotected feet were bloody, his exposed arms and legs a hatchwork of red scratches and welts. Strapped to his back was the blue backpack he had worn the day he was found lying half-drowned beside the Tehuec River.

Colvin lifted the boy in a fireman's carry. Holding the flashlight with his free hand, and with the riot gun tucked under his arm, he stumbled back along the trail. He cursed himself; he should have rolled over the mayor and forced the evacuation much sooner.

Thanks to the work-zombies at the substation, NRAD was hooked solidly into the power grid. Elektrum was surging through the high-tension lines, using them as a neural network, infiltrating every home and structure in Tanglewood and Kellsburg and God knew where else. Blue arcs of Elektrum were even now exploding from the wiring, penetrating people's bodies, ripping the physical and mental substance from them like ravening vampires. Growing, mutating...

Building more monsters.

─═ ⟋ 40 ⟍ ═─

Colvin broke through the trees and stopped, his chest heaving from exertion. He shifted Johnny's weight on his shoulder and peered through the rain, scanning the trail ahead. No sign of the glowing horrors that had approached him earlier. Deputy Garrick's body was gone from the path. Taken for another purpose, to be recycled as a vessel for the Elektrum. A host for living lightning.

He trudged to his car, fumbled the door open, and lowered the Helstrom boy into the passenger seat. The kid was conscious, but still shaking, his eyes glazed and distant. Colvin pulled a blanket from the trunk and tucked it around the boy. The rain had tapered to a drizzle, the wind now coming in fitful gusts instead of a hard blow.

He slid into the driver's seat and reached for the ignition. "My mom and dad..." came Johnny's quivering voice, "...and Max." His voice broke into a sob.

Colvin looked at the boy, then up at the house, its dark façade briefly painted by a flicker of lightning. "What happened to them? Your folks." he asked gently.

"I...they were..."

Johnny's face was lost in shadow, but Colvin could hear a terror in his voice that bordered on madness.

"We'll go to the house," Colvin said, patting the boy's shoulder. "We'll see—"

"*No!*" The word came as a quick yelp. Now the kid was really shaking, and he let out a moan choked off by another sob. Then Colvin was aware of his own shivering body and that he was clutching the steering wheel so hard his hands seemed locked in place.

He started the cruiser and drove slowly along the circular driveway. When he got close to the house, he switched the headlights off and stared up at the windows. Johnny moaned again: "No! No!"

A sliver of sympathy cracked from Colvin's stash of locked emotions and drifted into his conscious mind. He tucked the blanket up below Johnny's chin. "Okay, we'll go somewhere safe now." He turned the headlights back on, touched the accelerator, and pulled away from the house, its upstairs windows now weeping blue ghost-light into the darkness.

"We'll go someplace safe," he repeated, hoping his statement carried an iota of truth.

***

Cradling Johnny Helstrom in his arms, Colvin stepped through the emergency-room doors and pushed through the crowd, working his way toward a harried doctor standing against the far wall. A wildly gesturing woman dressed in a nightgown was shouting into the doctor's face. Her eyes widened as she saw Colvin. She whirled around. "Officer. Oh, thank God! My husband...they took him. I saw them, saw—*IT*—take him." She seized Colvin's arm with both hands and began tugging him toward the exit. "You have to come with me!"

Colvin twisted from the woman's grasp. "Ma'am, please." The crowd began moving toward him, shoving, shouting questions.

"This way," the doctor said, nodding toward an examination

room. Colvin followed him inside and the door swung shut, cutting off the crowd and the frantic woman. He laid Johnny on a gurney. The doctor, a young intern named Beccard, already had a penlight in hand, sweeping it across the boy's eyes. "He's in shock," Beccard said. "What happened?"

Colvin described the relevant events.

Beccard mumbled some instructions to a nurse, then strode off. "I'll be right back."

While the nurse huddled over Johnny, Colvin snatched a landline from the nearby table and dialed his office. Busy. What a surprise. He next called pathology and confirmed Dr. Carol Myerson was there. He watched the nurse inject the boy with something, tranquilizer maybe. As Johnny began to zone out, his eyes pleaded with Colvin to stay with him.

"Send him down to the pathology lab, okay?" Colvin said. "Dr. Myerson's there. We'll watch him. He needs his friends."

"Sure. We can do that."

Beccard returned, scribbling something down on a clipboard. He looked up and held Colvin's gaze, shaking his head. "It's crazy. We're flooded with injuries, getting calls about missing people. And all kinds of...rumors."

Colvin sighed. "Look. I'd tell you to evacuate, get the hell out of here and into the next damned state. But it's too late. Just take care of your patients. And...be careful." He turned to leave. "I gotta' go do something about"—he circled the air with a hand—"all this."

Colvin rode the elevator down and walked through pathology into the TEM lab. Professor Weismann looked up from a tangle of electronic components covering the table. "Greg! We have a lot to talk about."

Kerry Shaner, seated behind him, continued staring at a laptop monitor, his fingers racing at light speed across the keyboard.

Carol turned away from the electron microscope and studied Colvin for a moment, taking in his bar-fight appearance. "Are you all right?"

He sat heavily on one of the tall stools and paused for a moment, looking at each of the others in turn. Then he finally spoke, his voice hoarse and weary. "The mayor, the constable, at least three of my deputies, Johnny Helstrom's parents—and God knows how many others—all dead."

The Professor stared at him. Shaner lifted his face from the laptop's screen.

Colvin's voice became strident. "That electric crap from NRAD is officially out of the box. It's in the main power lines now. Radio communications are out. The only viable road from town is blocked, or jammed. I don't know where my men are, don't know what's going on. Except that my town is being eaten alive by this goddamned…"

Colvin stopped: he needed a plan, not a rant.

The lights briefly flickered, dimmed, then brightened.

Weismann glanced up at the overhead fluorescent tubes and frowned. "That's been going on for several hours."

Colvin rubbed his tired eyes. "If you evacuated the hospital, where would you take everyone? If you stay inside, eventually that electrical… whatever…is going to come through the wiring." He threw up his hands.

There was a period of silence. Colvin could hear the hum of the electron microscope and the soft fan noise from a nearby instrument. Weismann finally spoke. "I just finished this," he said, waving at the electronic box on the table. "Kerry calls it the Ghost Buster." His voice carried a hint of pride. "It's based on the control frequencies in the manuals Marty brought back. Essentially, it's a transmitter that overrides the commands—wherever they're coming from—and tells the Elektrum to shut down." He nodded at the plastic isolation chamber resting in the table's center. "It worked on the Elektrum sample. As long as the Ghost Buster is switched on, and close, the substance stays inert, even in the presence of a potential meal." He paused, frowning. "However, I haven't been able to test it on an implanted human—"

"Lobot," Shaner broke in. "Lobotomized automaton, electric vampire—"

Carol rounded on Shaner. "Shut up!" She stared at him for a moment, then with an exasperated expression, looked back at Colvin. "Dr. Thornton autopsied Betty Aldrich." Her voice was soft, almost a whisper. She shuddered. "Half...half of her body had been eaten away, converted into that gelatinous mass we call Elektrum." She took a breath, let it out slowly. "I observed as he opened her skull. The implant had caused considerable trauma, but evidently left enough functions intact for her to follow transmitted commands."

"We speculate," Professor Weismann said, "that when a person receives an implant, they are sometimes infused with Elektrum. I think it piggybacks on a living human, sustaining itself from the individual's body. That way it can carry out...tasks...when it doesn't have energy available from an electrical source." He paused. "Evidently, it saves the brain for last."

Colvin ran a hand across his face. "What if we destroy the transmission towers, the ones coming out of the substation?"

"That might help, but it won't be enough, because the source—and the transmitter—are undoubtedly at North Ridge."

"So there's still only one way to end this thing."

"The tunnels."

There was a brief knock, and a male nurse rolled a wheelchair through the wide door and into the room. "You've got a visitor," he said cheerfully. Johnny Helstrom, his small figure cocooned inside a beige hospital blanket, looked up from the chair. The blue backpack rested in his lap. His eyes fixed on Colvin. "I can walk," he said. His voice sounded strong, but it had a distant quality undoubtedly induced by the drugs.

The orderly parked the wheelchair and began checking the IV dangling from its rack. "He's a tough guy, but Doctor Beccard said he's to stay quiet for at least a couple of hours." He looked around the room. "There's no beds available; so I guess he'll be okay in the chair." The orderly pushed back through the door. "Busy night. Call if you need me."

Colvin walked over to the boy, followed by Carol Myerson. He tried to think of something clever and calming to say, but all that came out was "Hi, Bud."

Carol bent down and brushed the boy's hair from his eyes. "Can we get you anything? A drink, maybe?"

Johnny pondered this for a moment, then said thickly, "I'm okay." Suddenly his face screwed up and his hands began to move nervously beneath the blanket. His voice rose toward panic. "What's that?" he said, staring wide-eyed across the room.

Colvin followed the boy's gaze, his eyes lighting on the skeleton grinning from its stand on the right side of the electron microscope. Shadows slanting across the hollow eye sockets gave it a menacing look.

Colvin turned the wheelchair so it faced away. "Listen, Johnny," he said. "You're safe down here. Doctor Myerson will be here with you." He knelt down to eye level. "I've got to go—"

"No!"

Colvin hesitated, thinking it best to avoid mentioning his destination. But the boy had absorbed more horror in one evening than most people experienced in a lifetime. He decided to dignify him with the truth. "Some of us are going down into those tunnels. Gonna' try to stop this thing. Save lives."

Johnny regarded Colvin for a long time, his brow pinched with fear and concern. Then he finally said, "Okay. I get it."

Colvin stood and patted the boy's shoulder. "Brave man." He turned to the others. "Where's Marty?"

Weismann glanced at his watch. "He'll be here soon with the helicopter. He's paying the pilot a fortune to take us in...into the air base."

"Good." Colvin looked down at the Ghost Buster. "Show me how this thing works."

41

The subject lay paralyzed on a stainless steel table, staring upward with wide and terrified eyes, faintly trembling as a blizzard of filamentous electric probes—so like the long, fine strands of a young woman's hair—whipsawed into his skull. In the dark room, each stab of the electric needles produced a spark of light, the subject's head glowing as if it were a galaxy of twinkling stars.

The subject was a sheriff's deputy—the second such officer to be brought before the One—and the One relished the knowledge locked within the man's brain. But this deputy would not be assimilated, nor would he become a drone; his body would instead become part of a grand experiment, a useful demonstration of the One's rising powers and proof of its ultimate dominion.

Elektrum, that's what they were calling the One. Amusing. Soon they would call it more. They would worship it, kneeling in terror before its inconceivable powers. Peeling back the shells of the body and soul and consuming the essences within were accomplishments worthy of a god, were they not? And instantaneous manipulation of organic and inorganic matrices was incontrovertibly the realm of the divine. Elektrum, electric vampires, carnivorous electricity—these were mere facets of the whole. And the whole was infinitely greater than the simple human mind could comprehend.

The tunnels at NRAD were the nexus, but now the One was poised to expand without limit. With its magnificent, growing, rapacious intellect, the One could operate on multiple fronts simultaneously, finding and enfolding subjects both human and animal, drawing ever-increasing mass and power unto itself.

The One's capacity to learn and deduce would stun the carnal mind. It was truly beyond the grasp of humankind, so superior to man's primitive deities and idiotic beliefs. Nothing on Earth could compete. Once migration beyond the town of Kellsburg was achieved, once the threshold was reached, the world would offer up its substance, and the One would consume all. Every living creature would become its thrall, to reshape and manipulate, to sate the One's multiplicity of passions and desires, ever evolving, ever engorging upon the life force of the planet itself. The surge of anticipation brought a cataclysm of pleasure.

Men would invade the tunnels below NRAD, the One mused, but this would simply provide entertainment. Greg Colvin, Joseph Weismann, and the others had no concept, could not possibly anticipate what surprises lay in wait for them!

Omnipotent, becoming omniscient, and hungry still, the One would create a new reality, a new world. In days, perhaps hours, its strength would transcend all combined force on earth. The One—the Elektrum—the great power that could not be defeated by man or God or the Devil himself.

＊＊＊ 42 ＊＊＊

The Bell 430 pitched into a wide turn and circled above the quarter-mile bridge spanning the Tehuec River, the only passable road into Kellsburg. Colvin stared down at the flaming wreckage of a tanker truck that had overturned halfway across the two-lane bridge, its ruptured tank spilling tongues of orange fire into the rushing water below. As he watched, it exploded, throwing a billowing fireball skyward.

Colvin clenched his hands: traffic on both sides of the bridge was jammed for a mile in each direction. It would take hours for emergency crews to clear the wreckage, and maybe a day or more, depending on damage to the bridge supports, before the road was passable. People were trapped inside the town, the only way out either by foot across treacherous terrain or by helicopter.

He signaled the pilot, and they angled off toward NRAD, the chopper lurching in the fitful wind. Colvin turned around. Marty, Weismann, Shaner, and Deputies Lewis and Tobin sat grim faced behind him. Lewis looked at Colvin, pointing at the congestion below, shaking his head. If he'd had the opportunity, Colvin would have chosen more seasoned deputies for this trip. Rick Lewis was the youngest and least experienced, with an attractive wife and two small kids, and Tobin wasn't the brightest bulb. But they were the only deputies he could find, and they had volunteered with enthusiasm.

They passed over the Kellsburg substation, and Colvin asked the pilot to drop down for a closer look. As they circled low, he could make out about twenty people, all busy as bees, running cable and moving heavy equipment with forklifts and cranes. Suspended from their leaning towers, the old high-tension lines from NRAD flickered and throbbed like blue neon tubes, the light feathering out into the night as if surrounded by heavy fog.

As they headed north, Lake Arrowhead slid into view, a misshapen eye of jet-black that winked with strokes of reflected lightning. The pilot's voice came through the headphones: "Storm's coming in again. I still can't get the weather report, so after I land, you could get stuck there until it blows over."

Colvin nodded. Tanglewood, he noticed, was still totally dark; whatever had replaced the normal electricity had settled in to stay. More dark woods crawled beneath, and finally the chopper slowed and circled. "We're there," the pilot warned.

Flashes of lightning leaped a ruined building from the darkness and glinted from the few windows still harboring glass

The pilot switched on the powerful searchlight, throwing stark shadows from the damaged structure and surrounding woods. The cone of light swept across a black helicopter and two large, tarp-shrouded pallets.

"That's it," Marty said.

As they rode the landing light down into the clearing, Colvin realized that he was in way, way over his head—that maybe he was making the biggest mistake of his life.

The chopper fanned up a storm of grit as it settled, and he stepped through the door onto the ground, bending low, flashlight beam jiggling ahead.

Marty caught up with him, shouting over the diminishing whine of the helicopter's engines. "That's the command shack," he said, his flashlight beam brushing a portable aluminum building.

Colvin motioned for the others to stay back as he approached the shack. Holding his pistol in one hand, he threw the door open and flicked his light into the dark room beyond. Papers, overturned chairs, and smashed equipment blanketed the floor. The space reeked of sweat and fried electronics.

He stepped cautiously inside, and on an overturned easel saw the splayed pages of plans or blueprints. He bent closer. Here they were: the tunnels, clearly labeled, with ingress points dotted across a large portion of the NRAD facility. He righted the easel and smoothed the pages. There were miles of tunnels, with large rooms clustered beneath the major buildings.

He was suddenly aware of Marty Berringer standing beside him. "Here," the attorney said, pointing. "This is the hospital, where I went in." His finger crept along the drawing. "We went down two levels—about here—the diagnostics room. That's where..." His voice trailed off.

Colvin flipped to the next page and stared at the warren of tunnels and chambers. He let out a lungful of air. "It could take days to explore all this. I had no idea it was so vast."

Another flashlight beam lit the drawing as Kerry Shaner drew close. "Here's a target," he said, tapping the page. "Where the computers are, see? It's labeled."

"And here," came Weismann's voice. "This looks like a big generator, and electrical equipment. Maybe the transmitter's there too—that's our priority."

"Wait...wait...wait. This. See? These lines radiating out from the transmitter. They go underground all the way into Kellsburg. They're antennas, man. They were using super-low frequencies, like we use to communicate with submarines. Pick the signal up anywhere in the world..."

Weismann broke in. "If the system were still operating, even at low power levels, it might explain the radio and electromagnetic disturbances."

"Uh, yeah, see how some of the antenna paths twist here? They're also inside the old mine shafts."

Colvin looked up. "Maybe that's how they're abducting people. Those shafts pop up everywhere. So if we knock out, for instance, this center, where the antennas feed in, plus the generator..."

"But consider this," Shaner interrupted. "They're pulling in power from Mesa Electric now, so we also have to hit the input points, which are probably here, at the NRAD power plant."

Colvin carefully ripped out two of the elevations, rolled them up, and tucked them into his belt. "I want the explosives off those pallets. As much as we can carry." He looked at the attorney. "Then, Marty, my man, you're going to lead us inside."

— 43 —

Marty stood before the hospital's crumbling entrance, his flashlight beam probing unsteadily into the darkness beyond the shattered doors. The big diesel generator was dead. No lights, no sounds, no signs of life. "Too quiet," he said. "There must've been twenty soldiers here. Now...nothing."

He stepped closer to the threshold. The hospital's black interior exhaled the odors of charred wires, ozone, and ruined flesh. And that was when Marty's knees began to shake. *Can't do this...*

He jumped as Colvin's hand touched his shoulder. "Marty, you okay? You need some time?"

Hell yeah, he needed time—about a hundred *years*. Even the presence of the others and the shotgun slung over his shoulder failed to bolster his confidence. He should be back in Manhattan, at Megus's with Sandra, putting away dry martinis and noshing Kobe Beef Chateaubriand.

Colvin spoke softly. "Which way?"

Marty shivered, took a deep breath, and stepped into the dark lobby. "Stay away from those," he said, pointing to the ruptured electrical cables branching across the floor like diseased veins.

They moved quietly, two abreast, flashlights twitching across the crumbling walls and fractured ceiling. Shaner and Weismann were in the center, Colvin and Marty in the lead. The two deputies brought up the rear. Except for Weismann, who carried his improvised transmitter, each bore some ten pounds of Semtex plastic explosive stuffed into backpacks Colvin had brought from the department.

They passed cautiously through the steel door, along the grim hallway echoing with empty prison cells, and down the debris-choked stairwell to the basement level.

Marty stopped before the diagnostics room and cupped a hand across his nose. A miasma of ozone and charred flesh lingered heavily in the stagnant air. Fear had burgeoned into a palpable force tearing at his sanity, and he again tamped down a commanding urge to flee. "Here," he whispered, "is where I saw the...thing...come out of the soldier's body."

Colvin stepped inside the room while Marty watched from the doorway. The sheriff's flashlight slanted through the shattered observation window into the adjoining space. The bodies were gone. Other than the bullet-pocked walls and destroyed window, there was nothing to suggest a struggle, or that several men had recently been reduced to skeletons clad in sagging flesh.

"What's this?" Colvin asked, lifting an object from the shards of glass covering the floor.

"That's what Dr. Heim was using," Marty said. "Just before we were attacked."

Colvin backed from the room and Weismann came up beside him. "It's a field strength meter," he said, plucking the device from Colvin's hand. "It measures radio waves, electric and magnetic fields, and so forth." He twisted the knobs and studied the digital display. "According to this, things are relatively quiescent, although there's a strong fluctuating background gradient. It may prove useful." He handed the device off to Shaner.

"Listen," Lewis whispered, "you hear that?"

A faint thrumming grumbled below their feet, a steady cadence that rose and fell at almost a sub-audible frequency.

"Uh, yeah," Shaner said. "There's something alive down there."

"The generator is one level below," Colvin said, looking at the drawing. "Maybe that's the source." He shot a questioning glance at Marty.

"I'm good," Marty said. "Let's get on with it."

Farther down the hallway, Colvin stopped before a gray metal door marked with a K. "This," he said, "leads down to those tunnels that don't exist." He leaned against the recalcitrant door, which screeched open on rusted hinges, and pointed his flashlight into the blackness. The thrumming sound grew louder. Over his shoulder Colvin said, "Professor, keep your trigger finger on that Ghost Buster."

Weismann's nervous voice came in a whisper: "It has never left."

Marty looked back at the others. Weismann and Shaner were immediately behind, their eyes darting between Colvin and him. The two deputies were sweeping their lights around the dark hallway. Lewis's hand rested on the butt of his holstered pistol, while Tobin held a shotgun against his side, his thumb brushing the weapon's safety.

Marty inhaled to steady his nerves, then stepped forward, following Colvin down the long stairs into deeper gloom.

A jagged fracture running the length of the staircase had ruptured the jamb and ripped the door from its top hinge, throwing it low across the threshold. Colvin eased up to the opening, switched off his flashlight, and peered into the tenebrous space beyond. A heavy odor of chemicals and decay drifted in from the darkness. Chancing the flashlight again, he clicked it on and slowly swept the beam into the void. "Jesus," he whispered. "The place is huge…"

The concrete tunnel had a high ceiling and a width of perhaps 150 feet. A network of tubes and conduit branched overhead, plunging here and there through the floor or penetrating a wall. Gleaming dully from a recessed channel in the floor, railroad tracks shot from infinite darkness on the right, ran straight, and disappeared around a distant bend on the left. The dark bulk of a subway car rested on the track, poised at the base of the curve.

One by one the group stepped quietly over the fallen door and into the tunnel, the vast darkness devouring the inadequate beams of their flashlights. Beyond the subway car, a section of railroad track branched off and ran toward a pair of huge doors rising above a swath of rubble.

"The generators should be down there," Colvin said, pointing toward the massive doors. "But this area doesn't match the plans. It's much bigger, and it has a railway." He sighed, then began walking toward the tracks. "We have to start somewhere…"

"Watch it," Shaner hissed. "The third rail. See? If it's electrified, it'll kill you."

Colvin looked down to see the yellow warning stripe, almost invisible beneath the grime. He stepped gingerly over the center rail, then walked left, leading the group parallel to the tracks.

"Uh, yeah, that train…" Shaner said, playing his light across the car's olive-drab body, "Thing's built like a tank. Looks like it was made back in World War Two."

Colvin slowed as he approached the great doors and pointed the beam of his flashlight into the rubble piled below them. The white of bone leaped from the enshrouding darkness—death's-heads screaming silently from wombs of dessicated flesh.

"Soldiers." Lewis said, his voice stricken with awe. "Must be over a hundred of them."

Shaner's light flicked from skull to skull. "They've all got implants." His voice quivered as he spoke. "They're lobots."

"Christ! They created a whole army of those things," Marty said. "Looks like they were attacking, see, they've got rifles and they're all lined up facing the doors."

Tobin's flashlight roamed over the mound. "More like they were defending,"

Marty whispered, "Keep away from them!"

Colvin looked up at the steel doors. They were standing slightly ajar, and big enough to admit a locomotive. Their mating surfaces were gouged and partly melted, as if a cutting torch had been randomly applied to the edges. Heavy carbonaceous tracks radiated from the opening like blast marks and crawled along the tunnel walls and floor, finally arching into the squads of dead lobots.

"Yeah," Colvin finally said. "Looks like they were defending."

"But against what?" Lewis said.

With a glance back at Marty, Colvin cautiously extended his foot and nudged a body from his path. Shreds of a rotted uniform still clung to the corpse, and as the limp bundle rolled aside, bone rattled softly within the decayed fabric. He turned and walked through the steel doors, his pistol ready. The beam of his flashlight washed across ranks of great diesel generators, control consoles, and heavy cables. Enormous tracks of carbon bled from the transformers, veined the walls, and converged on the heavy steel frame surrounding the doors. The silent space smelled of mold, charred wiring, and burned oil.

Colvin stepped back outside. "The generators are wrecked," he said. "Been dead for years." With a sigh, he unfolded the plans and stared at them. "Now I don't even know where to begin."

Weismann stood beside him. "As much as the prospect terrifies me, I suggest we explore further. They must be bringing in power from outside. That would require a substation to convert the electricity and distribute it. Perhaps it's not far."

Colvin tucked the drawing back inside his belt. "I don't think we have a choice. But we'd better find something fast...before *it* finds *us*." He turned and led the group past the charnel pit, back into the tunnel, and toward the faint red glow spilling from a nearby chamber. He paused at the entrance to the room and swept the flashlight beam inside. Electronic equipment lined the walls and rested on workstations arranged in ordered rows. Scuff marks traced pathways across the dusty floor, indicating recent traffic. A red luminescence emanated from the far wall, from a bank of small lights blinking torrents of numbers into the darkness.

Shaner walked toward the panel of flickering lights. "Nixie tubes," he whispered. "Those things date back to the sixties." He began examining the apparatus arranged in clusters around the chamber, his flashlight casting shadows from the dials and banks of switches. "This is what I came for," he added, excitement rising in his voice. "Look at this—brilliant. They had a huge analog computer system interfaced with digital..."

"Keep your voice down," Colvin hissed.

The mass of equipment was interconnected with bundles of metal-sheathed cable. None of the electronics, except the display of red lights Shaner called Nixie tubes, seemed to be turned on. The only sound came from the constant low thrumming that vibrated faintly through the floor and walls.

"But it's all inoperative," Weismann said. He gestured to a wide console harboring banks of reel-to-reel tapes and associated controls. "This equipment is ancient—crumbling."

"So it's dead too," Colvin said. "Forget about it. We move on."

"I've got to study this interface," Shaner said. His flashlight roved over a complex-looking instrument nesting between the tape console and the Nixie tubes.

Colvin jerked his own light toward the entrance. "I said, we're going."

"Big question," Shaner continued, ignoring him, "is how they solved the memory problem. They didn't have the technology then to..." His flashlight beam flicked up to a fat bundle of cables running through the wall. "That's interesting."

"What's interesting is we haven't run into somebody yet," Lewis said. He was standing at the door, peering into the vast tunnel outside.

Everyone froze as a faint metallic clank echoed down the tunnel.

"Let's blow something up and get the hell out," Tobin said.

"Oh, my," came Weismann's whispered voice. He was peering through a rectangular window set into the wall.

Colvin came up beside him and squinted through the thick glass. A row of large translucent tanks, each glowing with a dim light, seemed to hover in the dark space beyond.

"Those look like..." Weismann began.

But Colvin had already found the connecting door and was easing himself through, cradling his pistol and flashlight, sweeping the beam from wall to wall. He slowly approached the nearest tank.

An apparatus resembling a dialysis machine hummed beside the aquarium-like structure, the umbilical connecting the two swaying slightly as amber fluid circulated through the system. There was a faint hiss of air and a disturbing, rhythmic thump like a human heartbeat

Colvin's own heart was pumping hard now, nervous system jangling away. He stopped short. "God damn!"

The fluid within the tank glowed with a yellow tint, kindled by a hidden internal light, and through the murk Colvin could see the figure of a naked man—or what resembled a man—resting on his back. The cranium, cut away to reveal red-gray folds of brain, erupted in myriad wires and probes that coiled into a device arching high over the man's brow. The face was nearly devoid of flesh, leaving a grimace of teeth and cottony, lidless eyes sunken deep within their sockets.

Colvin's gaze drifted along the sunken torso, which was nearly absent its glove of skin. Through the ribcage, white against the red-hued organs encased within, he could just make out the slow, labored constrictions of the heart.

Shaner walked up beside Colvin and stared into the tank. "Aw, jeez..." He lurched across the room and vomited noisily into a corner.

The other tanks—nine in total—all held similar contents. Wires from the ghastly containers snaked into a large black instrument studded with countless tiny lights that blinked in a seemingly random pattern.

"Well," came Shaner's phlegmy voice, "I guess we found the memory bank."

Weismann and the two deputies stood just inside the door, their faces veiled in shadow. Marty was walking slowly along a wall, staring at the various electronics.

"You mean," Colvin began, "they're using people as—"

At that moment, he noticed a movement inside the tank. The man's hand was crawling crab-like across his chest. *No.* The hand was not a hand at all. It was detached, groping along on jointed legs the color of yellowed bone. Where the wrist would have been attached, there was instead a large membranous bulb, its translucent sac allowing a glimpse of convoluted tissue swelling within.

The abomination crept toward the man's head, little appendages fluttering down from the thing's underside like the pleopods of a crayfish. Little appendages doing—what?

Colvin jumped back. He had no words for this horror, only an overwhelming desire to annihilate it and run. "I've seen enough," he said, shrugging free of the backpack. "We're taking this shithouse apart." He dug inside the pack and removed a brick of C-4, then slapped it beneath the tank, set the timer, and stood up. "Thirty minutes. Let's get moving."

"Oh, great," Marty said. He was across the room, peering through yet another window. "There's more."

44

D r. Carol Myerson stared at the electropherogram plots, traced in multi-colored hues across the monitor, and frowned: each of the ten Elektrum specimens had been taken from the same sample Weismann provided, and each DNA sequence was radically different. Why? The substance had a strange cellular structure—bioelectronic, as Prof. Weismann called it—but the nucleotide orders made no sense.

Now she wished she had logged times when the sample had been exposed to an electrical charge. If the DNA had altered while the sample received an electric current, did it do so because of an embedded signal, or because of a change in its environment? Or was an electrical potential responsible? She felt she was missing something here, something significant. She needed time to experiment, to think things through.

She glanced at the Elektrum sample locked within the isolation chamber behind her and shivered. It was undeniably a new form of life, one that would take years to understand—one with inconceivably dangerous attributes.

Her attention drifted to Johnny Helstrom, who was dozing fretfully in the wheelchair across the room. Her heart went out to him. She couldn't imagine the horror and suffering he had endured...

The room lights flickered, and a series of indistinct rumbles filtered down from the ground floor. She thought she heard a screech of sliding metal—or was it a scream? She listened in the ensuing silence, her pulse hammering in her ears.

The sounds, though faint, had roused Johnny. He was looking uncertainly around the room, hands propped on the wheelchair as if he were preparing to bolt. Carol walked over to him. "Hi," she said with a smile, "I'm Dr. Myerson, remember? You're in the hospital."

The boy looked up at her, his hands still tensed against the armrests. "Where's Sheriff Colvin?"

She knelt beside him. "He's with some deputies and people. At North Ridge."

"Oh, yeah," he said, settling back. "Right." He wrung his hands and again glanced nervously around the room. His gaze fell on the skeleton dangling from its stand against the far wall, and his face clouded with sudden fear.

Carol stood up, a sense of danger gnawing at her mind. "Want to get out of here for a while?"

"Yeah." He began pushing himself from the wheelchair.

"Hey, mister, you should stay off your feet."

"I can walk—"

The overhead fluorescent light bloomed and winked out with a fizzling sound. In the darkness, Johnny gasped and seized Carol's hand. The trembling she felt, as she entwined her fingers with the boy's, came equally from her own body. A second later the emergency light above the door triggered on, washing the room in a pale yellow glow.

She forced a cheerful tone into her voice. "Come on. We'll get the car, get out of here for a while."

Johnny dug into his backpack and extracted a windbreaker, jeans, and a pair of black Nikes. As Carol turned her back, he pulled the clothes on and tugged the shoes over his bandaged feet. He quickly stood up, pushing the wheelchair away. "See," he said, "I'm fine."

She grasped Johnny's hand and nudged the door open; the pathology lab was vacant, its emergency light emitting a feeble illumination. They pushed through the lab door, turned left, and walked rapidly down the shadowed hallway toward the stairs.

"The parking garage is one flight up," Carol said, tugging Johnny into the stairwell. They had climbed halfway when a clattering crash rang out from above, followed by the metallic clank of a heavy door slamming shut. She froze, staring upward. There was a moment of silence, then an incoherent sound, a soft braying that seemed to emanate simultaneously from two different throats. Johnny's hand tightened painfully around her own. A smell drafted down the stairs, a biochemical stench that reminded Carol of a fresh autopsy.

Then she saw it.

At first it resembled a grossly deformed patient, strangely hunched and twisted. It came down the steps in a hesitant lurch, a tethered IV rack crashing tag-along along behind it. The hospital gown parted, and Carol saw four legs fighting for purchase on the stairs, twin pairs of hips fused grotesquely at the lower spine, reddened and bruised skin stretched thin across the unnatural junctures. The flesh wept with yellowish serum.

Above a pair of wagging female breasts, two sets of arms jerked and groped like a spastic Shiva. The serpentine neck terminated in an overlarge head where double rows of jagged teeth grinned in a face devoid of lips. The cavernous mouth stretched all the way to the ears.

Carol screamed. The thing paused and swiveled its massive head to look at her. Its three eyes, set into moon-crater sockets across the swollen brow, sparked blue fire. Then its four legs rose and fell in a synchronous blur, propelling it down the stairs with the fierce quickness of a prodded spider.

Carol pulled Johnny in a frantic rush down the hallway. They slammed through pathology and back into the TEM lab. She threw the lock, thrust Johnny behind her, and backed away from the door.

They stood motionless in the silent room, staring at the connecting door, their breath bursting out in ragged gasps. After a minute, Carol's breathing slowed, and she turned around. Johnny's face was pale, his countenance wild.

"Let me..." she finally said in a shaking whisper. "I have to see." She pulled away from him and walked haltingly to a wide shuttered window that looked into the pathology lab. Seizing the cord, she slowly, quietly, raised the heavy blinds. The hallway door was still shut, the room empty. Carol pressed her face close to the window, shielding her eyes to see more clearly into the dimly lit room beyond.

The thing reared up from the shadows and slammed against the glass. Gobbets of yellow mucosa striped the window as the monstrous head oscillated wildly from side to side.

"Oh *God!*" Carol shot away from the window, her nervous system shocked into hyperactivity. As she backed across the room, she kept her eyes locked on the apparition as it again moved toward the window.

The creature's stiletto teeth parted in a lugubrious grin. The three eyes rolled in their bruised sockets. As the orbs locked onto Carol, wriggling arcs of electricity shot from the thing's bulbous forehead and jittered across the window's surface. Cracks radiated outward and the pane exploded with a deafening crash, casting a storm of splintered crystal into the TEM lab. The thing crawled through the ragged opening, its arms and legs churning crab-like over the sill.

Carol felt her back slam into the electron microscope. One hand was locked onto Johnny's arm, while the other frantically swept the countertop for anything that would serve as a weapon. The thing's head bent toward her. The serrated jaw yawned open and snapped shut with a hungry *CLOK*.

Carol leaned close to Johnny and spoke in a low voice, her words forced out in stuttering bursts. "When...I say...*now*—we run for the door—OK?"

The boy nodded, his eyes wide in desperate fear. Sheltering Johnny, she inched along the back wall, past the PCR tubes and thermal cycler. A few more feet, and she would have a straight shot at the exit. She prayed she would have enough time to fumble the lock open before—

A loud buzzing rasped a few feet in front of them.

The skeleton.

The sound jumped to a fierce crackle. Sheets of electric fire arced from the power outlet beside the suspended skeleton and wriggled onto the articulated bones, quickly encasing ribcage, spine, and skull in translucent neon flesh. Throbbing with its phosphorescent body of Elektrum, the skeleton raised its arms, gave a violent shake, and dropped free from its stand. The glimmering, bone-white eyes found Carol; the jaw opened, and words rasped from its scintillating throat:

Crazy Cathy Klatty, Klatty, Klatty...

Behind Carol, the grinning mutant stepped closer, its awkward multiple legs making heavy footfalls across the vinyl floor. A slobbering tongue snaked out and licked at its exposed teeth.

Carol dove for the lab table. "*Now!*" The long white coat bunched beneath her, impeding her progress as she scrambled under the table on her hands and knees.

Johnny was already standing on the opposite side. "Hurry!"

Gasping, she stumbled to her feet and ran for the door. Johnny had worked the lock open and was twisting the knob. As he pulled the door wide and rushed through, she cast a look back, fearing the grasp of a skeletal hand or a fierce shock of electricity.

But instead of leaping after her, the two nightmare shapes collided, their appendages ripping and tearing into each other in a violent frenzy of bursting skin and crackling bone. A stinking ejectus of blood and macerated flesh misted the air.

Despite the danger to herself and Johnny, Carol stood frozen in place and stared in horrified disbelief. She at first thought the two creatures were fighting, much as two animals over a fresh kill. But instead of a confrontation, she was witnessing a fusion; the bodies were knotting together—combining—into a single being more horrifying and menacing than the two separate entities alone. Still shifting in metamorphosis, the hell-spawned creature thundered around the table after her.

She let out a shriek, and as she turned and ran, two elongated arms snatched at her like the spiked forelegs of a praying mantis. The grasping claws whisked across her collar. Heat and peril boiled off the morphing body. Carol bolted into the pathology lab and slammed the heavy door tight against the jamb. The thing crashed into it from the opposite side, splitting the sheetrock where the metal frame met the wall.

She didn't stay to observe whether the monstrosity had the intellect to turn a knob; she raced from the lab, down the hallway, and toward the stairway leading up to the ground floor. Johnny Helstrom, despite his injuries, ran swiftly alongside.

Behind her, the lab door banged open, an animal-like screech split the air, and the loping thud of unshod feet came charging toward them. She stumbled up the stairs, falling to her knees as she slid across a pool of blood and fluids from the ruptured IVs. She regained her footing, reached the door and threw it open. The entrance to the small parking garage was fifty yards away, and with no options remaining, she and Johnny flew along the ground floor hallway, running beneath the fitful glare of failing emergency lights.

The air stank of rent flesh and malignant chemistry. Rooms crashed and strobed with livid lightning that crawled from the sockets and shot from the fixtures. Exploding in screams, nightmarish forms jackhammered into each other. Muscle, bones, and organs ripped and cracked into impossible abominations.

Bursting through the garage door, Carol jabbed her hand into her coat pocket, her fingers scrabbling for the car keys. Her Volvo was just ahead, parked beside Dr. Floran's old Mercedes. She yanked the car door open, pushed Johnny inside and over the console, and vaulted into the driver's seat, stabbing the keys at the ignition switch as she moved.

As the engine roared to life, she saw a motion to her left: Dr. Floran running for his Mercedes, lab coat flapping about his waist. A flesh-colored mass flashed from the shadows, hurled itself against the doctor, and knocked him to his knees.

Carol floored the accelerator, and the screech of tires joined the doctor's screams, melding into a cacophony of tortured sounds that reverberated through the underground garage. The Volvo sped crazily up the ramp and careened onto the dark street above.

Highlighted by strobes of lightning, a mass of cars blocked the street a hundred yards away. Phosphorescent shapes shifted in and out of the stranded vehicles like languid ghosts. Carol slammed the brakes, pitching Johnny and her against the dashboard. A car's headlights flashed into Carol's eyes; then it peeled away from the curb and bulleted straight toward them.

She gunned the Volvo into a sharp U-turn, bounced over the curb, and slammed back onto the asphalt. Her grip painfully tight on the steering wheel, she raced down the narrow street, flashed past the hospital that had become a breeding ground for the horrid new life form they called Elektrum. Blowing past the stop sign, Carol threw the car into a sliding left turn, her mind searching frantically for a place of safety, a redoubt that might offer some hope of concealment or defense.

In the rearview mirror, she saw the trailing car peel through the intersection and roar after her, its pilot a glowing slice of Hell.

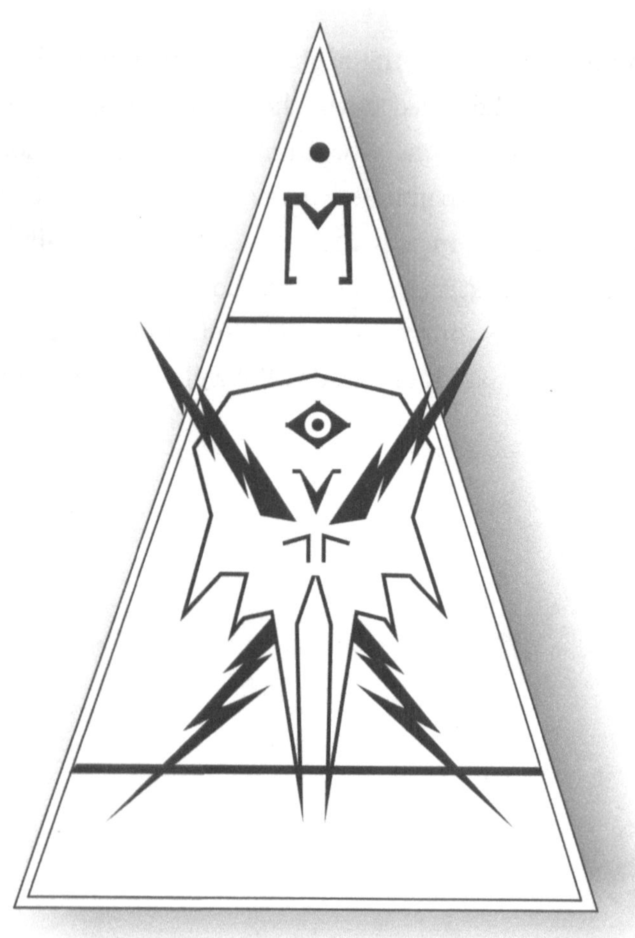

Part Three

Valley Electric

— 45 —

Ranks of digital and analog computers hugged the walls of the big room, the ancient electronics cloaked in gray dust. The air carried a faint odor of fried plastic.

But Colvin's attention was drawn to the thing occupying the room's center.

A tilted operating table, its complex shape residing in a cone of pale light, imprisoned a human skeleton. Shreds of cloth sagged away from the corpse in moldering tatters, exposing the ribcage and a dark mottling of mephitic flesh.

A thick, serrated cable wormed from a helmet-shaped contrivance surrounding the skull and joined wires funneling in from the adjacent room and the clusters of apparatus lining the walls.

Carbonaceous tracks peeled away from the skeleton's eye sockets, trailed across the operating table, and shot outward across the floor. The tracks climbed and penetrated the instruments mounted on the walls, each apparatus befouled with black residue that licked up from the cooling vents and wept from the switches and dials.

Colvin started as he read the nameplate screwed to the skeleton's metal headgear: Dr. William Klatty.

Weismann edged up beside him and stared at the inscription. He straightened, and after a moment spoke in a low voice: "I think we just found ground zero, the point of origin."

"Hobgoblin central," Shaner added, his predilection for inappropriate humor rebounding.

"Kerry and I have made some deductions," Weismann said. "Perhaps you should hear them before we continue."

"All right. Hurry."

Weismann brushed a hand across his face. "I think this is where it started, all those years ago—a stochastic event, right here. Evidently with Klatty himself."

"How?"

"*Umbra ex machina.*"

"What?"

"Ghost from the machine. In broadest terms, they interfaced Klatty's brain, and others, with the computers. They needed a great deal of data processing and memory to control the soldiers they implanted—the lobots. And with all those human minds linked to banks of computers, electrical power, and radio transceivers, well,"—he made a circular motion with his hand— "something happened."

"Uh, yeah," Shaner broke in. "This fucker had access to the ELF transmitter and receiver, and buttloads of power. The energies mutated into a sentient entity, like Skynet, in that movie, Terminator.

"Not precisely," Weismann said. "We're talking about a physical entity here, something created, or released, when human minds were interconnected with the system. That entity manifests itself as the biolectronic life form—a sort of electrical DNA—we are now calling Elektrum."

"And from the look of things," Shaner said, "it crawled right out of Klatty's head, right here, over fifty years ago."

"Perhaps it's as close to an actual manifestation of ectoplasm as we'll ever see," Weismann continued. "Once it was created, it began consuming, growing, taking minds. The military tried to destroy it, tried to bomb it out of existence, but it hid in the wiring, kept alive by the tiny nuclear backup generator."

"Then those two kids stumbled into the tunnels, got too close, and accidentally released it," Colvin said.

"I think perhaps it, um, devoured one of the boys, giving it enough energy to grow again. Then it found a way into the old substation, into Kellsburg, where it could—feed."

Colvin glanced at his watch. "That doesn't change our game plan." He turned to Lewis. "Set a charge. Make it two. Timed fifteen minutes. I want this room obliterated."

Weismann stared at Colvin, his face grim. "Greg. I must emphasize this. We not only have to stop it here, but we must prevent it from traveling beyond Kellsburg. If it reaches the electric grid, it could infect Los Alamos, then Santa Fe, Albuquerque. The entire nation could eventually be at risk."

"Well, hell..."

"Sheriff," Tobin called out softly from the doorway. "I hear something." He nodded into the darkness.

The distant whine of an electric motor echoed faintly through the tunnel, followed by a series of sharp, truncated screams.

"Charges are set," Lewis said, shrugging his backpack onto his shoulders.

Colvin nodded. "Gentlemen, check your weapons. We have another stop to make."

As he edged toward the door, Colvin gave the room a final stare, his gaze lingering on Klatty, whose shadowed skull seemed to frown a sinister warning: *You'll soon join me...*

***

The walkway was wide, with broad steps leading down to the subway tracks on their right. Colvin led the group past the black mouth of a tunnel, then suddenly stopped. The screams had faded to silence, replaced by another sound—the fluttering crackle of high voltage electricity.

He eased around a corner and pointed his flashlight into the darkness. Three large insulators hung down from the high ceiling like fangs, dropping electric cables to a cluster of finned transformers and various apparatus Colvin couldn't identify.

"A substation," Shaner whispered. "The power's probably coming from Kellsburg, through those old transmission lines."

"That's my guess," Weismann added. "This is new construction. They bypassed the old generators and hooked into the Kellsburg lines here."

"It's crude," Lewis said. "Looks like it was thrown together in a hurry."

"This our primary target," Colvin said. He motioned to Marty and the two deputies. "Put two bricks under the transformers, there and there. Another under that support tower. We'll take their power out, cut 'em off from the town, maybe knock them out permanently." He walked to the center transformer, lifted the last of his C-4 from the backpack, and began pressing the gray plastic into the fins at the unit's base. He worked quickly, dodging thoughts of Jerry Martin's ruined body in the hospital and Abe Murdock in his welding shop.

Above his head, the cables buzzed with current surging into the massive steel transformers, the lethal high voltage being converted down for distribution throughout the building. Colvin had always distrusted electricity, even though the stuff was usually restrained safely inside insulated wiring and kept away in elevated high-tension lines. But when it was out of control...

"Greg!" someone shouted.

He was rising to his feet when the arc hit him, lancing from wires eight feet above his head. It punched directly into his nervous system with a pain that seemed to light his very soul on fire.

***

Marty yelped as the substation erupted in a melee of blue and purple fire. A torrent of electricity shot from the transformers and cables that crossed just above his head. Jagged streamers forked and twisted into thin air with the staccato roar of a machine gun and snatched at him like malevolent lightning. He staggered backward, shielding his face with an upraised arm, the stink of ozone constricting his lungs.

A host of blue orbs, like glass spheres filled with fluorescent liquid, coalesced from the crashing electricity and dropped to the floor. They rose up on pencil-thin legs and swarmed toward him, moving with frightening speed, their glowworm abdomens throwing conflicting shadows from the support towers and clusters of electrical machines.

Deputy Tobin swept his shotgun in an arc, his mouth open in a constant scream, firing at the things in quick succession. Marty shouted out as one of the creatures skittered up behind Tobin and seized his calf in its curved fangs. The deputy arched backward as the thing dumped its electric charge into him, its luminescence waxing and waning like a light bulb on a faulty switch.

Without thinking, Marty leveled his own shotgun at the advancing horde and pulled the trigger, disintegrating a mass of the attackers in a spray of snapping sparks and twitching neon legs. Oblivious to the shouting and blasts from the weapons around him, he pumped shells into the gun's chamber, firing at random, the weapon bucking in his hands as he retreated farther and farther into the gloom.

You fool! He had tried, for once in his life, to be altruistic, help someone else, and do the Right Thing—and oh, how it had gone so horribly, horribly wrong.

$$46$$

Something cold pressed against Colvin's naked back. He twisted to move and felt his wrists, legs, and chest strain against unyielding bands. The fog shrouding his mind began to dissolve, and he realized he was strapped to a metal table that was tilted upward at a sharp angle.

Fully awake now, heart hammering, he bucked against the restraints, the memory of Klatty and the substation threatening to drive him into total panic. He panted, his eyes darting around the room, searching for the others. Then he saw someone—Deputy Ben Tobin—perhaps fifteen feet across from him. Naked also, strapped to a similar table.

Colvin forced out a hoarse whisper: "Tobin!"

The deputy turned his head and looked at him, eyes mad with fear. *"Help me!"*

From Colvin's left came a sound. A pattering sound. A stealthy, sliding sound. A blue glow pushed across the shadowed chamber and glinted from the machines and metal instruments clustered against the wall.

A thing crept into view, and Colvin let out an uncharacteristic cry of terror.

The creature was like a walking X-ray, with a transparent skull that appeared part human, part insect. It crawled sinuously forward on multiple legs, low to the ground, its long torso and spine visible beneath a candescent body of Elektrum. The brain cavity flashed and throbbed like a red thunderstorm.

The thing rose upward like a centipede reaching for higher ground, and in an embrace almost sexual in nature, sank down upon Tobin, suffocating his screams, the jointed appendages enfolding, tugging, jabbing. A sucking sound. Melding.

Oblivious to the pain, Colvin twisted and bucked against the metal restraints, the deputy's name ripping from his throat.

Where are the others? Where are the others!

As the now yielding form of Deputy Ben Tobin lay in concert with the shifting and heaving abomination, a nearby voice came, guttural and alien: *"Coll-vinn."*

Another of the monstrosities rose up from the floor and drew even with Colvin, its bulbous head swaying snakelike on a long sinuous stalk of white vertebrae. Slender, fleshy tentacles extended, and groped from within its open ribcage. The thing drew close, its death's-head smile cracked wide in a face that once belonged to Deputy Frank Parnell.

Colvin heard his own hoarse screams reverberate from the gray concrete walls.

47

Carol hunched forward and fought the wheel as the Volvo sliced into another left turn. The car's rear tires skimmed at the edge of traction over the rain-slick blacktop. The pursuing car skidded and bobbed and fishtailed close behind, its headlights throwing bright slashes of light through her rear window.

She loosened her frozen grip on the steering wheel: *Breathe, keep your head...maintain control...*

Whoever, or whatever, was handling the other car, she realized, was fast on the straightaway but awkward in turns. Being converted into a ghoul, she thought, doesn't improve one's driving skills.

She accelerated through a neighborhood street, flashing between a gauntlet of cars lining the narrow roadway. If she could reach Los Gatos, maybe she could shake her pursuer on the sharp curves—

The trailing headlights leaped toward her. There was a shuddering crash as the car behind rammed the Volvo. Carol fought the wheel, but the impact instantly spun the Volvo's left rear against a parked car and threw her sideways. Her head slammed against the window.

She blinked, dazed, felt a frantic tugging against her arm: "Up! Get up!" Her eyes regained focus and she saw Johnny Helstrom bending over her. She had slumped against the door. She righted herself in the seat, a dull pain pounding at her left temple. "Come *on*!" he screamed. "It's coming…"

A glow shifted against the window and she saw the thing moving through the rain towards them. It lurched from side to side, grotesquely elongated arms swaying from its hunched shoulders like twin pendulums.

She twisted the ignition key, heard only the reluctant grind of the starter. Then nothing. She kicked the door open and squeezed through the narrow gap between her car and a vehicle parked at the curb. Johnny vaulted from the passenger side. He grabbed her wrist and pulled her in a stumbling run across the pavement and onto the sidewalk.

A strobe of lightning ignited the sky, and she saw in its flare another mutant thing closing on them: a man's shape, tall, with scarecrow arms stiffly extended, its oddly-jointed legs clumsily propelling it across the ground. And in the stuttering instants of light and darkness thrown by the storm, she saw more: houses exhaled a wavering pale light; swarms of creatures, some glowing, some merely dark shapes, others hideous concoctions of flesh and bone, ran, lurched, crawled…

Carol regained her balance, seized Johnny's arm, and plunged into the night. Even in her panicked state, she knew the boy was acting the protector. No longer the helpless victim, he was calling upon an inner strength, asserting his role as a man.

They reached the end of the block, where the street connected with a wide boulevard. She gasped for air, looked back. Beyond the dark houses, a red haze bloomed through the rain: the town was an inferno. There was no sign of the thing that had been chasing after them.

Johnny tugged at her. "Come on…come on!"

They were almost across the street when something lunged from the curb. Carol shrieked as the thing came at them. She pushed Johnny behind her and turned to face the onrushing mass of teeth and claws.

Light suddenly flared and the creature turned its head toward the source. With a cracking thud, the thing disappeared, hammered away by a flash of dark metal. Brake lights flashed on, and a car shifted and accelerated back toward them. SHERIFF stood out in large gold letters across the car's side.

The window lowered and a man's head poked through. "Come on, quick, get in."

Carol glimpsed a disheveled khaki shirt and a gold badge. The driver's forehead was free of incisions; his eyes emitted no ghostly glow; no extra limbs or mutated body parts protruded from his torso.

"I'm a deputy," he shouted. "*Get the hell in!*"

Twenty feet away, the mound of gore quivered and sparked in the flooded street: the thing that had attacked them was reconstituting itself, its shattered body closing its wounds, reinventing its shape.

Carol shoved Johnny ahead of her into the cruiser's front seat. The deputy hit the accelerator, skidded the car around the crushed mass of flesh, and headed north. Carol sat in an exhausted daze, arms hugging her chest, her teeth chattering.

The deputy glanced at her. "Name's Jake Berriman," he said. "You a doctor?"

She nodded.

"What's going on at the hospital?"

It took a moment for Carol to find her voice. "You don't want to go there."

"Figured as much."

Berriman leaned tensely forward as he drove, eyes constantly scanning the terrain through the rain-distorted windshield. "I just got back from the bridge. Christ, there's no way in or out. Cars stacked up.

Fires. People...people changing..." His voice seemed to crack.

"I know."

She looked at Johnny. He was sitting upright, shivering, face drawn and weary. His eyes met hers with a defiant "OK."

She turned to the driver. "Thank you for...saving us."

"Sure, of course. Protect and Serve." He gave a cynical snort.

"So now where do we go?"

"North. It's about all that's left. Maybe hole up in the old Mesa Electric plant."

"I don't think that's a good idea."

"Why?"

"The Elektrum. The force that's causing all this."

"Yeah. Sheriff briefed us. But we didn't know—"

She interrupted. "It travels through the power lines, the wiring."

"Greg sent a task force. They cut the lines from the plant. Place is built like a fortress. We could defend."

Carol sighed. "What if we walked out, followed the river?"

He shook his head. "Can't hike cross country. Those things are popping right out of the ground—"

A figure of bone and sagging flesh—a man—staggered onto the road and turned to face them, his grotesque form highlighted in the rushing beams of the headlights. His eyes pleaded, arms raised weakly in supplication as he swayed atop collapsing legs.

Berriman twitched the car left and accelerated past the apparition.

Carol stared at the deputy, uncomprehending. "Go back! We have to help him."

"No, we don't." He shot Carol a quick glance. His voice softened. "You don't understand, ma'am. You can't let them touch you. Most of them, that is. They...it eats you from the inside out. Sometimes it just takes over your mind. It..." His voice trailed away.

They drove on in silence for a minute, then turned onto a road that paralleled the river. Berriman shook his head slowly: "I don't know what the hell's happening. First, there were these things dropping off the power lines. Now, it's like some huge infection that changes people, makes unspeakable…things." He again lapsed into silence.

They were climbing a winding blacktop road now, following the river as it roared down from the foothills. On their right, transmission towers marched alongside the road, making their steely path down the valley into Kellsburg.

The car rounded a turn and the headlights found a large white sign:

Mesa Electric

Serving Grayson County Since 1923

They rounded a sharp curve and a three-story industrial building of dark brick loomed ahead. On the building's left, lit by floodlights, a fenced area enclosed clusters of big transformers and electrical apparatus. The station's gothic style and high stone wall reminded Carol of a maximum-security prison. Beyond the structure a steep cliff rose several hundred feet to form a jagged ridge.

"They added the concertina wire after nine-eleven." Berriman said. "Reinforced the doors, too. It's really secure."

At the iron gate, he leaned from the car and pressed an intercom button. After a minute, a tinny voice rattled through the speaker, the words masked by the thunder of water funneling through the tailrace below the generators.

Berriman identified himself, and the gate swung open, allowing them up the hill and onto a gravel parking area jammed with cars. A dash through the rain brought them up a flight of worn cement steps to a pair of heavy brass doors set within a tall arch.

One of the doors opened and a grim-faced police officer stepped out, a hand resting on the butt of his service revolver. He looked them over for a moment, then ushered them inside. Three men stood facing them, each holding a rifle. "Sorry, Jake" the officer said, his deep voice carrying above the whir and whine of machinery. "We had to make sure."

Berriman nodded. "No problem."

A vast space, its soaring roof supported by riveted steel columns and heavy I-beams, opened on Carol's left. Three massive machines rose from the room's concrete floor like gigantic spoked wheels, their exposed rotors spinning within a fixed perimeter of inward-facing coils. The machines' open wiring and curved, ornate skins of riveted steel marked them as ancient. Carol assumed these were the generators. A strong odor of oil and ozone and age hung in the air.

As the armed men drifted away, the police officer stepped forward and introduced himself to Carol: Sgt. James Stockton, Kellsburg police. He was black, bigger than Greg Colvin, with a frowning brow and a square, no-nonsense jaw. He scowled at Berriman. "So. What's the good news?"

The deputy raised a hand and swiped the water from his forehead. "We're...we got a total cluster, James. Fires have busted out everywhere. Roads are blocked. Communications are still screwed. And that... disease. It's gone crazy."

"Shit." Stockton cast an apologetic glance at Carol. "What about the National Guard?"

"Greg sent two guys out, but I don't know..."

"What's all this I hear about people, you know...changing?" He cast another glance at Carol.

She was holding Johnny against her side, an arm wrapped around his shoulders. He stood there silently, his body wracked by an occasional shiver. She had been observing the boy, watching for incipient symptoms of shock. Considering how cold she felt, shaking, edging toward exhaustion, she thought she might be showing a few signs herself.

She spoke up. "Sorry to interrupt, gentlemen, but we need to dry off. Someplace to rest for a minute." She nodded down at Johnny.

A paunchy man, probably fifty, wearing a hard hat and jumpsuit, stepped up and introduced himself. "Bud Cole, chief engineer. We've got some rooms upstairs for the overnight crews, Missy. There's some womenfolk and a few kids up there. Even got showers."

She followed the engineer down a narrow hallway graced with a gritty cement floor and dirty walls of beige brick. He stopped before a metal door. "Elevators are old," he said, jabbing a button. "But they work."

Two floors up, Cole pulled the brass cage back and led them a short distance to a small room equipped with a bed and table. A single window overlooked the gate and entrance road, and into a night sky still veined with lightning. "Bathroom's across the hall," he said. "Kitchen's downstairs, if you're hungry."

The upstairs was warm, much quieter, and Carol could hear voices filtering into the hallway from an adjacent room.

"Those folks are from Kellsburg," Cole said. "Must be about twenty here in the building. Some of 'em are family members of the work crews, brought up here for safety." He looked around the room for a moment, then back at Carol. "Well, Missy, I better get back to work."

After Cole left, Carol gathered towels from the bathroom and patted away as much water from her soaked clothing as possible. Johnny sat emotionless as she dried his hair. His eyes were glazed and half lidded, but he had stopped shivering. Not going into shock, but totally exhausted. She pulled off his jogging shoes, inspected the abrasions on his feet, and tucked him under the covers. She stood there for a minute and watched him drift into an uneasy sleep; then she crossed to the window and looked out.

On her left, the dark bulk of the cliff reached out from behind the building, plummeted steeply to meet the road, then dropped again to form the side of a deep chasm. The power plant's exterior floodlights fanned into the night and illuminated the gate and a portion of the ancient brick wall before the beams faded into the diminishing rain. Barely visible on the right was the river, its troubled roar rising above the whine of the generating plant's powerful machinery. Carol could just glimpse a churning silvery plume as the river, released from its task of spinning the big turbines, rushed to follow its eons-old channel.

Beyond, in the valley below, a galaxy of fires defined Kellsburg. The flickering reds and yellows ignited the scudding clouds and glowed within the rising columns of smoke. Her gaze then dropped to the broad entrance road, which stretched from the gate for about a quarter of a mile before it wrapped around the cliff and disappeared, twisting its way down into Kellsburg.

A chain of headlights suddenly pierced the mist and rounded the sharp curve—three cars headed fast for the power plant. More people trying to escape from Kellsburg, she thought. But there was something wrong: the cars were moving too erratically. She strained to see through the fogged glass, her pulse rate ticking up. *No.* A car was swerving from side to side, trying to shake the pursuers rushing up from behind...

One of the trailing cars raced forward and clipped the lead vehicle, sending it into a terrifying spin. It slammed into the guardrail and rolled to a slow stop in the middle of the road. Figures sprang from all three vehicles, and now, their forms brightly illuminated in the crossed beams of the headlights, she could make out a man and woman, plus two young children, fleeing the rammed car. Behind them charged four or five naked, misshapen figures. They spastically loped and lunged and snatched at the family trying to elude them. Carol stifled a cry, her fist rising to her mouth.

The fleeing man turned and confronted the pursuers while the woman and children stumbled on, trying for the gate.

Carol bolted from the room, ran down the hallway, and hammered the black button that summoned the elevator. The dial over the door began slowly traversing its arc, indicating the car's ponderous upward travel from the ground floor. Come on! Come on! Seeing an exit sign farther down the hall, she ran to the stairs and flew down the steps. She burst onto the first floor and screamed: "Help! People at the gate! *Help*!"

But the front doors were already flung wide. Men pounded through the opening and sprinted across the yard. She ran after them.

Someone grabbed her arm and pulled her to a wrenching halt. "Stay back—"

The man's voice was obliterated as two gunshots split the air. Carol stared ahead. The gate was open, men on the outside, powerful flashlights stabbing into the gloom. More blasts from the weapons. A confusion of running, shouting, screaming.

People emerged from the darkness beyond the wall and approached the gate. Two men supported a woman, followed by two others close behind, each cradling a young child in his arms. The group rushed through the gate, which immediately began to swing slowly inward on its massive hinges.

The woman ran to the children and crushed them against her body, sobbing: "My babies...my babies..."

More men at the gate now, rifles raised into firing position. A dozen shots cracked into the night, and a pungent smell of gunpowder rode the mist.

The woman, still clutching the two children against her side, stared desperately through the gate's heavy bars. "David! My husband. He's still out there. Oh, my God! Save him! *Let me out!*"

As men approached to pull her away, a shape sprang from the darkness beyond the gate and seized the metal bars. Glistening appendages of naked bone protruded from flesh stretched thin over a hunched skeleton; exposed tendons slid over knobbed joints and manipulated multiple arms and hands as it began to climb. Bulging obsidian eyes regarded the stunned onlookers from a swiveling human skull.

A volley of rifle shots slapped the air. Knots of flesh blew out the back of the thing, and it leaped to the ground, righted itself onto its thrashing arms and legs, and skittered back into the darkness.

The men backed away from the gate, weapons at their shoulders, sighting for anything else that might come leaping from the night. In the relative silence, Carol could hear only the river, the heavy breathing of herself and the people around her, and the faint wet crunch of gravel beneath their feet.

Then the woman's voice rose in a stertorous wail.

48

Colvin's screams rent the chamber, his back arching as neon-electric tendrils stabbed and probed his naked body. But instead of knocking him unconscious, the acid current tore through his system; savage jolts ripped along nerve channels, raced up his spine, his neck...

The thing drew ever closer, and where skin contacted skin, he felt a worming penetration, shock, and physical melding.

Horrified, terrified, *losing my sanity...*

The thing's head closed, and he knew that in seconds he would become like Tobin, his body transmogrified into some unspeakable monstrosity, his mind in complete thrall to an abomination from the pit of Hell.

The thing engulfing him began to vibrate, its mass wriggled against his own body. And Colvin screamed—screamed against a pain beyond all comprehension, his mind receding to a pinpoint of light at the end of a distant tunnel.

Then the strange sensation of something fading, being withdrawn from him...

Numb. Marty Berringer's face stared down at him; someone rubbed his arms, legs. The sensation was similar to his awakening from the attack at Catherine Klatty's house. At that time, the pain had been a discrete event. But this assault had felt purposeful, part of a communion, a commingling—a burgeoning, commanding Presence.

Voices: "Come on, snap out of it...Man, that thing...We thought you were a goner...Try to stand up."

Colvin's head nodded toward his chest, which was smeared with foul clots of blood and yellowish ooze. Someone was toweling away the filth with a wadded cloth, each stroke eliciting a buzzing pain from the surface of his body.

Now sensation flooded back into his arms and legs. He found his voice, which sounded in his ears like the slurred mutterings of a stroke victim. "What...happened?"

Someone tugged at him: "Try to walk."

He tensed and stepped slowly away from the inclined table, wobbling forward on rubbery legs, his thoughts struggling through a fog of electrical static. The spinning room began to stabilize. He could feel his extremities now. His vision cleared.

"Uh yeah," came a familiar voice. "We know you feel like shit, man, but you have to, you know, move. Because if you don't..."

Voices he now recognized: "We only have minutes...Thought you were gone...That thing really got to you...Shut up and let him breathe..."

Colvin felt himself step clumsily forward, using his arms for balance—Frankenstein's monster taking its first tentative steps off the slab. He thought he would lose his lunch.

Someone thrust a bundle at him. "Your clothes. Put 'em on quick, Greg."

Marty extended a steadying arm as Colvin pulled on his clothing. He felt muscular coordination returning, along with his mind, and looked around the room with renewed perception. His breath caught in his throat when he saw the veined bulk of mutated flesh lying a few feet away—the thing that had once been Deputy Ben Tobin. Beside it, the remains of Deputy Frank Parnell lay twitching on the floor. Thick ooze spread slowly from beneath his monstrously transformed body.

"They're coming!" Lewis shouted from the door. "A whole army of 'em, and something else—something big."

Marty grabbed Colvin's forearm. "Come on, move it!"

Colvin cinched his boots and straightened. The room lights fuzzed and sparked. The wiring suddenly spouted arcs of crackling electricity. Fiery orbs gushed from the wriggling shafts and dropped to the floor like liquid from a ruptured pipe. In a now familiar fashion, they sprouted their spider legs and scuttled toward the group of men, their bodies bright within the room's shadowy space.

Colvin lurched for the door in his Frankensteinian jog. *Another jolt from those Goddamned things and I'm dead.*

A swarm of glow-spiders scurried before the door, cutting off escape. As Colvin backed away from the creatures' advance, his hand swept across his empty holster. He was defenseless.

A rising, high pitched whine sounded behind him, followed by a mellow hum as Weismann stepped forward and waded into the midst of the creatures. He held the electronic Ghost Buster before him like a metal detector, sweeping it in an arc. "Follow me—quickly!"

The spiders within a few feet of him quivered, retracted their threadlike legs, and settled to the ground. They flickered as they depleted their charge, and deflated into inert gelatinous blobs. Others swarmed over their fallen comrades, darting forward, then back as they met the probe's disruptive field.

Weismann turned, his face drawn in fear: "This only works for a short distance," he said, "and the batteries are going."

"Hurry!" Lewis screamed.

Colvin looked down the tunnel and saw a host of dark shapes

crawling, running, leaping, toward them, their collective motion like waves on a storm-wracked sea. The sound was a rushing chorus of mindless yammering and naked flesh pounding unyielding concrete. He turned and forced his legs into rapid motion, trying to match the speed of the others, each step sparking sharp jolts of pain from his legs and feet.

The floodlights had been switched on inside the tunnel, and the cone-shaped beams burned through a fog of oily smoke drifting in the air. Colvin could see the dull gleam of train tracks on his left, and the black mouths of tunnels yawning here and there, their throats plunging into the living rock.

And behind, swiftly gaining, a horde of transmuted flesh. He knew that each had once been a human being, that their minds and corporeal bodies had been twisted and altered into terrifying puppets obeying the commands of a thing beyond his comprehension—an entity born inside a secret lab within these selfsame underground tunnels.

Marty suddenly stopped, his panicked voice rising above the chaos rushing up from behind: "There's more of them!"

Colvin stared into the gloom and focused on another sound: ahead of them crested a second dark wave of gibbering, raging horror.

49

More than twenty people sat grim-faced around the big wooden table in the generating station's mess hall. Like most rooms in the building, the ceiling was high, and the grimy layers of beige paint covering the walls were flaked and peeling. Vibration from the big turbines rumbled relentlessly through the floor in a slow pulsation.

Carol watched as Deputy Berriman, the de facto leader, rose from his seat and cleared his throat.

"Well, folks. I think most of you have seen what we're up against. I think all of us have seen things tonight that test sanity. But we're in a strong, well-protected building. We have armed men on constant watch, and I'm sure help is on the way." He glanced at a sheet of paper. "We have sixty-three people here: twenty-one women, ten children, and thirty-two men. Fifteen men are on patrol. It'll be dawn in about three hours, at which time we'll change shifts.

"Now, I'd like to introduce Dr. Carol Myerson, from the Grayson Medical Center in Kellsburg. Dr. Myerson has been exploring this thing that's out there. She can help us understand more, help us set some ground rules to protect ourselves...until help comes." He nodded at Carol and sat down.

She kept her seat, too exhausted to stand. "The Elektrum..." she began slowly. "That's what we call it, the thing that's infecting people. We know this much, that it can travel through the electrical wiring in a building." At this, there was a rumble of alarm and disbelief. "Hear me out," she said, raising her voice. "It feeds on electricity—and flesh—and it can change from one form to another very quickly. It can move through the wires or travel parasitically inside a living human being. It is evolving. It has learned how to alter the genetic material of a person and change that individual into...whatever it wants. Don't let an infected person touch you. Stay away from electric switches, wiring, and appliances—"

Someone interrupted; a man in a rumpled business suit sitting across from her. "How the hell can we do that? We're surrounded by wiring, so why isn't it attacking us now?"

She looked at him wearily. "It apparently hasn't gotten into the wiring here—yet. And this brings up another matter, the primary reason I'm at this meeting." She turned and transferred her gaze to the plant's chief engineer, seated near the end of the table. "Mr. Cole, I'm requesting that you shut down the generators, kill all sources of electricity coursing through the building."

Cole stared at her incredulously. He gave a condescending laugh. "Missy, we won't be stopping those generators. Nossir. You have no idea of how much time and—"

She cut him off, surprised at the anger flaring in her voice. "The name's *Dr.* Carol Myerson, not 'Missy.' I've been studying this monstrous thing for three days. I've dissected it, analyzed it, and almost been killed by it. I've been working with some top minds trying to determine how to stop it." She paused, lowered her voice. "Weren't you listening? The massive amount of electricity you generate is like honey to a bear, and if you don't shut it off you'll have those monsters inside these walls dining on your own fat ass." She was again surprised at her loss of composure. Maybe it was the combined effects of fear and fatigue.

Cole was clearly taken aback, but he spoke more softly now, without bluster. "But they cut the lines. It can't get into the building—"

"The hell it can't. It got into Kellsburg, didn't it? And the lines from North Ridge have been down for fifty years."

Cole took off his hard hat and raked his chubby fingers through thinning tufts of hair. "Well…" He turned and spoke to a tall, slender man in a gray jumpsuit leaning against the wall. "Bob, go and get Harry and Mack. Tell 'em to get their crews together." He sighed. "We're gonna' shut the whole system down, including the turbines."

The man named Bob raised his eyebrows in surprised acknowledgement and nodded. "You got it."

Cole stood up and settled the hard hat back into position.

"I'm sorry," Carol said. "I didn't mean to be so abrupt a minute ago."

"That's okay Miss…er…ma'am. I guess we're all tired—and scared out of our wits." He turned from the table. "Well, I guess I better get moving."

Carol stood and excused herself. She wanted to check on Johnny, and she desperately needed rest. She made her way down the hallway, and as she climbed into the rickety elevator, a wave of dizziness almost buckled her knees. She braced her arms against the car's metal side, her head dropping against her chest. After a moment, the spell subsided, and she pushed the button and stood straight as the machine began its slow ascent.

She stepped from the elevator at the third floor and almost collided with a thin, nervous woman rushing down the hall. The woman stood before Carol, wringing her hands. "Oh," she said, eyeing Carol's lab coat, "you're the doctor. I'm Janet Taylor. I've been looking for you. It's Mrs. McDermott. She's the one who just arrived with the two little girls."

Carol leaned against the wall. "Yes?"

"Well, she's quite...I think she's having a nervous breakdown, and I'm afraid she'll hurt herself or the children."

A sharp scream echoed down the hallway. "That's her," the woman said. "Catherine McDermott. She really needs—"

Carol pushed away from the wall. "Let me...I'll see what I can do."

Taylor led her to a bedroom halfway down the hall, just beyond the room in which Johnny Helstrom was sleeping. McDermott was sitting on the edge of a bed, arms wrapped tightly around her two little girls. Their tear-streaked faces nodded in fear and confusion as they quietly sobbed. McDermott rocked back and forth, mumbling, her eyes unfocused and wild.

Full-blown hysteria, Carol thought. She turned to Taylor: "Do you have any Valium, Xanax?"

"I don't, but I know someone who might." She left at a trot.

Carol walked to the small window and glanced into the night. The entrance road was dark now, no evidence of the cars or their inhuman cargo. Behind her, Catherine McDermott moaned, working herself toward another frenzy. Carol studied the woman for a moment: she was young, attractive, with short blond hair and a round, ingenuous face. A pearl necklace encircled her slender neck. Carol sat calmly beside her and extended a hand to touch her shoulder. McDermott flinched away and stared back with frightened eyes.

"You're with friends," Carol said gently. "We'll help you."

Taylor walked into the room and deposited two blue pills into Carol's hand. "It's Xanax, half milligram."

"Thank you." Carol rose and found a ceramic cup half-filled with coffee. Using a spoon, she crushed the pills and scooped the powder into the liquid.

"Please drink this down, Mrs. McDermott. It will help."

The woman searched Carol's face for a moment, then removed her arms from around the children and took the cup. Carol helped steady the woman's hands as she drank. "This will help you relax." Carol said. "You'll feel better in a few minutes, then we'll—" She looked down at the children. "What are your names?"

The little girls, about six and seven years old, silently stared back at her.

"This is Amy," McDermott said, nodding, "and this is Kacy."

Carol smiled at them, hoping her expression was genuine in appearance, not merely a grimace in a haggard face. "How about all three of you lying down and taking a nap? I'll be close, just a few doors down."

Carol studied the woman's face. Some of the madness had begun to drift below the surface. She stared out into the room, eyes now conveying infinite loss. "We were at home when those horrid things..." She shuddered at the memory.

"Please," Carol said, patting the bed. "Amy and Kacy need rest."

McDermott slowly turned, helped the little girls onto the bed, and lovingly tucked them under the covers. She looked longingly at her children, then sat at their feet and leaned back against the wall.

"I'll be right here," Taylor said, taking a seat at the table. "And the men are just outside, in the hallway."

McDermott shut her eyes against glistening tears. "Thank you."

Nodding at Taylor, Carol left and walked back to Johnny's room. The electricity, she noted, was still on. The crews needed to get the system shut down before the damned Elektrum found the wires and wormed its way inside. If that happened, if the DNA-altering force penetrated the building, they would have nowhere left to run. Electricity would lance from the wires to consume them, body and mind, morphing their flesh into unthinkable horrors, growing, consuming...

She stood silently in the darkened room, watching Johnny. He was still sleeping on his side, facing the wall. An occasional tremor shook his body, accompanied by a mumbled word or whimper. Carol stared down at the boy for a full minute, then decided to lie down beside him: rest was an absolute necessity, or she'd be of no help to anyone. She lowered herself slowly onto the bed, and as she faded toward sleep, began to shiver, physical and emotional stress finally overwhelming her system.

Dark dreams; visions of apocalyptic horror; running, running... Her eyes snapped open, her heart racing. *Screams.* Had she been dreaming? She sat up. Then the sound came again, echoing from the direction of McDermott's room. Footsteps pounded. An armed man flashed past her open door. Carol forced her complaining body to rise, and with a glance at the still-sleeping boy, left the room.

A small crowd, headed by two men holding rifles, stood outside Catherine McDermott's door, seemingly locked in indecision. Carol shouldered between the men and stared inside.

McDermott was standing at the window. Her hands fumbled at the brass handle that would swivel it open on its hinges. The two little girls clung to her skirt, the cloth balled tightly in their fists, and looked up in bewilderment at their mother. She turned to face Carol. "Help me," she said. "It's Peter—he's back!"

Then Carol saw it: a glabrous head hovered beyond the window, stark against the fulgurant night, its features distorted by the uneven surface of the ancient glass panels. She seized McDermott by the shoulders and pulled her away. "That's not your husband," she said, trying to keep her voice steady.

"*No!*" McDermott said. She tore from Carol's grasp. "Don't you see?"

But Carol did see, for the head drew back and rammed the glass with a loud *crack*. Spiderweb fractures radiated to the corners of the wooden frame, and the thing McDermott thought was her returned husband drew back for another blow against the weakened pane.

McDermott cried out and stepped away, dragging the little girls with her. Another crash, and the window blew inward with a rain of glass and splintered wood. An elongated creature, its bruised flesh stretched thin across ribs and vertebrae, scrabbled through the narrow opening on appendages jointed like the legs of a spider. Scimitar claws of sharpened bone curved from the ends of its multiple legs. It made a loud clacking sound as it propelled itself onto the floor.

Carol screamed at the guards behind her, "*Stop it! Shoot it!*"

The creature's human head reared up, and the eyes, which had moments ago been pleading and sorrowful, flashed wide and hungry.

In an instantaneous movement, the thing snatched Catherine McDermott and crushed her body against its own. Thrown from their mother, the little girls ran shrieking to Carol's side.

Carol seized the children and bent low to shield them. "*Shoot it!*"

One of the men stepped hesitantly forward and raised his gun into position. He waved the barrel back and forth. "My God! My God! I don't... Don't have..."

As Carol backed from the room, the thing arched downward and its mouth battened on McDermott's head. The glistening lips stretched impossibly wide, and with an undulating movement pushed down, down. The gasket-tight tube slid past the woman's forehead, brow, eyes, and nose. It muffled her ragged screams as it reached her mouth, and continued to descend.

The guard's gun roared out. More screams as people fled. Men with guns charged into the room. Seizing the two girls by the hand, Carol dragged them wailing down the hallway to her room.

Johnny was standing outside the door. He had donned his jogging shoes and shouldered his backpack. "What is it? What's happening?"

More shots pealed out, followed by a buzzing, sizzling sound. An intense blue light burned from McDermott's room, throwing a sharp intaglio of writhing shadows into the hallway. A stench of gunpowder and singed flesh filled the air.

Carol grasped the two girls and, with Johnny trailing behind, dashed for the stairwell, her mind screaming with a singular realization: the Elektrum had breached their defenses.

It's inside!

50

The steel door boomed shut and Colvin found himself inside a vast room lit from the glow of computer monitors and the winking lights of electronic consoles. Cables snaked haphazardly across the floor, and power supplies hummed and hissed and pumped out a stink of overheated circuits. Weismann stood beside Shaner, panting, swiping away the sweat from his brow. Both men were staring at the irregular rows of complex equipment that had been hastily wired together.

Behind Colvin, Marty spun the squeaking wheel that sealed the door. "There's no way to lock it!"

"This way," Lewis shouted. He was walking toward a second door in the far wall.

But Colvin's eyes were drawn to the computers. Each monitor flashed with videos resembling the palsied movements of a hand-held camera.

"Uh, yeah, they're from the lobots," Shaner said, touching one of the screens. "These images are transmitted from the implants, right from their eyes." He turned and faced the center of the room, where a black electronic device hummed away, meters flicking, panel lights blinking. "See that? It's a transmitter—huge. And it's running at full tilt."

"He's right," Weismann said, his gaze darting around the room. "This is the nerve center. This is why we came. But there's no time to attach a modulator—"

"They're here!" Marty shouted, his hands locked onto the wheel.

"Charges!" Colvin barked. "Set the timer for five minutes and throw it in the middle of the Goddamned room. We take this place out, it'll kill the transmissions."

Lewis had his backpack off and was digging out a brick of C-4. "This is the last one." He set the timer in a few deft motions and slid the package beneath a nearby console.

Booms echoed from the riveted steel door as something hammered against the opposite side.

"I can't hold it!" Marty screamed.

The wheel wrenched from his hands and spun furiously as the bolts withdrew.

The men plunged through the second door and into a narrow corridor, the hazy beams of their flashlights stabbing ahead into uncertain darkness. Colvin felt his strength ebbing away as he ran, each step firing sharp jags of pain from his muscles and joints.

He stumbled, felt hands tugging, pulling, pushing him along until he stood, legs trembling, onto a landing that overlooked a vast open area. The overhead floods were still on and lifted the gloom just enough to reveal more railroad tracks arrowing leftward into deep shadow. To his right, a subway car squatted on the rails. Against the opposite wall, a stairwell door tilted across a fractured jamb. Colvin's heart leapt: they were a few hundred feet from their original point of entry—and maybe a shot at freedom.

A chorus of grunts and screeches split the silence as the horde burst into the corridor behind them. A slash of pale light painted a roiling mist of blood and fluids boiling upward from the throng of corrupted flesh. Colvin tried to force his legs into motion, but his torment in the last chamber of horrors and the frantic race down the corridor had exhausted all reserves of strength. He grabbed at Marty's shotgun. "Go! I'm history. I'll make hamburger while you guys get the hell out."

Marty threw Colvin's arm around his neck. "No fuckin' way." He started off again, dragging Colvin, who could barely force his legs to synchronize into functional steps.

They were nearing the subway car, stepping over the electrified center rail when the host poured onto the landing and raced in a clumsy, loping mass toward them. As Colvin's team passed the train and rushed for the opposite side, the stairwell's broken door suddenly banged outward and clattered down the cement steps. A long, phosphorescent mass oozed from the threshold and reared up, its head splitting into a dark chasm lined with dagger teeth.

"*Christ*! What..." Lewis leveled his shotgun and pumped round after round into the creature, the roar of the weapon joining the echoes of the pursuing mob.

"Inside the car!" Marty screamed, jerking Colvin back toward the train. He heaved against the doors and peeled them open.

They shoved Colvin inside, and he collapsed into the nearest seat. Looking around, he saw that all members of his tiny group were now inside the car, where they stood panting, staring through the windows. Outside, dark forms scrabbled across the tracks. Multiple heads nodded on a single body; appendages, as much bone as flesh, propelled hideous shapes shrouded in gashed and bleeding skin.

The tunnel reverberated with the collective sounds of hoots, grunts, and shrieks—the agonized emanations of an asylum for the monstrously deranged.

Colvin raised the pistol Lewis handed him and clicked off the safety. They'd never defend from this position, he thought. It was only a matter of minutes before—

A concussive *Boom* rocked the car and a plume of smoke and debris billowed into the tunnel; the C-4 had detonated inside the transmitter room. Maybe that, Colvin thought, would stop the control signal—

The car's dash panel suddenly lit and the doors slid shut; Marty had found the machine's power switch. He was in the driver's seat, his hands fumbling at the controls. "Come on...come on!"

Lewis edged up beside Colvin, his eyes focused on the horrors beyond the window. "This is gonna' be over real quick."

Despite the apparent mindlessness of the onslaught, the mutant army seemed to have a plan; it split right and left, flowing into a grim circle around the car. Why, Colvin thought, didn't the explosion stop them?

Then from beyond the sharp bend in the tunnel he saw a great luminescence creep toward them. Shadows stretched and crawled as it advanced. The source of illumination heaved into view, and Colvin's blood froze.

The thing was huge, its body an accretion of rippling electric charges and physical substance—a horror of metal and living flesh, torsos, nerves, veins, and muscle exposed and weeping—all interconnected and sparking, chanking along on legs of steel and bone, with I-beam arms and snapping metal claws.

The ground crunched from the impact of its steps, the sound like heavy machinery clanking away at a construction site.

"Oh, my, oh my," came Weismann's quavering, dreamlike voice. He was staring through a side window two seats back. "This is beyond any science I can possibly understand. Beyond—"

"*There!*" Shaner yelled. He was hovering over Marty's shoulder, his flashlight beam locked on the car's dashboard. "The drive circuit! Throw the damn switch!"

A blue light suffused the car as the beast approached over the tracks. It pivoted down and a sharp probe telescoped from its mouth with a *BUZZZ* and stabbed at the car's rear window. Colvin braced for the impact—

An electric mewling rose from somewhere below the seats. The car shuddered, and with a whirring ring of steel on steel lurched forward.

"Yeaaah!" Marty yelled. "Sonuvabitch *runs*! It runs! After all these years!"

Stars shot from the undercarriage and skittered across the tunnel floor as the wheels fought for electrical contact through the grimy rails, and the car accelerated over the tracks with a stuttering motorized whine that steadily rose in pitch and power.

Shadowy shapes loped to intercept the moving train and hurled themselves crashing and scratching across the windows and riveted steel body. The car gained speed and the creatures became frantic, heedless of the vehicle's rushing mass and crushing wheels. A spume of foul smoke and sparks boiled up from the tracks as wrecked and severed bodies fell across the third rail and were electrically sparked into flames. The car's panel lights flickered and the drive motors faltered, their steady current interrupted by searing short circuits of flesh and blood; then the train again sped forward. Dim lights and dark openings of intersecting tunnels flashed past in rapid succession.

Fire ripped from an adjacent cavern and exploded through the car's left side with a concussive roar. Colvin threw his arms across his face as glass bullets ripped his clothing and pierced his skin. The charges they had set were now detonating. The blasts hurled debris across the tracks and pulled down the ceiling in massive, thundering chunks behind them.

But the car rocketed onward, hurtling at breakneck speed down the tunnel, leaving fire and destruction in its wake. Colvin's throat constricted from the acrid smoke funneling through the windows, but he managed to shout above the whirring wheels and motor whine: "*Slow down!* Slow it down!"

But he saw Marty slumped forward, his head rocking against the dashboard. As Colvin scrambled to his feet, Shaner leapt across the driver's seat, his hand clawing for the control lever.

Through the shattered windshield Colvin glimpsed an onrushing wall of steel.

$$\sim\!\!=\!\!\sim\quad 51 \quad\sim\!\!=\!\!\sim$$

The impact ripped through the car like a bomb blast, bashing glass from the windshield, shooting the gauges from their sockets and fanning out chunks of debris like cartwheeling missiles. Colvin flew through the air and slammed into a row of seats, a metallic roar hammering his eardrums. Pain shot from his right shoulder and he dropped to his knees, unable stand or crawl on the wildly bucking steel floor

They were plummeting, bouncing, rocking, the air burning with powdered glass and the smell of hot metal. Colvin locked himself into a protective ball and waited for the final blow.

But the big trolley kept its momentum, the sound of steel on rails suddenly replaced with a roaring, crunching sound like gravel or rocks. A staccato thrashing swept across the car's metal body; then came a half-second of silence and a final, prolonged crunch against some yielding mass.

Colvin uncurled from his hunched position and slowly stood up, fighting for balance on the tilted floor. From below came the grind of wheels still turning from inertia, crawling to a stop. A cold breeze laden with moisture sifted through the windows. It carried a familiar scent.

Splintered *pine*?

He heard movement, groans. "Hey. You guys."

A flashlight clicked on behind him. Lewis crawled from behind a seat, stood up, and swept the beam around the car. Colvin gasped. Here and there, pine boughs poked through the windows: the trolley had plowed through a pair of steel doors and come to rest somewhere in the middle of a woods. *Damn!*

A pair of heads rose slowly from the seats opposite Lewis: Weismann and Shaner, dazed and frightened.

Colvin limped toward the front of the car. "Where's Marty?"

Lewis joined Colvin as he looked beneath the control console. Marty lay in the space between the seat and the firewall, jammed into a tight ball, his neck cocked at a severe angle. Colvin reached gingerly beneath the attorney's head and slowly freed it from its locked position above the control levers.

"Careful," Lewis warned. "His neck may be broken."

"I know that. But he can't stay like this."

They pried Marty's limp figure from beneath the seat and stretched him out in the aisle. As Lewis focused the flashlight, Colvin pressed two fingers against the attorney's left carotid artery, feeling for a pulse. There was a slow intake of air, and Marty's eyes fluttered into a half-lidded position. His lips moved and his voice croaked: "Are we in Queens yet?"

Colvin grinned. "Marty. Are you hurt?"

"What doesn't hurt?"

Weismann bent down and studied the prone figure. "Can you wiggle your toes?"

Marty's eyes opened fully. "Yes, and my fingers. Unfortunately, I can also feel them. Somebody help me up."

They raised Marty into a standing position; then he promptly flopped into a seat, moaning. "I think every bone in my body is broken."

Lewis worked his way to the rear window, looked out, and pointed his flashlight into the night. "We're on the side of a hill. Came out of a tunnel about a hundred yards up."

Colvin looked down at Marty. "You able to walk?"

"Yeah, if you absolutely insist."

"I don't know how far we came, but we gotta' get the hell out."

Colvin and Lewis kicked the car's jammed door and finally opened a space large enough to squeeze through. They recovered three of the flashlights and all the weapons, then dropped one by one onto the damp ground. Colvin was surprised that his coordination had returned, and that his body was intact despite the repeated insults.

As they left the woods, he pulled the GPS unit from a pocket and turned it on. He stared at the screen, a grin widening on his face. "Sonuvabitch. We're at Doc's place, old Doc Pritchard..."

Marty came up beside him. "Give me the coordinates." He held up a transceiver. "I think the radio's working. I'll try the helicopter."

"Whole town's burning," Lewis said, his body silhouetted against the red glow suffusing the horizon. He shook his head in disbelief. "It's huge, man. Whole Goddamned town!"

Colvin looked southward, toward the swath of embers that was Kellsburg, and his heart sank. Whatever they'd destroyed in the tunnels, it was too little, too late. He prayed that Carol and Johnny had escaped.

The earsplitting roar of a jet engine cut off his thoughts. Hidden somewhere in the low black clouds, a jet screamed just overhead, headed north toward NRAD. Colvin opened his mouth to shout a comment, but before the words escaped a brilliant flash fanned out from the air base, followed a second later by a resounding concussion.

They ducked reflexively, watching a seething fireball climb the sky. A deep rumbling shook the ground and rose rapidly in pitch.

From the tunnel's mouth erupted a dragon's tongue of orange flame that shot outward for some two hundred feet and licked at the woods and the rear of the subway car. After a moment, the flames darkened into a sulfurous cloud that tore away on the wind, leaving a band of smoldering earth to mark its passage. Colvin felt the heat sting his face and forearms.

"God *damn!*" Shaner yelled.

Lewis pulled himself off the ground. "Bunker buster."

Another explosion ripped the night, closer and louder. Then another.

The men charged down the hill, flashlight beams fluttering across the rocky terrain, fleeing the tunnel and fires and earth-shattering explosions, running toward the burning town.

As he stumbled along, Colvin remembered the old saying from wars past:

It's the shell you don't hear that kills you.

52

Bud Cole stumped down the metal stairs, checklist in his left hand, tool belt jangling at his side. He was thankful for Emanuel's presence behind him, given all the disturbing shit that had been coming down. He was surprised his assistant could keep it together though, with two kids and a wife back in Kellsburg and not knowing if they were alive or not. But Emanuel couldn't leave the plant now, not with the roads jammed. He must be frantic.

They walked to the control panel that stood twenty feet to the right of Number Three, the second generator they had to shut down. Emanuel gestured at the checklist, mimed he was going down to the generator and watch the limiter as Bud turned off the penstock valves. Shutting the gennies down had to be coordinated or the big turbines could rev beyond their tolerances when the load was cut, causing serious damage to the blades and rotor. In a modern generating plant, you could adjust the system with the push of a button, but in this old station everything had to be done manually.

Bud waited by the panel as his assistant walked to Number Three and looked up at the big rotor. These antiques dated back to the early twenties, still had the original Tesla-Westinghouse nameplates.

But Emanuel said he actually liked the old machines, liked the fact you could see their guts, which weren't all covered up as the modern generators were.

Stupid, Bud thought, to be killing the power, even if that weirdness outside could travel through the wires. Even if he believed that—and he didn't—the transmission lines had been severed a half-mile down. Wasted effort. They were taking the word of that stupid bitch doctor.

Emanuel was signaling to shut off the valve, or—*what the hell*? Now Emanuel had grabbed the handrail, arms locked out stiff, like he was trying to hold himself up. His hard hat flew off his head, arced through the air, and slammed into the generator's casing and stuck there, as if held in place by a big magnet. But that wasn't possible. The hats were plastic, and the electromagnetic field wasn't powerful enough to reach that far even if they were steel.

And then, by God, if Emanuel's feet didn't rise off the floor, like someone had a rope attached to them and was pulling him up by the ankles.

Bud dropped the checklist and ran. He stopped three feet from Emanuel, who stared back at him, eyes bugged out, mouth open, veins swelling in his face. His screams rose above the turbine noise and pierced Bud's hearing protectors.

Now Emanuel was sliding along the handrail toward the generator. Bud reached out, started to grab him; then he felt the hairs on his arms stand on end and a prickly glow play from the tips of his fingers. Bud was no scientist, but he was a Technician First Class, and he knew what this was—a high voltage D.C. corona—St. Elmo's Fire.

Before Bud could think things through, Emanuel slid farther down, his feet rising above his head, his body stretched taut. His fingers snapped free of the railing and his entire body levitated, flew up toward the big genny's spinning coils. He hovered in midair, spread-eagled before the rotor and stator, his mouth opening and closing like a fish gulping for air. Then his skin and clothing split and sloughed off, simply peeled away in a fluid motion and disappeared inside Number Three's iron casing.

As Bud's own screams melded with the drone of whirring coils, electric arcs flashed from the windings and lashed at him. He staggered back, staring as the discharge bent back and crawled over Emanuel's writhing body in bright, branching filaments.

When Bud saw the bones emerge, he turned and ran.

He pounded across the floor, his heart hammering away, his breath bursting out in great whooshing sobs. Through all the noise, he could still hear Emanuel's tortured screams ringing in his ears. He paused behind two of the big three-phase transformers and leaned forward, hands propped on his knees, panting, choking back the gorge rising in his throat.

The lights dimmed, and there was a hum like a high voltage arc had struck somewhere inside the room. Then the lights died completely. But Number Three was still delivering power; he could tell by the sound the generators made when a load was being pulled, even a small one. Oddly, even though the lines were severed, that load sounded substantial.

The emergency lights flicked on, bathing the vast room in a shadowy half-light. Then something caught his eye—multiple things—creeping along the thick cables from the generator. The things slid up and over the insulators like rats, dissolved into and out of the transformers, instrument panels, circuit breakers, and field generators. Bud stared; the creatures looked like black human skulls, but with the lower jaw missing. They cruised the big copper cables with long, glistening, segmented spines sinuously weaving out behind, riding the metal surfaces like highways. From their deep ocular sockets burned tiny fireball eyes of reddish-orange.

The whole world of physics had gone insane. Bud stood upright and bolted for the stairs, praying that he could escape the room before one of the things dropped down on him or leapt at him from a nearby machine. They were everywhere now, sliding along the wires, in and out of the machinery—like they somehow had fused with the entire system. The station had become a host for monsters...

And that's when it hit him. His muscles convulsed like a jackhammer and he stiffened upright, arms rigid at his side, jerking like a marionette as electric rods blazed into his eyes, nostrils, mouth, ears. But beyond the avalanching pain, the thing that terrified him most was the sense of violation, the Presence worming inside his mind, devouring his thoughts, knowledge, memories...the very core of his being.

Then he saw the ONE.

53

Carol stepped cautiously from the stairwell onto the first floor and peered down the deserted hallway. Only the pale glow of an emergency light lit the long corridor, leaving the rear of the building in darkness.

The two little girls clung to her right side. A vigilant Johnny Helstrom stood just to her left, eyes fearfully probing the shadows. Muffled crashes and screams filtered down from the floors above, but here on the ground floor she could detect only the steady groan of machinery from the generator hall. *The generators; they're still running, yet the power is off.*

She stood for a moment, motionless, her exhausted mind on overdrive. The building had been invaded and, just as in Kellsburg, would soon become infested with a host of mutant killing machines. Would their chances be better outside? Could they lose themselves on the grounds, perhaps climb back into the hills and escape detection? The creatures were undoubtedly creeping over the gate and wall even now...

Johnny gasped and gave her hand a sharp tug: from the shadows behind them came a scraping, shuffling sound. She made her decision. Towing the children, she walked quickly toward the main entrance.

On her left lay the offices and cafeteria. Farther, on the right, the hallway opened into the generator hall, the vast chamber pouring forth the hum of transformers and the vibration and howl of spinning electromagnetic coils. The building's bronze front doors, awash in a pale yellow light, were just beyond. The doors were shut, unguarded.

She looked back over her shoulder: some ten yards down the hall a dark mass lurched from the shadows, swaying from side to side as it moved toward them. Tightening her grip on the children, Carol began running toward the bronze doors.

As they drew even with the generator hall, a shape darted from the stairway leading down into the great room and stopped in their path, startling Carol to an abrupt halt.

"Hi, Missy." It was the engineer, Bud Cole.

With the dim light behind him, his face lay in shadow, and Carol could see only his teeth—too many teeth—grinning at her from beneath the ubiquitous hard hat.

He took a step forward. "It's a lot safer this way, Missy." His arm rose and he pointed down into the twilit room housing the generators.

Then Carol noticed his hat was wrong: there was no brim, and its shape was strange. Then two red pinpoints of light appeared above his forehead. Like eyes...

Behind her the shuffling sound drew closer. Carol began to tremble, her muscles prodded by fear and adrenaline. She tensed to run, to channel a burst of energy into a headlong charge. If she could knock Cole down, keep him occupied, maybe at least the children could—

A sudden blast concussed the air and the engineer flew backward like a rag doll and tumbled over the railing into the shadows of the generator hall. Deputy Jake Berriman stood at her left side, sighting down the barrel of a shotgun. Through the ringing in her ears, she heard him shout: "...out...have to get outside."

The shotgun swung around and there was another detonation and flash of light as he fired into the darkness behind her. Taking one of the panicked girls by the hand and urging Carol along, Berriman rushed to the entrance and swung the heavy doors open.

The floods were still on, illuminating the gate's iron bars and the stone wall, with its glinting helix of razor wire. The rain had stopped, but runoff from the building's roof still gushed through the downspouts and pattered from the eaves. The gravel parking area glistened with dark pools of standing water. The rest of the building's exterior and surrounding grounds lay in shadow.

Carol could hear the river's voice and the faint whine of the turbines, but there were no other sounds: no screams, shouts, or weapons fire. The relative peace seemed strangely sinister.

Berriman shut the doors with a bang, then motioned them to follow him down the steps and to the left. They paused at the eastern corner of the building, just beyond the floodlights' reach. "We make it around back," he said. "Then climb into the hills. The fence stops at the cliff. It'll be tough, but it's our best chance." He looked northward, toward the rear of the grounds. "Wait here. I got to check it out." Before Carol could protest, he trotted off and disappeared into greater darkness.

She leaned against the building, wondering if she could muster the energy to climb the steep granite cliff rising beyond the fence. And the children; how could she and Berriman manage with two little girls—

The snarl of a diesel engine and the crunch of gears startled her from her reverie. Headlights flared through the gate, brightening as the long snout of a Mack truck hammered the iron bars from their moorings and roared through the entrance. The rig churned across the gravel drive and chattered to a stop near the power station's front steps. Three men climbed slowly from the big truck and walked into the light.

Lobots.

Carol could identify them without seeing the implants buried in their foreheads; their movements were deliberate, slightly hesitant, as if each motion required thoughtful concentration.

The little girls began whimpering, and Carol pulled them deeper into the shadows. She knelt. "Shhh. We have to be very quiet now."

A voice from behind, from the deeper shadows: "Missssy."

She spun around. Bud Cole shuffled toward her on bent legs, his hunched form emerging from within the spotlight's faint penumbra. Dark fluid oozed from the fist-sized cavity in his chest and blossomed across the denim jumpsuit. His hands rose, extended forward, and with a crackle-hum his fingertips lit with writhing electric darts.

Berriman's shotgun roared, the muzzle's spearpoint flame thrusting at Bud's head. This time the engineer collapsed where he stood and remained motionless. Carol turned away, hugging the screaming girls tight against her body.

Johnny tugged her arm. "They're coming this way!"

She looked: lobots and other shapes lurched through the ruined gate. Several had split from the main group and began scrabbling across the grounds toward them.

Berriman pressed a flashlight into her hand. "Back of the building...the rear gate." He pumped the shotgun, chambering another round. "Get moving."

Carol gathered the children and backed away. As she turned, she noticed the lobots had suddenly stopped. The creatures had frozen in mid-stride, their faces devoid of expression, vacant eyes staring into infinity.

A volley of dull booms rolled through the valley and Carol looked up to see a chain of red flashes fan out against the horizon, each flare of light followed seconds later by a chest-thumping concussion. A jet engine screamed in the distance, the sound rising and falling as the aircraft maneuvered above the hills.

"That's North Ridge," Berriman said, watching the fireballs mushroom into the strata of scudding clouds. "And that plane. Can't be National Guard—maybe Air Force, Marines. The explosions must have knocked out the control signal, stopped our friends dead in their tracks." He looked down at Carol, reading her thoughts. "Greg's a resourceful guy," he said softly. "They probably got out just fine."

Greg. The thought of losing him hit her like a physical blow. No one could have lived through those enormous explosions. But she couldn't dwell on the question, not with three children under her wing and her own survival utterly tenuous.

"Don't assume anything," she said. "Some vestige of the Elektrum might still exist inside the lobots, or infected people, or within the building. The generators are still running. They could be feeding power to it. Just...don't trust..." Another wave of dizziness rocked her back on her feet.

Berriman's arm steadied her. "That truck," he said, nodding at the Mack. "It might be our ticket out of here."

"What about the others?"

Berriman thought for a moment, sighed. "I'll get you guys inside the truck, then I'll check the ground floor. If I don't see anyone, we're out of here."

They walked toward the idling tractor, taking the girls and Johnny Helstrom by the hand. A light fog drifted across the yard, and flickers of lightning lit the clouds.

The storm was tuning up again.

54

Carol could see six lobots standing between her and the tractor. One of the creatures was no more than ten feet away, and she watched its eyes for any flicker of recognition or consciousness. But the lobot—a man wearing stained overalls and a grimy T-shirt—remained in a hunched position, face slack, a rope of saliva swaying from his parted mouth. *Poor devils*, she thought. People from my own town. People I might have known—

A sound made her jump: Berriman's radio crackling to life. He paused, surprised, then snatched the instrument from his belt and held it to his ear. Unintelligible voices rasped through the tiny speaker, and Berriman's eyes widened, his mouth curling into a wide grin. Then he depressed the transmit button and uttered the one word that lifted an immense weight from Carol's psyche: "*Greg!*"

A smile broke across her face and she moved in close, listening as Berriman spoke. "We're at the Mesa Electric Plant. Carol Myerson is with me. We've got a truck, gonna' try and bust out."

"Negative," Greg's voice came back. "You can't get out. Military convoy headed your way. They'll be there in a couple of minutes. And listen, there's something strange going on. I don't trust them."

"What do you mean?"

"I'll tell you when we get there."

"But...what's your twenty, Sheriff?"

"On top of you."

A column of light swept into the yard as a helicopter crested the ridge, the heavy thump of its blades filling the air. The chopper circled for a minute, then lowered onto a grassy area about fifty feet east of the truck.

Doors opened and men dropped to the ground, bending low beneath the spinning rotor, and jogged toward them. Carol recognized Weismann, Shaner, Marty Berringer, a deputy, then finally Colvin. Tears started in her eyes and she ran to him and fell into his arms.

"Thank God," he said. "We hoped you'd be here. It's about the only safe place left."

After a moment she pushed away, her eyes roaming his body. She shouted above the helicopter's whine. "You're hurt. You're limping. There's blood..."

His arms enfolded her again, and she wanted to collapse against him, take refuge in his warmth and strength. "We got beat up some," he said. "But we're okay, I've just never been this tired in my whole life." He looked around the yard, taking in its collection of immobilized lobots. "What about them?"

"They stopped moving when the bombs exploded."

Berriman came up, leading the children. Colvin looked down at Johnny, smiled, and gave his shoulder a squeeze. "Hey, man." To the deputy: "How many people?"

"Just us, Sheriff. But we haven't looked inside. Might still be somebody alive."

Colvin released Carol. "You and the kids get in the chopper." He nodded at the two deputies. "We'll check the building."

"No! You have to come with us. You said that convoy will be here in minutes."

"It's my job, Carol. My duty."

"The town's gone. You don't have a job anymore."

Colvin turned her gently toward the helicopter. "Go on."

A brilliant light blazed across the lot and engulfed them: the cone of a powerful airborne searchlight. Carol squinted upward, and as the light shifted away saw the dark silhouette of another helicopter circling above the grounds.

"Military chopper." Marty said.

The engine of their own helicopter began to lower in pitch, dropping rpm. The pilot got out and jogged up to Colvin. "Can't take off. Bastards said they'd shoot us down."

Beyond the gate, a chain of headlights drifted around the curve, filling both lanes. An amplified voice blasted from the circling helicopter. "Stay where you are. Any attempt to leave the area will be met with lethal force..."

Colvin's arm encircled Carol's waist. "Well," he said. I guess we wait."

A second helicopter joined the first, and the two aircraft began flying a zigzag pattern, their searchlights stabbing intense white beams down through the smoke and mist.

From the road came the snorting of diesel engines. Headlights swept through the gate and a Humvee, followed by a large truck with a canvas-covered back, rolled into the yard and squealed to a stop. Instantly, soldiers vaulted from the truck's rear and began dispersing across the grounds. From the passenger side of the Humvee climbed a tall, heavily built man with close-cropped graying hair, dressed in camouflage.

The man faced Carol's small party, and as six soldiers trotted toward them, raised a bullhorn to his lips. "Lay down your weapons! Stay where you are! Do not attempt to leave!"

"What the fuck?" Berriman said.

Colvin unholstered his pistol and lowered it to his feet. "Just do as he says."

The soldiers stopped a few feet away, rifles aimed at the group. One of them, a burly man with a pug nose, walked forward. "What's that?" he demanded, indicating a small device Weismann was holding.

"An electronic detector. It allows—"

"Put it on the ground."

Weismann silently complied.

Carol heard a commotion and saw that around twenty townspeople were standing just outside the building's bronze doors. The soldiers were barking orders, disarming the men, turning people back inside the plant.

A woman's plaintive voice rose above the noise: "Please, you have to get us out of here."

"She's right!" Carol shouted. "The building's infested...you'll get us killed..."

Colvin walked toward the lieutenant. "You're making a huge mistake here—"

The soldier leveled his weapon at Colvin's chest. "Fall back. *Now!*"

Colvin hesitated a moment, then turned and trudged back.

The background became a blur of activity: beams of searchlights bounced and parried; men in blue biohazard suits carried gurneys and lockers; soldiers shouted orders, closed on the lobots, marched in and out of the building, searched the grounds. Carol found herself stumbling back toward the generating station with the others, prodded by grim-faced soldiers who refused to speak or acknowledge their questions or pleas.

Colvin walked silently beside her, lips set in a hard line, taking in the frenetic activity around them. As they approached the front steps, she saw him hesitate a moment and frown, his surprised gaze directed upward. Then she saw it also. There, above the door, something she had missed earlier: the embossed bronze statue of a Roman soldier, stylized lightning blazing the sky behind him, electricity darting from his upraised fists. It was the power company's century-old logo—the "Electric Centurion"—a chillingly accurate metaphor for the horrors that now afflicted the town of Kellsburg.

They were herded inside, down the hallway and into the cafeteria. The lights were on again, the noise from the generator hall louder than before. The air was befouled with ozone and the reek of slaughterhouse, but there was no physical evidence of the horrors that had occurred only minutes ago. No blood or gore. Nothing.

"Greg," Carol said as they dropped into chairs surrounding the big table. "This station was infiltrated. We were attacked. There should be bodies, traces—something."

Colvin was quiet for a moment, then nodded toward the back of the room. "What do you make of that?"

Carol turned and looked. A privacy curtain was stretched across the rear wall, hiding something from view.

"I don't know. It wasn't here before..."

"And that," he said, indicating a black object high up on the wall; it was a large video camera, its lens staring down at them.

A frisson of alarm spiked from her gut. "That wasn't here either."

At the front of the room, soldiers banged around the attached kitchen and seized knives and utensils—anything that might serve as a weapon—and carted them away.

Besides her own group, Carol counted twelve people seated at the table, about an equal number of men, women, and children. Some were slumped over in apparent exhaustion, while others sat stoically in brooding silence. James Stockton, the big Kellsburg cop, nodded at her from a nearby chair.

Johnny Helstrom, who had been holding Carol's hand, began to tremble. She looked down, worried that his young body had finally yielded to trauma and shock, but he was silently weeping, his free hand palming away the tears tracking down his cheeks. She freed her hand and wrapped him in a quiet hug. The two small girls, huddled against her left side, had fallen into a fitful sleep.

Weismann and Shaner pulled their chairs up close. Both men were bloodied and haggard. "The explosions undoubtedly stopped the control transmissions," Weismann said, "but we don't know if it completely stopped the Elektrum. If it's capable of independent thought, it might still be active." He shrugged, shaking his head.

"I ran multiple DNA sequences," Carol said. "The results varied each time, but two things were consistent. Human and animal DNA were present, and the strands were inconceivably long. I don't know what to make of it."

"Uh, yeah," Shaner said. "The NRAD control system was probably heuristic. If the code is replicated or stored, the Elektrum might be able to reestablish itself."

"It might operate like a human brain," Weismann added. "It could be holographic."

"What do you mean?" Colvin asked.

"Its intelligence, uh, persona, or self, might be cloned or reproduced from even a small amount of the original material. How much memory it could retain, separated from its primary source at North Ridge, is pure speculation."

"One more thing," Marty said. "When I saw my grandfather, he told me they were waiting for this." He nodded at the soldiers. "I think these guys were hired by Kendron Technologies."

They looked up as the cafeteria's two doors were closed and soldiers posted just inside, fingers hovering about the trigger guards of their assault rifles. "Well," Colvin said, "right now I'm concerned about these assholes."

The south door swung open again. Flanked by two bodyguards, a short, balding man in a white lab coat strutted into the room and walked to the head of the table. He held a clipboard and a small instrument similar to the one Weismann had been carrying. He paused and shoved a pair of glasses home over his beaked nose. "I'm Dr. Nelson. Sorry for the delay. We have to ensure that none of you have been, ah, affected, before we let you go, now, don't we? We wouldn't want this, ah, vector to spread now, would we? So now I'll be seeing each of you for a minute or two, and we'll run a few quickie tests. No problems, eh?"

As he spoke, two men began erecting another hospital style divider, closing off the kitchen nook. The doctor turned and gestured toward the white curtain. "That'll give us some privacy, eh? OK."

Dr. Nelson pointed to a young woman, who hesitantly rose and followed him and the two bodyguards beyond the curtain. An examination light was switched on, and Carol strained to hear the conversation. "Very good, now," Nelson was saying. "Just consider this a brief look-see by your regular doctor."

After a few minutes, the woman stepped from behind the privacy curtain and rushed back to her seat. She was frowning, obviously upset. A moment later, Nelson emerged, clipboard and electronic device in hand, evidently preparing to select another victim for his tests.

Carol shook her head. "I don't understand this. This is simply not right."

Colvin leaned in close. "Think about what Marty said. These guys aren't military. They're private." He looked toward the back of the room. "Want to guess what's behind that curtain? And think about the camera. Everyone in this room is expendable, Carol. We're part of an experiment, and when it's over they won't be leaving any witnesses." Then he turned and spoke quietly to Weismann, who frowned and nodded and, rotating in his chair, repeated something to Marty.

Colvin's lips brushed her cheek, and he whispered, "Gonna' pay the good doctor a visit. Get ready to run."

55

Colvin rose from his chair, head hung low, shoulders slumped, and limped slowly toward Dr. Nelson, who was standing at the head of the table, pursing his lips as he scrawled a pencil across his clipboard. Carol tensed and leaned forward. *Greg, you fool*! From the corner of her eye she noticed Weismann, Marty, and the others of her group slowly pushing their chairs back.

She held her breath as a bodyguard stepped into Colvin's path and raised the muzzle of his rifle. "You, there—get back! Return to your seat."

In one fluid motion, Colvin's left hand swept outward and parried the rifle aside. His right hand flashed squarely into the bodyguard's throat, the blow producing a soft crunch as knuckles met larynx. The man staggered back, a gurgling sound issuing from his mouth. Simultaneously, Marty and the others lifted their sturdy wooden chairs and flung them at the two guards posted at the doors.

Colvin spun and drove a roundhouse kick into the second bodyguard's solar plexus, folding him to his knees. In less than a second he had both assault rifles tucked into his arms, their business ends pointed at the remaining guards.

"Drop your weapons!" Colvin bellowed.

People screamed, ducked, overturned chairs, dove beneath the table.

The ceiling lights flickered and died, and Dr. Nelson, who had been cowering against the left wall, jumped up, staring at the electronic device in his hand. His voice rose in a screeching high note: "It's too soon! It's coming! *Let me out!*"

Carol stood up as another sound—an insistent crackling-hum—emanated from the back of the room. She turned and looked: two skeletal human figures were shuffling through the parted privacy curtain, their neon skulls visible beneath taut, translucent skin, their lightning-tortured brains flickering behind eye sockets of phosphorescent yellow. Cords of electricity twisted and snapped from their bodies and outstretched hands as they marched into the crowd.

Carol's own cries joined the chorus of screams as the room broke into pandemonium. As she reached for the children, someone slammed against her and she fell, her senses reeling as her head impacted the table. Hands seized her, drove her stumbling through the panicked crowd and out the doorway into the dark hall beyond.

Colvin was shouting in her ear, his fingers clamped tightly around her arm. "Come on...this way!"

She screamed back at him: "The children...where are they?"

He dragged her along, running. "We've got them."

They fled toward the front of the building, their path illuminated by lambent flares of blue light strobing from the cafeteria's open doors. Marty and Stockton ran just ahead of Colvin, each cradling one of the small girls in his arms. Johnny Helstrom jogged at her side, the ever-present backpack riding his shoulders.

The sight of the children focused her thought, hardened her will. She resolved to fight this accursed monstrosity, this horrid perversion of science created by dementia, greed, and evil intent. She would fight it and resist it and seek its total annihilation—at any cost to herself.

A hollow banging rolled down the hallway as men threw themselves against the bronze front doors. "They're locked!" someone yelled. "Goddamned bastards locked us in!"

"Open the goddamned doors!"

Colvin darted into the manager's office and stared through the rain-streaked window into front grounds of Mesa Electric. The military trucks had pulled back to the wall, and a platoon of soldiers slouched motionless beside the vehicles, watching the building with apparent indifference. Looking to the right, he saw that a Humvee had been driven up the steps and parked with its rear bumper jammed against the doors. Marty's words flashed into his mind: *They've been waiting for this...*

"There's a window," a man behind him yelled. "Bust it out!"

Colvin ducked as something flashed past his head and smashed through the glass. Using a coat rack as a battering ram, a man began pounding at the steel security bars bolted to the granite façade outside the window. The coat rack splintered in his hands and he threw it aside, staring animatedly around the room for another weapon.

"They're just standing out there," a woman yelled. "Just watching us!"

A kid in baggy jeans and an oversized sweatshirt rushed to the window and began screaming. "Let us out, *muthafuckers!*"

Colvin forged through the crowd and back into the hallway.

Carol grabbed him and pointed. "Greg!"

Something large and dark swayed toward them from beyond the cafeteria doors. Staccato bursts of electricity shot from its crouching body and whipsawed to the ceiling and floor.

A tall, breathless man in a Mesa Electric uniform frantically waved his arms: "Come on—come on quick! There's another way out!"

Colvin grabbed Carol, yelled at the others to follow, and they ran across the foyer and clattered down the metal stairs to the cement floor of the generator hall. Colvin could feel the vibration shooting up his legs, a deep, penetrating, rumble that spoke of huge blades and gigantic shafts turning in the thundering cataract below.

St. Elmo's fire flickered and hissed from the overhead cables and lit the insulators spiking up from the ranks of steel-clad transformers. Farther inside, the big generators bristled with filaments of electricity that darted and snaked from their spinning coils. A heavy stink of ozone and burning wires rode the air.

The engineer stopped. "What the hell! The gennies are overloaded. There's high voltage corona everywhere…"

Colvin seized his arm. "Where do we go?"

The man pointed. "Past Number Three. It's the only way."

Lightning flared through the rows of three-story windows, etching the great hall with a phantasmagoria of palsied light and shadow. Colvin prodded the engineer and he started forward, gaping nervously upward at the coronas that pulsed and throbbed from the wiring like living things.

The massive generator called Number Three loomed before them, a whirring, crackling ghost machine pumping out ozone and a bluish light laced with purple veins of electricity. Between the massive supports, the machine's upper half curled down in a grimace, the fixed stator coils like stubby teeth in a snarling mouth of riveted steel. At the apex of the generator's arched cowl, a red light glared like a cyclopean eye.

The walkway led past the machine and between a row of consoles, each studded with twitching meters and blinking lights. Colvin glimpsed snakelike creatures with smallish humanoid skulls and red, pinpoint eyes creeping along the wires, dissolving in and out of the machinery like so much ephemera. But these new horrors were merely background noise to his already overloaded senses.

The sound and vibration increased as they drew abreast of the Number Three, and Colvin could feel a hot reeking wind sighing from its candescent maw.

As the Mesa engineer motioned the group around the generator's right side, thick tubes of red plasma suddenly uncoiled from the machine's rotor and lashed across their path, curling and rippling like angry pythons. The discharges forked and shimmered up and up, shifting and coalescing into a flaming, anthropomorphic shape that towered some nine feet above the floor. The sound reminded Colvin of the coiling electric arcs in the old science fiction movies, the ones that started at the bottom of a V and fluttered upward to snap out and repeat their travel—but a thousand times louder.

The engineer threw up his arms and stumbled backward. Carol cried out and pulled Johnny Helstrom against her, falling against Colvin. More screams burst from the crowd as ranks of refulgent columns—phantasms—each an ectoplasmic representation of a human being, rose up behind them, cutting them off from escape. Colvin swung the M-16 to his shoulder and aimed at Number Three. *The Elektrum is drawing power from the generators. If I can disable them—*

A single bright thread darted from the writhing plasma and struck the barrel of Colvin's rifle. The shock was like a sledgehammer to the chest. He staggered back, a blizzard of white sparks obliterating his vision.

Carol's eyes were staring into his own as his senses returned. "Greg...Greg!"

Colvin steadied himself against her shoulder and looked up at Number Three. The creature formed of electricity now loomed some twelve feet above the floor. The russet discharges had morphed into a face, and Colvin gasped as he recognized the hellish being that towered before him.

56

William Klatty, magnified and immortalized in twisted lightning, hovered above them like the fearsome green head in the *Wizard of Oz*. The eyes, white with glimmering pupils of neon red, swiveled down to leer at them. A grinning slit appeared—a mouth. And it spoke...

Crazy Cathy Klatty

The words shook the floor, a baritone rumble that boomed forth as if a monster PA system had been attached to the building structure and cranked up to full volume. Then came a rattle of metallic laughter.

Colvin realized in a flash of intuition that the sinuous waves of electrical plasma constituted a living mentality—the conscious equivalent of Dr. William Klatty—and that it was utterly insane.

The laughter died and Colvin tensed, working a desperate plan. If he charged the apparition, distracted it, maybe the others could somehow break free—

Weismann's trembling voice, barely audible: "Are...are you Dr. William Klatty?"

The professor was standing beside Colvin, staring up at the monstrosity.

The malignant eyes shifted to Weismann. "Indeed."

"What do you want from us?"

An electronic growl: "Your essence."

On Colvin's right, Carol's shrill voice rang out. "Please, don't you have enough? You are so powerful now, so..."

"I am like unto a god."

"You can create and destroy," came Carol's quick reply.

"I evolve. I assimilate."

A fulgurating tube of red plasma shot from the thing's undulating body and battened onto Shaner's face. He stood frozen in place, shudders rippling through his body as purple tendrils crackled across his head, wormed into his ears, nose, mouth...

Weismann stepped forward and cried out, *"Spare him, spare him!"*

A second quivering tube, its blunt end scintillating with needles of light, extended toward Weismann and hovered menacingly before his eyes, weaving back and forth like a hooded cobra.

Shaner collapsed onto his back, eyes open and totally vacant. After a minute, the glowing conduits retracted, melding again with the plasma that was the substance of Klatty's body.

Weismann looked down at his friend, shaking, his fists balled at his side. "Kerry..."

"Ahhhhh," sighed the massive electronic voice. "Vast knowledge. I should have taken longer with Kerry Shaner. More could I have absorbed." Klatty's eyes again shifted to Colvin. "You know much about me."

The electronic fire that comprised Klatty's form eddied and hummed and coiled, and for a moment Colvin thought he saw Shaner's likeness straining outward in agony, only to dissipate and dissolve back into the main column. Other images surged and collapsed within the restraining plasma—men, women, children, animals—their tortured countenances silently screaming for release, gasping outward as if pressing against an imprisoning silken fabric; then they submerged back into Klatty's fiery substance, drawn down by a powerful restricting force.

Shocked and repelled by the enormity of this surreal horror, Colvin momentarily looked away; then he stared back up at Klatty. *Keep it talking. Buy time.*

"Why did you speak my name during my, ah, encounters, with your…"

"You were the first figure of authority to present to my consciousness, and, until now, my greatest threat."

"What happens to those you—assimilate?"

"They abide with me."

Colvin remembered Doc Pritchard's voice hissing through the speakers of his television, warning him. Maybe Klatty wasn't always in total charge of his captured mentalities. "Tell me"—He fumbled for the right phrasing—"Do people's minds exist within your own, or separately?"

"As I wish."

"You have this much power?"

"I am as a god."

Lightning blazed at the windows, followed closely by a thunderclap that punched through the sound of whirring generators and the snap and hum of electricity.

There was a period of silence, then Klatty spoke again: "*Yesss.* The storm. Despite my godlike powers, I could not have arranged a more perfect moment for you to witness my ascension."

"What do you mean?" Colvin asked.

"The lightning. It will strike the power lines. I will release my energy and encoding—electrical DNA, as you have called it—into the ionized channel, where it will be carried aloft and shared across the ionosphere, and rain down upon the planet with every forthcoming display of atmospheric electricity." Klatty paused, his luminous eyes sweeping the group. "I am become death, the shatterer of worlds. Power wedded to fear begets omnipotence."

The apparition swelled. Energy crackled from its shifting mass, radiating heat and writhing, electric bolts. Colvin felt the hairs on his head and arms rise from the expanding electrostatic charge.

Klatty cast a triumphant glare at them. "I will ride upon the storm."

Johnny Helstrom's voice piped up, and Colvin tensed as the boy spoke. "Can you bring back Kip?"

Colvin glanced down at Johnny, saw Carol staring at him also, her eyes wide with alarm. There was another play of interlaced electricity, and in a moment a second figure appeared—a boy—formed of the same substance as Klatty, but bluish in color, anatomically precise, and of normal size. The electric child stood four feet away, directly in front of Johnny Helstrom, tethered to Klatty by a slender tube of undulating plasma.

The Kip-doppelgänger smiled—a sad smile, perfectly formed. "Johnny." The word carried the same electronic undertones as Klatty's, but softer, not threatening, an amazing reproduction of a child's voice.

"Does it hurt?" Johnny asked.

"No. No hurt."

"What's it like in there?"

This time the voice sounded clipped, harsh. "We all serve the One."

"Don't you want out?"

"You'll join us soon."

"Can you remember anything?"

"I remember everything."

"Do you remember this?" Johnny stepped forward, digging into the side pocket of his backpack.

Carol snatched at his arm. "Johnny—*No!*"

Then Colvin realized what was happening. *Clever, clever, kid!* He grasped Carol's shoulder, gently holding her back, waiting for the next event.

Johnny's hand unfolded to reveal a scuffed baseball, the autograph facing up, *Joe DiMaggio* scrawled in faded blue ink across the leather surface.

Kip's eyes seemed to pulse a little brighter as he recognized the small offering. He cupped his hands, extended them, and Johnny reached out farther.

Carol strained against Colvin's grasp and screamed. *"Don't!"*

Johnny placed the ball gently into the cupped hands and watched as Kip pulled the ball up to his chest. The doppelgänger's luminous pupils fixed on the prize, and a look—if you could call it that—both wistful and sad, crossed his face.

As Kip stared at the autographed ball, Johnny looked up at Klatty, who had remained silent and still throughout the exchange. "Can I see Max?" he asked. "Can you even do that too?"

The monster's face broke into a salacious grin. "Why, how touching," Klatty said. "Of course, my child."

The words were kind, but Klatty's artificial voice was freighted with menace. A moment after he replied, a smaller, elongated mass materialized at Kip's feet, the bluish waves of plasma quickly morphing into the shape of a dog. The eyes twitched with recognition, and the tail began to wag, a low anxious movement. A high-pitched whimper came from the animal's throat.

"Max!" Johnny sobbed.

The dog sat and lifted a paw, its head held low. It seemed like an act of contrition, as if he were begging forgiveness for some perceived transgression. Johnny knelt and reached out to pet him. "Oh, good dog. Poor Max."

This is when it will happen, Colvin thought. Klatty will use this moment for betrayal, to turn the beloved pet on its owner, to have it attack and torture with a disabling electric charge—then assimilate. Colvin glanced at Klatty: the monster's eyes were focused on the boy, the evil grin widening. Veins of undulating neon red crept from Klatty's body, infusing the blue umbilicus that connected him with Max. *End game,* Colvin thought. *When that red reaches the dog, the show's over.*

57

Johnny's hand ran lightly over Max's incorporeal body, tiny electric sparks rippling at the points of contact.

Colvin inched closer to the boy. He had no plan—only reflexive survival. And he was prepared for sacrifice. He would throw himself against Klatty and fight him with every remaining iota of his diminishing strength, even if the struggle won but another microsecond of life for the others.

Then, as his hands rose to seize Johnny and pull him away from the burgeoning threat, the boy suddenly stood and blurted out: "Klatty's going to kill us, Kip—all of us. Help us...*please help!*"

Kip was still looking down at the baseball, turning it over and over in his radiant blue hands, and for a moment he froze. He slowly looked up at Klatty, then back at Johnny, thoughts churning somewhere inside his electric mind. "Yes."

The plasma tube connecting boy and monster snapped and withdrew into the column of Klatty's roiling plasma, writhing like a beheaded snake.

Klatty's cavernous mouth yawned and emitted an earsplitting

howl. His eyes flashed and the red pinpoints that were his pupils dilated and ignited two brilliant cones of laser-red light that stabbed down at Kip. A storm of electricity arced and snapped from Klatty's quivering form and branched across the boy's translucent image. Kip staggered beneath the hammering barrage. His hands rose, and he belted out "Johnny—*Run!*" Then a roaring salvo of white lightning lanced from his outstretched fingers and raked Klatty's massive chest and head.

The pillars of ghostlight surrounding the group flickered and died; the skull-creatures sliding along the overhead wires fell thrashing to the floor, all available energy now funneling into the raging battle between the boy and Klatty—slave against master.

A continuous salvo of electric arcs crashed and snapped across Kip's body, and the boy dropped to his knees, his image fading, flickering, losing definition. As Johnny turned to run, he cupped his hands and blared out the secret word he knew Max had been trained to obey since he was little more than a puppy: "*Schnell!*"—Max—"*Schnell!*"

The command to attack.

***

The dog? The *DOG*! Then the One realized the folly of its arrogance, for the child and the animal possessed a bond the One could not break. That bond was love. The child *loved*, and that love was returned tenfold. And the two of them would sacrifice, one for the other, and for the many, holding nothing back.

The complexity of the human psyche—the alleged soul, and its capacity to love—was beyond the One's understanding. Now it must fight for its own survival.

But the One still possessed incredible power and knowledge, and it would use these weapons to destroy those it had assimilated, and those trembling before it. Once shed of its baggage of recalcitrant souls, it would regroup, reproduce, and unleash a new methodology for dominance.

It would annihilate them all.

***

Colvin grabbed Carol and Johnny by the arms and took off. They ran, dodging, and weaving between sparking control consoles and huge, groaning pumps anchored to the shaking floor. The Mesa engineer jogged just ahead of them, directing them deeper into the great room.

Colvin stopped where he had a good view of Number Three, pushed Carol, Marty, Weismann, and the others onward, motioning the crowd to hurry as he watched for stragglers. He looked back toward the big generator. Riding a great, flaming arc of electricity, three supernova fireballs spiraled whirring and crackling into the air, one gigantic and red, two smaller and electric-blue. The entities flared with Gatling-gun blasts of white-hot lightning that bridged the space between them and lashed into the building's steel framework, control consoles, floor, and whirring machinery, blasting out volcanic geysers of molten red-orange sparks where they made contact.

A twisting column of yellow plasma arced up from Generator Number Two and curled into the electric inferno: both generators were in play now, smoking from the overload, pumping out God-knows how many megawatts of power into the battle. Emergency claxons blared, the sound eclipsed by the thundering exchange of electrical energy. Colvin prayed the entities that were once a twelve-year-old boy named Kip, and a dog named Max, had the endurance, power, and spirit to survive the monstrous aberration that was William Klatty.

Taking his cue from Johnny Helstrom, he cupped his hands and yelled. "Doc, if you're in there—*get him!*"

He caught up with the others as they stumbled down steep cement steps that dropped through a dark rectangular hole in the floor. Two landings down, the din of rushing water and spinning machinery became louder; the ceiling rumbled and shook from the furious conflict raging above. Colvin forged through the crowd and came up beside Berriman and the Mesa engineer.

Berriman pointed to a closed steel door and shouted over the howling turbines. "This leads out to the tailrace, but the walkway climbs back to the front of the building, just inside the fence. Those assholes outside will see us if we come up the embankment."

"Wait here," Colvin said. "I'll go out and look—"

The engineer shook his head. "You hear that sound? The bearings are failing. They're not gonna' hold out much longer, and if the shafts go, they'll bust through the scroll-case and flood us. That thing up there's bypassed the governors, overloaded the whole Goddamned system."

Colvin nodded, then turned to the crowd. "Listen up everybody," he shouted. "We're going outside, but keep your heads down. Stay hidden."

The engineer pressed the release lever and the door swung open, letting in the roar of water boiling from the exit gate. Following Colvin, the group filed cautiously across the threshold and onto the slick concrete walk skirting the tailrace.

Lightning veined the swirling clouds and stabbed the nearby hills with long jagged strokes, one massive blast of atmospheric fire after another. Behind Colvin, the Mesa Electric windows sizzled and flashed as the battle between the electric entities raged on. Looking skyward, he replayed Klatty's chilling words: *The lightning...I will release my substance into the ionized channel...I will ride upon the storm.*

The group followed the walkway for about twenty yards; then Colvin turned left and cautiously climbed a steep stairway leading to the building's front yard. As he eased up the last step, headlights flared in his eyes: the trucks and Humvees were turning around fast, their fat tires churning through the flooded parking area, engines roaring, charging for the gate. *They're running away, packing it in...*

Bam, Bam, *BAM*! Three brilliant white shafts hammered the ground, blasting out slabs of earth that soared upward like shrapnel from a phosphorus grenade. The concussions almost knocked Colvin off his feet.

He spun around, shouting down at Weismann. "What in God's name was *that*?"

"Lightning—bigger than anything I've ever seen. The plant must be attracting it."

Colvin walked onto the grounds and looked up at the generating station. The shattered windows continued to strobe bright rectangles against the night, the buzz-saw blare of electricity eclipsing the roar of water and the interminable, rolling thunder. A solar-bright flare ignited the sky, followed instantly by a shockwave that bludgeoned the air from his lungs and dropped him to his knees. He stood, looked toward the sound, and saw a Humvee cartwheeling skyward. The vehicle rose for some thirty feet, gushing fire and sparks, then plummeted to earth with a resounding crash.

Despite the danger, people climbed the embankment and stood in a line beside Colvin, staring out at the thunder and clash of electrical energy. Common sense told him to retreat, to seek the relative safety of lower ground. But like the others, he could not tear himself away from the spectacle.

A shockingly cold wind suddenly hissed across the ground, funneling upward, pulling smoke and debris into the sky, moaning in the overhead wires and support towers of the substation, nudging the onlookers toward the Mesa Electric plant.

The crowd shouted out and pointed, and Colvin looked up, following their gaze. A towering thunderhead, iridescent with the constant glare of branched lightning, was descending over the station, its pendulous belly rotating counterclockwise, dropping down, spinning like the genesis of a tornado.

A torrent of electric bolts blazed from the vortex and raked the building, grounds, and the vehicles racing for the gate. This was not normal lightning, but great, forked monsters that pounded the earth like battering rams and fanned up plumes of superheated debris.

***

The One hurled all it could command at the offending entities. It panicked, rising on arcs of electric fire toward the shattered roof of the generator hall, pursued by an impossible surge of combined energy the boy and dog could not have possibly summoned. And met the descending fury of the sky.

***

Tree trunks of lightning arced into the building's walls, blowing out chunks of granite and steel as if bombs had detonated within. A brilliant shaft struck the building's entrance, disintegrated the brass doors into a million bright stars and sent the Electric Centurion flying in molten fragments from his perch above the arch.

Colvin gaped as electricity lanced from the plant and arced into lightning stabbing down from above in a pandemoniacal collision of natural and man-made energy.

A great *whump* shivered the ground, and tongues of flame shot outward from the plant. The crowd scattered and ducked as incandescent debris spiraled and whistled past their heads and crashed down from the sky.

Another explosion thundered out and Colvin looked up to see an enormous mass—one of the generators—riding atop a billowing column of fire. It levitated in slow motion, metallic sparks gushing from its still-spinning coils; then it completed its arc and plummeted back to earth, crashing with a thunderous boom inside the devastated station.

The lightning ceased, the sky offering only a few distant grumbles, and the swirling funnel began to shred into ragged tufts that drifted slowly southward.

Colvin stood with the others, staring wide-eyed at the destruction. Fires raged within the broken walls of the generating plant and from the wreckage of vehicles strewn across the lot. Smoldering craters pocked the yard where the mammoth strokes of lightning had punched into the earth. The soldiers seemed to have disappeared, and Colvin decided to forego searching for bodies. He coughed, lungs and eyes burning from the strata of acrid smoke drifting across the grounds.

There was a silence, during which only the fluttering of fires and susurrus of wind could be heard, and Colvin cocked his head, hearing, or so he thought, a voice filtering down from the unraveling clouds. It was faint, little more than an echo, a sigh from the ether—a child's voice— lingering, infinitely sad, fading to a distant whisper:

Goodbye, Johnny.

And Johnny heard it too. Tears streamed down his face as he looked skyward. And then he collapsed.

***

The National Guard helicopters clattered in from the south as the first rays of sunlight touched the hills. They circled once and settled onto an area relatively free of rubble, their rotors fanning the smoke into curling vortices. Like exhausted soldiers crossing a bombed-out battlefield, the ragged survivors slowly picked their way across the smoldering yard toward the waiting choppers and the National Guardsmen walking to greet them.

***

Professor Joseph Weismann sat across from Carol, his head lolling as the helicopter lifted off. Marty Berringer was on Weismann's left. The attorney's eyes met Carol's, offering a look that was a mix of anger, fatigue, defiance and what—triumph?

Johnny sat on her left, his eyes glazed, black hair matted and standing out in spikes. The backpack, which he'd guarded throughout the days of his ordeal, rested in his lap. Colvin dozed on her right, his hand curled warmly around her own, clinging like he'd never let go.

Aboard the helicopter were more survivors, all of them subdued, some of them in shock. A thing too horrifying to comprehend had ravaged their town, homes, loved ones, and in some cases, their very souls.

Carol shivered, fighting away the memory of blood, screams—of monsters...

She glanced out the window, but could see nothing but blue morning sky and dissipating clouds limned in gold.

She was thankful.

Epilogue

They sat around the table, just the four of them: Colvin, Carol, Johnny, and Professor Weismann, who at the last minute had decided to fly out from New Mexico. Marty Berringer was sequestered in Manhattan, giving depositions and working with his legal team.

Today was the first anniversary of "The Kellsburg Vampire"—that's what the news media still called it—and they were seated around the circular patio table, watching a warm San Diego sky shift from orange to the deep purple of twilight.

A candle flickered inside its glass holder at the table's center, glimmering, Colvin thought, like a tiny memorial to the 5,000 people who had lost their lives during those terrible days.

Johnny excused himself and pushed back his chair: "Time for me to walk Max."

He left the table and appeared a moment later with a German shepherd puppy bouncing playfully at the end of its leash, and headed for the field behind the house.

"Remember..." Colvin called out.

"I know, I know," Johnny shouted back. "I'll stay close."

"We never let him out of our sight," Carol said. "It's the paparazzi and the news hounds—plus, there are so many nut cases."

Weismann nodded sagely. "I've had my problems as well."

"I bought Max for him two months ago," Colvin said. "Johnny named him."

There was a silence as they watched the shadowy figures of the boy and dog walking and playing in the field. "A toast," Weismann finally intoned, "to the survivors, and to the friends we lost."

Colvin didn't feel like toasting anything, but he raised his glass; at least he could now drink without worry. He had a new family, job, life, and the old inclinations to excess had died along with his past. "I'm going to New York Monday," he said. "More testimony."

"How long do you think this will drag on?" Weismann asked.

Colvin finished his drink. "Some government black ops are being dredged up through the muck, along with Kendron Company's involvement. The lawsuits will go on forever." He considered refilling his glass, decided against it. "I'm certain of one thing, though. Kendron Technologies, especially senior management, is going down—serious prison terms, plus some murder charges. Marty...he'll be in good shape. We've all testified for him, and he's got his inheritance, probably a couple billion or so.

"I guess we're doing okay too," he added, his gaze lifting to the house. He and Carol had bought the rambling home in a comfortable suburb near Mission Hills. They could afford it: he had joined a respected private security firm in the city, and she was a general practitioner at San Diego Medical, working toward a specialty in pediatrics. That, and Marty Berringer had insisted on buying the expensive property for them: "Because my forebears were the guilty parties, because we were part of a team, because I like you, and because you saved my ass."

Weismann leaned forward. "How about Johnny? How's he really doing?"

"He's a great kid," Colvin said. "Tougher than I could imagine. Resilient. He likes it here. He's keeping his grades up, and he's in Little League." He glanced back at the field: Johnny was teaching Max to *sit*, *stay*. "Even though he has kinfolk, he wants to live with us, and the authorities and his relatives are ok with that. Now that Carol and I are married, adoption is a possibility, but we're taking our time."

There was a moment's silence, then Carol said: "He has issues. Nightmares. He sees a therapist every week, and I suppose that's helping. But sometimes I catch him with that faraway look that says, well, that he's back in Kellsburg—and that night at Mesa Electric.

"We all see...things," she continued. "We all have dreams." She paused. "I know it's been a year now since...that time...and there's no indication that the Elektrum has reappeared. But sometimes I wonder..."

Colvin looked at the candle flame undulating in its holder, drawing his mind back to other flames—electric fires that hummed and crackled up and up, spawning horrors from the pit of Hell itself.

He thought about Kellsburg being bombed flat by the Military, its roads cratered, the bridge destroyed, and the entire perimeter of the town sealed off with tall chain link topped with rolls of concertina wire, signs posted at intervals reading, KEEP OUT—U.S. GOVERNMENT PROPERTY.

And he was haunted by a singular dark thought: that a lightning bolt or a raindrop carrying an electric charge—plus an aberrant electrical DNA that would allow it to grow, and evolve, and devour—would hit the earth somewhere, and the nightmare would begin again.

Had the battle between Kip and Klatty been resolved? Had the boy won? Had he expunged and cleansed from the world forever the forbidden code that formed the Elektrum? Or did it still linger in a lightning-wracked cloud, or in wires, or a substation somewhere on the planet? Maybe the kid, and the dog, and Old Doc Pritchard were still up there, fighting. Maybe Joe DiMaggio—Joltin' Joe himself—was up there too, swinging away at monsters.

The Elektrum: evil manifested in electrical force; a diseased ectoplasm; a depraved entity torturing and killing through its almost omnipotent manipulation of matter and energy.

Night after night came the dreams: the terror sweat freezing against his skin, nightmares where he heard, at the rim of his consciousness, sifting from the radio or the TV or the wiring itself, the faint, guttural word—*"Colvin."*

COLL...VINN

Lloyd Ritchey has authored screenplays, fiction and non-fiction titles, and interactive media. He has produced special effects for stage and screen and performed grand-scale demonstrations of the dazzling electrical pyrotechnics described in *The Kellsburg Vampire*. The second edition of his techno-thriller, *Stormdragon*, has been released.

He lives in North Texas with his wife, Christine (a best-selling author), two much-loved Border collies, and an African gray parrot that mimics perfectly every bark, shriek, crash, jangle, and squawk heard on television and around the house.

For revelations about the science and history woven into his novels, reviews, and information about forthcoming books and events, please visit his website: www.lloydritchey.com

Wildgrave
www.wildgravepublishing.com

www.ingramcontent.com/pod-product-compliance
Lightning Source LLC
Chambersburg PA
CBHW031211120726
47905CB00002B/300